The Trouble with Girls

Jonny Cox

Published by New Generation Publishing in 2012

www.newgeneration-publishing.com

 New Generation **Publishing**

The only way to get rid of temptation is to yield to it.

OSCAR WILDE: *The Picture of Dorian Gray*.

He who cannot resist temptation is not a man....

HORACE MANN: *A Few Thoughts for a Young Man*.

Part 1 – PARADISE LOST

"All of my resistance, lying on the floor..." Way Down - Elvis Presley 1976.

1

"The trouble with girls," said Tiny, "is that they crease your shirt."

"My trouble with girls is that I can't resist them."

"Well, they do it on purpose," he grinned. "They're marking their territory to say to other girls: *Look, this one's mine, I've creased his shirt already.*"

"Perhaps, but she knows I have a girlfriend."

Tiny let the working parts of his rifle spring forward with a clang, silencing the insects that buzzed around us.

He stood and put a big hand on my shoulder.

"Don't worry 'bout it, sir, you're in the middle of the jungle, no one will know." Then he went to run a training exercise and disappeared into the dense undergrowth.

I sat alone in the camp. Tiny was my platoon sergeant and, as a new infantry officer, I valued his judgement. He was also on his third marriage and considered an expert on girls. His advice in this case was of little consolation, however, for I was determined to resist the one girl who had suddenly appeared in the jungle.

But I liked his euphemism. It reflected the irony that I was in the jungle precisely because of my trouble with girls: joining the army was just running away and she was a difficult mistress, alluring, unfaithful, and a real bitch.

My regiment was deployed to Belize to protect the border from Guatemala and now I was sat in the permanent twilight under the jungle canopy, drenched in sweat with scarcely a breath of wind to dry my skin. The constant hum of insects rattled inside my head like the voices of evil children.

"Ha, ha, Billy-boy, you'll never last in here, go back

where you belong." Martin Sheen was right; the jungle does send you mad.

We built a permanent training camp in the jungle and stayed there for many weeks. Initially, living among the snakes and spiders for which Belize is famous seemed daunting but we got used to it quickly and the reality of it was good fun and high excitement.

I found it particularly satisfying because my position in the army food chain was elevated from lowly subaltern[1] to Jungle Warfare Instructor. This allowed me to compensate through physical capability for the lack of social compatibility that I had endured in the Officers' Mess.

We made beds from bamboo poles and diverted a stream over a small cliff creating a shower. After a day's training, we sat around a campfire telling stories and drinking warm beer, serenaded by the orchestral insects, dreaming of home. The jungle canopy formed a natural ceiling, reflecting the light from the fire and it felt like we were sitting in a cave.

I wrote long letters to Emily Fisher, my long-suffering girlfriend. She was sweet and beautiful, with tumbling auburn hair and a slender, sensual elegance. We met at university where she saw through my reserve and claimed me for herself.

"Come with me, Billy," she said with a coy determination that awakened me from my clumsy shyness. Emily tried to ignore my inconsistencies but even she eventually lost patience and dumped me.

I missed her a lot, her gentle laugh and cool skin, and my letters grew increasingly reminiscent of times that we had never actually shared. My father, a veteran of the Korean War, had warned me not to make

---

[1] Subaltern is the lowest officer rank: Euphemistically referred to as "Red-arse" because of the abuse that the other officers bestow on them.

promises that I would not keep once I was back in the real world. It was sound advice for I grew very lonely in the jungle.

Emily wrote suggesting we get back together and I agreed enthusiastically. Being with her would provide the stability I desired, a steady, comfortable life, free from the Army Bitch; I just needed to resist temptation.

"Stop dreaming of distant lovers, Hanson and come play Scrabble," said Charlie Young, a senior captain, one evening. "She'll be getting it from Leroy Brown by now anyway."

"Besides, she's probably a dog," challenged Tom Dantry, another overbearing captain.

"No she isn't," said Tiny, "I've met her. She's lovely: looks like Daphne from Scooby Doo."

Dantry was suddenly interested.

"What's she doing with a numb nuts like you, then?"

"I don't know," I said. I really never did understand what Emily or any other girl saw in me.

In the boredom of a jungle evening, Scrabble became addictive. It also became contentious.

"You can't use a double word score twice, you cheating bastard!" spat Charlie.

"Well you didn't say that before we started," snarled one of the sergeants with equal vigour. "Besides, colour has a "u" in it!"

"We're playing American rules 'cos Carl's playing." Charlie pointed to our US exchange officer.

"That's not fair," said the Sergeant Major.

"It's my fucking game," said Charlie, packing it away. We played the following night but the arguments continued because we needed an outlet for our competitive male egos, besides doing press-ups. We had to give up playing at night because our torches attracted swarms of flying insects.

9

I had a portable bug killer. I tried it in my room before we deployed into the jungle and I watched with fascination as a fly was drawn to the light, then got zapped with a satisfying sizzle. It was intended for enclosed spaces but I turned it on in the jungle camp one night and every bastard bug in Belize swarmed to it and the thing exploded instantly.

"Should have read the instructions," said Collins.

The Scrabble mania was broken when Tiny caught a tarantula. It was a black beast of a spider such as is normally only seen crawling up James Bond's arm. Then another guy caught one.

"Ten bucks says my spider is harder than yours," challenged Tiny and the poor tarantulas ended up in a large box being urged to fight by bored soldiers.

Tiny's spider lost its first fight, which was also its last since it was then dead.

"Don King you are not," I said.

Tiny wandered off into the jungle and came back clutching a box.

"Now we'll see who has the hardest beastie." He opened the box to reveal his prize-fighter. It was a scorpion. Not that big but as mean as a pub full of Celtic fans.

Despite my moral objections, I was intrigued to know which little beast would be the hardest. It was the scorpion. The sight of its claws cowed the tarantula, which had to be coaxed out of its corner, straight into scorpion-induced death.

Then everyone wanted a scorpion and disappeared into the bush to seek them out. That was quite dangerous but we grew blasé about the jungle, becoming increasingly detached from society's norms, not shaving regularly to save water and giving up things like soap and deodorant. Our pupils, new to the jungle, would stand aside from us, not believing that the Guatemalans could smell synthetic aromas or cigarette smoke.

I imagined that I had an affinity with the jungle.

"See how that leaf is facing slightly away from the others? The dew has been brushed off." I instructed my troops with enthusiasm. "You can track people through the undergrowth quite easily." I lost the need for a watch, instead relating to the arc of the sun through the leafy canopy that governed everything. My comrades regarded me with unease.

"Good Lord, Billy, what the fuck are you doing?" The Honourable Montesque Ford-Bryce was a cavalry officer and we were at opposite ends of the Officer Corps' social spectrum. Monty thought it odd that I called my soldiers by nicknames. I thought it odd that Monty wore velvet slippers in the jungle. I was eating luncheon meat straight from the tin with a penknife.

"Having my lunch."

"But...aren't you going to put it on something?" I regarded the pink mess, gelatine runny in the fierce heat.

"Truth is, Monty, the crackers are all done." He declined my offer to join me but I received a tin of Carr's Water Biscuits in the post a few days later.

Life in the jungle was uncomfortable but it was uncomplicated and we enjoyed it simply because of that. We trained hard, we were adept at jungle warfare and there were no girls. It was paradise, like Adam in the Garden of Eden.

So, inevitably, Eve came and shattered the cohesion of our monastic Utopia in the form of a young girl called Debbie Miller. She came offering temptation and we realised we were naked.

Debbie was a TA officer on attachment to the regular army. She was in her early twenties, modestly pretty, blonde hair and pale skin made more appealing

11

by the contrast with our own leathery appearance. To our fevered minds, she was more beautiful than Andromeda.

She also made it obvious that she wanted to get laid.

"That was impressive, Billy," she said as I dropped off the pull-up bar that we had placed between two trees.

"I can beat that!" Collins heaved himself up on the bar, grunting like an ape. Several other officers joined in the impromptu competition and it was pathetic to see men, steadfast in military duty, pandering to the whim of a young girl. Debbie, however, took great delight in our rapt attention.

"You're all very sweaty," she said with a smile.

I quickly withdrew from the arena of Debbie's attentions, having no desire to ruin my fragile professional reputation or betray Emily's trust for the sake of a quick shag.

But my reticence seemed to intrigue Debbie who spent most of her time hanging around me, much to the annoyance of my older comrades. She was actually quite engaging, bright and inquisitive, and her easy laugh was infectious. I began to succumb to her presence, despite my high intentions.

A further complication was Debbie's baggage. Ben was also a TA officer and one of life's losers.

"So, what's with you and Ben?" I asked Ms Miller as I was showing her how to make a basha[2].

"Oh, nothing, we're just friends."

I looked at Ben.

"He doesn't seem so sure."

Debbie spared him a glance.

---

[2] A shelter to sleep under made by suspending a poncho or tarpaulin over a sleeping mat or hammock.

"He'll get over it. Nice and cosy," she said looking at her bed. "I don't suppose I'll need my pyjamas."

I suppressed my arousal and went to see how Ben was getting on with his basha.

"How's it going?"

"Fine, I've managed on my own."

I winced. The young officers had ignored Ben as they vied for Debbie's affections. I gripped his bed frame.

"Seems firm enough."

He shrugged.

"It's a good idea to rub mozzie rep on the straps," I suggested, trying to establish some rapport, "it stops ants and things crawling under the net."

He nodded silently. We worked together as I tried to build some mannish bond.

"How are you finding the jungle?" I asked.

"Lonely."

"Aye, it takes some getting used to." I was a bit lost as to what to say. "Are you missing a girlfriend?"

He looked at me incredulously.

"No, we just broke up."

"Why, what happened?"

He seemed keen to talk and looked over at Debbie.

"We were together for most of our first year at university," he paused briefly, "but when we got over here she said that we needed a break. Then she began shagging one of the captains in the headquarters."

There was silence between us, which Ben eventually broke.

"Fickle bitch. She even suggested we get back together when we go home."

"You not interested in that?" He looked at me again.

"Yeah, right. I may not be as butch as you infantry guys, but I still have some pride."

He offered me a mixture of pathos and defiance and

I felt some sympathy for him, for the way in which he had been marginalized by the whim of a girl and the lust of stronger men.

Near our camp was a pool in the elbow of a river that wound its way through the jungle. There was a small beach and some large rocks where we sometimes lay like lizards basking in the heat when we had a break from training. I took some large inner tubes from the transport platoon so we could float peacefully in the water, drinking beer.

One afternoon I was there with Debbie, just the two of us relaxing in the sun. I had tried to avoid being alone with her but trouble with girls sometimes seemed inevitable. Debbie swam in a pair of my shorts and a T-shirt that she tied under her ample bosom.

When she emerged from the water, the wet cotton clung gratefully to the magnificent curve of her breasts, nipples pointed, appropriately, heavenwards. She was very friendly that day and I feared that I would not be able to resist her attentions if she turned them on me.

Lead me not into temptation but deliver me from evil.

Fortunately, some of the guys turned up in a Land Rover and spilled out into the pool, breaking the tension of the moment for Debbie and me. I took the keys to the Rover and walked quickly to the vehicle.

"Hey, wait for me!" Debbie called, "I want to go back, too. I want to wash my hair." We drove back in silence. I desperately tried to focus on driving rather than her undulating chest, which bounced every time we ran into a rut. By the time we got back to camp, I was sweating like a racehorse.

I parked up. Debbie went to collect her shampoo and returned from her basha without her shorts. The camp was deserted, all the guys were out training or down at the water hole.

"That's good," remarked Debbie, "I wouldn't want anyone to catch me in the shower." She smiled and walked away, glancing over her shoulder and stroking her spare hand across the back of her thigh, raising the shirt slightly so that her bum-cheeks glowed in the shady light.

I fought with the Devil. Shagging Debbie would threaten my rekindled love of Emily Fisher. It would betray Ben. It would be unprofessional to biff someone I was instructing. More importantly, I had made a personal commitment to resist Debbie's advances: She knew about Emily and it seemed like she was just trying to prove a point.

"Billy!" Debbie's sweet soprano drifted through the trees like the song of the Sirens luring Greek sailors to their doom. I could imagine her, naked and soapy under the jungle waterfall, dappled sunlight on her lightly tanned skin and nipples standing proud, enlarged by cold water and hot anticipation.

"Come on Billy, fuck me harder!" she would cry with breathless enthusiasm and a strong sense of triumph and for the rest of the afternoon I could release the pent up lust of weeks spent in the jungle.

Holy fuck!

But I could also imagine Emily Fisher, patient and trusting, her smile broadening as she held out her hand.

"Come with me, Billy."

So I turned away, dropped to the ground and started doing press-ups. I quickly lost count but kept going until the pain obscured my throbbing libido.

Afterwards, Debbie was tense.

"Am I not good enough for you, Billy?"

I could only shrug.

No, you're not Emily Fisher.

That night the fireside ritual turned into an

impromptu party. A lot of beer was drunk and Debbie very publicly led Tom Dantry into the bush. He followed like a grinning fool

I was confused. Turning away from easy sex contravened all my basic instincts but such weakness had previously broken my relationship with Emily and I realised that unless I could resist temptation, I would always be a slave to my own libido.

Debbie and Ben left the jungle shortly after that. Peace returned to the camp and we resumed our monastic life for a while longer.

2

Further along the track running past our camp was an archaeological dig. US academics ran the site, spending seven months of the year there during the drier season. It was a magnificent place called Caracol and it had been a thriving Mayan city about 1000 years ago.

I was fascinated by the prospect of discovering things in the jungle that had lain dormant for centuries and we often came across stone ruins lying under the bush. The limestone blocks were huge, with sharp edges and smooth sides and the skill of the craftsmen was evident from the close fitting joists and lintels.

It was part of our mandate to offer support to people in isolated positions and I was ordered to take a Landrover patrol along the 30 kilometres of the treacherous track that led to the site.

Our arrival created a welcome diversion for the archaeologists toiling in the dirt and heat. We had brought jerry-cans of fresh water, food, generator fuel and some bottled beer and the gratitude that we received made me feel like we had liberated Paris. It would have been merciful to donate our Scrabble game but there is a limit to every man's compassion.

We were given a tour of the site by Angela who smiled at us in that American "Hi, I'm your guide" sort of way and led us around the ruins. I had a genuine interest in the archaeology and anthropology and I also had a professional interest in maintaining congenial relations with our neighbours in the jungle.

However, despite myself, I also had an interest in Angela. She was tall, lithe and tanned and she had the alluring confidence of an intelligent woman who expects to be listened to.

"The Mayans are often considered to be the poor cousins of the Aztecs and Incas but, in truth, there was no real connection." Angela had obviously given this tour many times before to American tourists but her enthusiasm was still compelling.

"The zenith of their civilisation was around the time of your British Dark Ages. The Mayans lived in an organised agrarian society whilst Britain was mired in tribal conflict." She looked directly at me, as if it was my fault. She dropped her gaze and continued the lecture. "Mayan culture endured longer than that of other Meso-American peoples and this is often, albeit wrongly, attributed to their more war-like culture."

Being a soldier, this impressed me but Angela disappointed.

"The truth seems to have been that the Maya were actually quite a peaceful people." She was leaning against a tree in the middle of what once must have been a paved plaza. "They probably survived longer because their cities were in the more remote areas of the jungle and Yucatan Peninsula in Eastern Mexico." Angela was clearly an authority on the subject and I loved listening to her rhythmic accent.

She led us through passageways, halls and paved squares and showed us murals depicting the rise of the civilisation. She spoke with such relish about the Maya that I became immersed in their history. This was helped by the fact that when she bent down to indicate something of interest, her thin cotton blouse did little to disguise her unbridled bosom.

Night came quickly, ending the tour and my lecherous observations and I welcomed the release from temptation that darkness brought. We had a barbecue and the fresh food, beer and new company excited the Americans. I sat in the shadows staring into the fire, dreaming and feeling a little lonesome.

Angela sat next to me. She had a musky odour, the result of a lack of fresh water but, in the environment, it simply added to her charm. We chatted and laughed and I quickly warmed to her friendly manner. I found myself leaning close so that her hair spilled onto my shoulder. There was a sense of inevitable trouble about this scenario and I steeled myself to resist.

We talked about the Maya, their culture and civilisation and it was perhaps my genuine interest that attracted her to me. She may also have been really horny but, whatever the reason, she suddenly jumped up.

"Do you want to see the temple in the starlight?" She ran off into the darkness. That was a bit presumptuous really and perhaps Angela's libido was dominating her behaviour even more than mine. Equally, she may have just been more honest with herself but when you are in the middle of the jungle feeling a bit lonely and an attractive woman wants to show you her temple, it is a fair bet that most men will follow.

Angela led me through the central plaza of the ruin and climbed up the huge stone steps of a pyramid. The view from the top was magnificent. Below us the jungle canopy looked like a heaving sea. A warm breeze drifted over the trees and across the pyramid, caressing our skin. Above us, the stars looked like scattered tinsel; I had never seen so many stars in one sky.

She showed me around the temple. Her voice was hushed and I assumed that this was in reverence to the Mayan Gods.

"Mythology suggests that the Maya practiced human sacrifice." She indicated a stone bed resting on short stilts, which certainly looked like a sacrificial altar. Angela ran her hands affectionately over the smooth limestone of the plinth, describing how the living victim would have been tied down and had their heart cut out with a gold dagger.

"But I'm not sure about that," she continued in a low voice. "There is little archaeological evidence for it and I am more inclined to believe that they were into erotica and that this was an altar of ritual love-making." To a simple soldier, this was a combat indicator[3]. Angela could have focussed on the Mayan's revolutionary method of mixing mortar from clay and limestone paste but she did not and it seemed to me that she wanted to get laid.

I was reticent. I'd had enough trouble with Debbie but Angela was quietly determined.

"I imagine that smooth skinned girls were brought up here before an expectant crowd and stripped naked," she whispered. I could imagine it too and my reticence was evaporating accordingly. "There would have been beating drums and the crowd's anticipation must have been evident even up here. I imagine that the girls were tied down on the plinth and then taken, one after the other, by the religious leaders."

Angela's voice was thick with lust as she described this ceremony and, in order to ensure my participation in its re-enactment, she slowly undressed and lay naked on the altar, her soft brown skin an alluring contrast to the hard white limestone.

I reeled in confusion. Angela was literally laying it before me but I could feel Emily's arms around my shoulders and I tried to resist. Angela carried on with her narration, becoming breathless until she actually seemed to be praying to some Mayan deity.

You're in the middle of the jungle, no-one will know.

I stepped forward, hating myself, or at least trying to: Emily and I were not actually together yet, so

---

[3] Military term for an indication that engagement with the enemy is likely.

perhaps it was not really betrayal.

"Billy, you up here?" Tiny came looking for me, using my first name to make a point. Angela hid behind the altar and I stepped away with an apologetic shrug and an awkward hard-on.

In retrospect, I was not sure that Angela's narration of the sacrificial process was true but that was no excuse and I had to admit that without Tiny's salvation I would have given in to temptation. I was disappointed in my own lack of strength but, having taunted me so cruelly, the Army Bitch then helped me to briefly hide from self-recrimination by sending me to play soldiers in the jungle.

3

The atmosphere in the helicopter was tense. Engine noise preventing conversation so each man was alone with his fears of the jungle. Below us the canopy sped by in a blur of impenetrable green. We landed close to the Guatemalan border and jumped out of the helo with the rotors still turning. I needed the troops to be alert and ready to move but morale was low and the soldiers lacked motivation.

As the helicopter lifted off, the noise of the engines receded into the distance, taking with it our last link to civilisation. The SOP[4] for landing into an unsecured area was to clear the immediate vicinity, check all the equipment and move off as quickly as possible to conceal the presence of the patrol on the ground.

"Play football?" A young boy emerged from the trees clutching a ball. The clearing into which we landed was a village football pitch. Half my troops immediately dumped their kit and rifles on the ground and the rest sat down to tab up. We lost the footy, 2:1.

Eventually, I restored order and considered the team composition as they sat sweating on the ground before me. I had no second in command, or British NCOs at all, just a motley collection of soldiers culled from other duties to provide enough men for patrol team. No doubt my Company Commander was back in camp with his shorts and sandals on (with white socks) completely oblivious to the plight of his troops in the jungle.

I had two soldiers from the Belizean Defence Force and I addressed the first one who was of native Ketchi origin.

---

[4] Standard Operating Procedure

"What's your name, soldier?"

"Sanchez." He paused before asking, "Where we headed for, Boss?"

"Some village named Santa Rosa," I replied looking at the map.

The Belizean nodded.

"I've been there before."

"Can you find the way?" He nodded again. Things were looking up.

I addressed the second Belizean soldier, a corporal of Caribbean origin.

"And who are you, Corporal?"

"You can call me Wild Ting."

I stifled my surprise.

"I'm not calling you that. What's your real name?"

"That's my name. My mother calls me that."

"Let's stick with Corporal."

It was still only six months since I had finished my initial officer training but, having qualified as a Jungle Warfare Instructor, I could lead long-range patrols into the bush. This was the first real test of my leadership and I relished it. It was what I had trained for and there would be no trouble with girls; the sustained hard work and privation of the patrol programme would free me from my own libido.

The first patrol task hit me soon after we had moved out of the training camp and there was little time to prepare. I had a map, some rations and ammunition, 10 soldiers I barely knew and twenty-four hours notice. We had landed some distance from our start point because the sapless bastard of a pilot refused to put us down close to the border. This was not how it had been in training.

I sat on my bergen, a large rucksack I had bought myself, and read the map. It had been plotted from the air and was simply green, illustrating jungle, with no recognisable ground or water features. I was in the wrong place, unsure of my objective on a hostile and un-marked border, had an ad hoc patrol team and no deputies other than a self styled maverick called *Wild Ting*. The Army Bitch was smiling at me.

I should have set up camp in the village by the LZ where there was food, water and shelter and conducted short, daylight patrols in order to map the area. But I was dangerously young and keen and decided to lead the whole patrol into the bush to find Santa Rosa.

"Corporal." I stood up and showed him the map. "Do you know where we are?"

He pointed to himself.

"Man, I don't have a clue. Wild Ting is a cook." I could sense the Army Bitch laughing now.

We tabbed all day like beleaguered pack animals. We should have spread out along the track, two soldiers taking point, everyone alert and rifles ready to fire, but our bergens weighed over 100lbs, filled with radio batteries, ammunition, rations and personal equipment. The temperature and humidity were in the nineties and we were struggling to move, let alone maintain rigid patrol formations.

Periodically, I stopped to check my map; a frivolous exercise aimed more at convincing the soldiers that we were not completely lost, than actually navigating. Sanchez seemed confident of where he was going, so I concentrated on taking bearings and counting paces so that we could at least retrace our steps back to the LZ if things went wrong.

Night comes quickly in the tropics, so we pitched camp early. I sat down under my bivvy[5] to scoff and

---

[5] Bivouac: Temporary patrol shelter.

then took out the pipe that Emily had bought me and puffed smoke into the air. It was a strange gift for a young bloke but it was soothing and the thick smoke kept the mossies away. I sipped whisky from the hip flask that Emily had also bought.

My soldiers were sat around a small campfire. It was poor patrol discipline but I considered morale to be more important than security. Indeed, my own morale was very low and I wanted to join the soldiers around their campfire but I was the officer and therefore detached.

"That's why you wear your rank on your shoulder and not on your arm," the Company Sergeant Major told me before I got on the helo. My isolation was made all the more acute because that night was my birthday and, as I sat pondering whether it was possible to feel any worse, it began to rain: jungle rain, heavy, torrential, deafening.

I was disturbed from self-pity by the soldiers approaching my bivvy.

"Sir."

I looked up and tried to smile.

"We understand it's your birthday." It was Private Johns, a normally dour chap from Cumbria. I smiled fully then, assuming the Company Clerk had told them,

"Sure is. I'm twenty three."

"Yeah, we know. We got you a cake."

Private Medley held up a ration tin of fruit pudding. The tin had been opened with a pen-knife and the jagged lid was stuck up grotesquely and a thick army candle had been squashed into the middle of the pudding. It was not pretty but one of the soldiers had given up his rations and the generosity of it was nearly overwhelming.

"Thanks, that's really kind."

The soldiers all smiled and sat down around me on

fallen logs and dripped in the rain.

"Crap birthday, Boss," said Medders.

"Still, if you were back home you'd only be enjoying yourself in a bar somewhere," said another.

"Yeah, surrounded by birds."

"Hey, maybe you'd get lucky."

"Naw come on, it's his birthday, not Christmas." I was happy to be derided; it was better than being ignored. I removed the candle, stuck it in the ground under my basha and began to eat the fruit pudding. I passed my pipe to a soldier and he smoked it for a while before passing it on. I passed around the hip flask.

Next morning it was well after dawn when we eventually struck camp. Morale was still high until I inspected the bivvy site before moving off. There was rubbish everywhere; empty tins and fag boxes.

"Get this shit cleaned up!"

"Where are we gonna put it, Boss?" asked one of the more robust soldiers.

"In your fucking bergen like you've been trained."

He grimaced. Putting rubbish in a bergen is bad news as it attracts insects but, left on the ground, it would alert every local farmer, drug smuggler and Guatemalan that a British patrol was in the area. It was also bad discipline and when things got difficult later, discipline would be all I had to rely on.

Loss of temper in a commander suggests a lack of self-control and insecurity, but I led the patrol at a punishing pace. The soldiers began to stumble and curse and as I pushed them harder I lost the moral high ground.

Eventually, I called a halt and the soldiers collapsed on the ground, too tired even to smoke. As they lay panting and groaning I got my map out and pretended to navigate.

"Sanchez, spare me a minute, will you?"

The native soldier came over and looked at the map.

"I'm not good with maps, Boss."

I put it away.

"Okay, how far is it to Santa Rosa?"

He thought for a minute.

"Full day's march. Maybe more but this track leads right to it."

I made plans for a minute before addressing the soldiers.

"Fellahs, we're going to have to keep the pace up, I want to get to Santa Rosa before dark." There was no verbal response but I did get some very dirty looks.

"We can sleep in the village tonight," I added in a thin attempt to raise spirits.

We pushed on through the day. There was little water available and there was no cooling rain. We began to dehydrate, muscles became taught and headaches grew worse. With each step our bergens became heavier. There was no breath for talking and each man withdrew into his own private world.

There was no route marked on the map so I allowed Sanchez to lead us along the dirt path. The patrol reports that I had read did mention an unmarked jungle track and we were headed in generally the right direction so we slogged on through the mud. The border was indistinct so I hoped fervently that we would not meet a Guatemalan patrol coming the over way. We kept going: I did not know what else to do.

Eventually, the path began to lead downhill. We slithered down the steep track until we reached a stream. The soldiers gasped with relief but I made them put sterilising tablets in their water bottles and wait half an hour before drinking. The physical and psychological condition of the soldiers had deteriorated so much that every instruction I gave had now become a battle of wills.

Military discipline was a long helicopter ride away; there was just me and I was as knackered as they were. My feet were blistering badly, my head pounded and the straps of my bergen had torn the skin on my shoulders so that blood was trickling through the hairs on my chest. The camaraderie of my birthday party had long since been forgotten.

"Let's go," I said after precious few minutes rest.

"Aw, come on, Boss, let's at least have a fag."

I had to fight my temper with both hands and search my soul for some sympathy.

"It'll be dark soon and the village isn't far, we can rest there." It was a lie of course, I had no idea where the village was but I had nothing else to offer. The soldiers dragged themselves up and we moved on.

Mercifully, the trees began to thin just before dark and Sanchez came hurrying back down the track to indicate the huts scattered in a clearing. Columbus cannot have been more pleased to see the West Indies than I was to see Santa Rosa.

So close to the border, I should have formed a fire support base in the trees and approached the village with a well-armed escort but I feared that if the soldiers lay down now I would never get them up again. We moved into the village in blob formation and collapsed on the ground scattering chickens and children in all directions. I was so wracked with fatigue that I did nothing for several minutes other than lie on my back like a stranded turtle.

Then I eased the bergen from my shoulders, drank deeply of chlorinated water, chewed on a hard tack biscuit and, finally, got my map. The village was at the head of a deep L shaped valley that was so big I felt it must have been marked on the map.

I began to develop a deep sense of unease.

"Sanchez, where have all the children gone?" The soldier looked at me for a while and then slowly nodded. Normally when a patrol entered a village, children would gather around, expecting sweets and other gifts.

Got you, Boss." He looked around the village for a moment. " I'll go find some-one to ask."

I continued my desperate study of the map. The valley was clearly marked and, although the village was not indicated, I was able to pinpoint our position about half way up the western slope.

"Fuck!"

"What's up, Boss?" asked one of the more astute soldiers.

"Well….we're in Guatemala." All the soldiers were looking at me curiously then.

"That's not good, is it, Boss?"

"Not really."

"That would explain it," said Johnno.

"Explain what?"

"I saw a sign back there that said international boundary or something."

"Did you not think to mention it?"

"Well, you was all fired up, Boss. I didn't want to disturb you."

"Yeah, man, there's a guy in my regiment been up here before, ya know," declared Wild Ting. "Him said de Guats opened fire on dem."

"Why didn't you say so?"

"You was worried 'bout de rubbish dis morning. Besides, Wild Ting is a cook."

Sanchez ran back into the village like a·man with a bit-part in a bad play.

"Boss," he whispered in urgent gasps. "I spoke to this kid….a Guat patrol was here recently."

We frantically put our kit back on and moved down

the track, the soldiers needing little bidding from me. In the situation, I had three choices: stay and fight, stay and negotiate or run away. Since we were clearly in Guatemala, running away seemed much the better option. I led the way back up the track, stumbling in mud and panic.

I did not know if the Guatemalans would follow us or how big their team was but I decided it was best not to wait to find out. Besides, the soldiers were now near to exhaustion and, despite their adrenaline, could obviously not go much further.

Once we seemed safely back in Belize I gave the hand signal for a quick ambush. At least the list of my crimes at the court martial would not include infringement of international borders. The soldiers filed silently back through the trees parallel to the track and then took up firing positions facing the way that we had come. It was pretty slick; I was quite pleased despite my sense of panic.

Suddenly, we were silent, trying not to pant loudly. Adrenaline and beating hearts made it difficult to keep still and we were all completely soaked in sweat, hands slippy and fingers twitching over triggers. I prayed that no one would slip and fire their rifle for that would cause them all to open up and I would not be able to stop it.

A twig snapped further down the track. We waited forever. I wanted to scream. Then a Guatemalan soldier came into view. I felt my own troops stiffen.

Please, please don't open fire.

The Guat moved fully into our killing zone, followed by another soldier and then their commander appeared.

He was a cautious man. His troops were spread out and alert. In the diminishing light they looked ten feet tall. The lead scout was examining the ground and signalling to the commander; they had found our tracks. Surely, he must know that they were now in Belize.

We were likely to win a firefight. We were in cover, had the aim and would fire first, killing most of the Guats before they realised where we were. But there would still be dead people and it would be my fault.

The immediate danger passed, my soldiers would wait for me to fire first. I had the Guatemalan commander in my sights. Less than a centimetre of finger movement and he would be shot, followed quickly by his troops. The sweat ran freely down my face, tension made my shoulders and arms twitch, I was fighting to breathe properly, fighting to keep my finger off the trigger.

I wanted to go down on to the track and explain that it was all a mistake, a navigational error, but he might panic and raise his rifle which would cause my troops to open fire and I could not afford to break silence to brief them not to.

Of fuck!

In the interminable silence that followed it occurred to me how perverse are the machinations of men. How tragic would it be for men to suffer a violent and ignominious death over a disputed border that no-one could even find?

Eventually, the Guat commander called his troops back. He spoke in Spanish but his intention was clear to us too. He sent his soldiers down the track, away from danger, and stood alone in the forest. Then he turned and stared into the trees. We were not visible in the bush but I felt sure that he could see in to my eyes, into my soul. I lowered my rifle slowly and the man smiled, then turned and disappeared into the jungle.

We waited for a long time, not daring to move. Then I silently led my soldiers away from the border, deep into the jungle. I refused to let them erect bashas that

31

night and we slept on the ground. I ordered a double sentry, which meant less sleep for everyone.

When the patrol harbour was set, I began to relax. Then I began to shake. This had been a bad day. I sat on the ground in the dark and reached into my bergen for my hip flask. It was empty.[6]

Dawn brought little cheer. It had rained heavily during the night and we were soaked through and miserable. Spirits were low and the atmosphere was already tense. I should have ordered a hot meal and brew but there was no water to spare for cooking.

"Let's saddle up and move away from here," I said with no attempt at false spirits. The soldiers were slow to respond and regarded me sullenly for a few seconds before stirring themselves into action.

I called a halt after twenty minutes.

"Okay, let's rest here. Fag up, eat biscuit or cold rats and clean rifles in pairs. Sparks, see if you can raise Company HQ on the net." We all set to our tasks with varying degrees of enthusiasm and a complete lack of success. Hard tack biscuits failed to satisfy appetites, sips of tepid water did little to slake raging thirsts and the radio operator could not make contact with the Company HQ on the radio.

"S'no good, Boss, atmospherics, I think, I've tried both HF and VHF." I looked up into the sky that was swollen with dark clouds. I nodded slowly.

"Fellahs, we're going to have to walk back in."

There were unanimous groans of protest.

"It's miles and miles."

"Aw, Boss, we're dead beat."

---

[6] In retrospect, I realised that a fire-fight with the Guatemalans was very unlikely since border infringements were quite common in the dense jungle. However, I had not been briefed about this and to a brand new second lieutenant, the threat seemed very real.

I shrugged, which was not much of a commander's response but I was struggling to keep the patrol together.

"There's no alternative. We can't make the helo pick up now and unless we can raise the Company on the radio, we will have to walk." Exasperation lent me some vehemence but it did little to appease the troops.

"Bollocks to this!" Private Esher, who had already been demoted from corporal for insubordination, hissed at me. I had been dreading this sort of confrontation.

"What's your problem, Esher?" I tried to dismiss his outburst as a tantrum rather than overt aggression, which might incite the others.

"My fucking problem is that I'm tired, hungry, thirsty and fed up of being fucked about by you." He paused for breath or effect before continuing his tirade. "How can we walk in, it will take three days?"

"Well, what do you suggest?" I threw back at him, more to try and convince the others that he was being unreasonable than to appease his own tirade.

"I'm staying here," he said looking around to collect consent from the younger, more impressionable soldiers.

"You can't stay here, you've no water, no food, what will you do?" There was no reason for me to argue with him, an order should have sufficed, or so my Sandhurst[7] experience suggested, but the paucity of my officer training was becoming increasingly obvious. There had been no mention of how to deal with mutinous soldiers lost in the jungle, miles from military discipline.

There was an impasse then that I misjudged to mean

---

[7] Royal Military Academy Sandhurst; where all officers receive their initial training.

that Private Esher would follow my instructions.

"Okay, get your get kit on and let's move."

"Why should I?"

"Because I fucking said so!" My Yorkshire up-bringing was starting to compensate for my lack of military command. "And if you don't, I'll have you Court Martialled." It was an extravagant boast.

"Then you'll be known as the officer who lost control of his troops."

"And you'll be known as the troops who weren't man enough to soldier with Billy Hanson."

That had some effect on the group, so I pressed my advantage,

"Now get your kit on, stop fucking about and we'll forget this matter." I could see some of the soldiers shifting their loyalty back to me but Esher could feel himself losing face and he was not prepared to let that happen.

"How're you gonna make me?" He issued the ultimate challenge. I had few options now and, besides, sometimes it just does not pay to be a gentleman.

"Like this." I held up a fist. Esher laughed. He was bigger than me but as his attention was drawn to my clenched right hand, I hit him hard and fast with a left jab.

It was a good punch. The soldier collapsed like a sack of shit, blood gushing from his nose. I glared at the soldiers.

"Any more stupid questions?" There were none. I looked at Esher, fearful that he might come at me but he seemed stunned by the fact that I had actually hit him. He just nodded.

"Good point, Boss." He picked up his kit and moved onto the track. The others followed him.

"Sir, there's a BDF[8] camp 'bout a day's march from here. They'll have radio comms." Sanchez made the statement without fanfare but it was the sweetest song I had heard for a long time.

---

[8] Belizean Defence Force

4

I relished the challenges of patrolling in the jungle. There was something pure about being a soldier, about the lack of trouble with girls.

"Billy, you are to conduct a boat patrol down the coast and along the southern border with Guatemala," the Operations Officer used his map as he spoke. "It'll be a six day patrol, with the Gurkha Engineer Boat Troop." He continued with the detail and it seemed quite an interesting task. "You'll be accompanied by a legal officer."

"Why's that, are there complications about the border?"

"No," he said, almost apologetically, "she's on attachment and needs some operational experience as part of her qualification process."

"You're kidding me! I am taking another border patrol with no NCOs other than a Ghurkha engineer sergeant and you want me to wet nurse some prissy bird of a lawyer as well!" The vigour with which I decried the task belied the fact that I was still only a second lieutenant. I supposed it amused the Army Bitch to challenge me so.

When the lawyer turned up for my team briefing my dismay got worse. She was a small woman with a big attitude. Reputedly, she had complained to a company commander when attached to his unit because the blokes all leered at her when she went swimming. So for half an hour every evening, the soldiers were banned from using the pool, which had been provided by The Sun newspaper, so that one lone officer could have a swim.

The indulgent excitement of the patrol overcame my

reservations. We sat in three Rigid Raiders[9] idling along the river towards the sea. Once we had sufficient depth of water, the engines roared, making the boats rear up like startled horses and we lurched forward at thirty knots. We raced along the flat river and then burst onto the Atlantic, the boats leaping over the waves with adrenaline pumping power.

We charged south hugging the coastline until we came to the estuary of the river that formed the border with Guatemala. We throttled down and slid westwards along the river scattering birds, terrapins and one lazy crocodile lying on a rock as we turned a bend in the river's course. By mid afternoon we had reached an abandoned customs post that was to be our first night's stopover.

"Sergeant Gurung, please sort out your boats, Chaffs, send a SITREP[10], everyone clean your weapons and scoff up before dark." My instructions to the team were simply reminders of the tasks that each individual knew they had to do. We occupied the wooden customs posts and life was quite cushy.

"Sir, I've got nothing on the blower." Private Chaffer, the team signaller, looked well pissed-off. Our position was in the lee of a mountain and he knew that failure to transmit meant that we would have to climb to high ground to report.

"We'll climb up to the OP at Cadenas[11], at least we won't have to carry the radio." We spent two hours climbing up and down the mountain, sliding in the mud and tripping over roots. As we approached our patrol

---

[9] 5m long hard bottomed combat boats that were originally designed for amphibious beach landings. They were ideal for river patrolling but vulnerable in the open sea.

[10] A radio transmitted situation report to Battalion HQ.

[11] Observation Post on top of a mountain overlooking the Guatemalan border.

base on the way back I could hear laughing and shouting through the trees.

"WHAT THE FUCK IS GOING ON?" I bellowed with a force emanating from my boots. The boats were drifting about on loose moorings, there was a pile of kit and clothes by the riverbank and a bundle of weapons lay unguarded in the grass. In the river were the Ghurkha engineers and all my soldiers cavorting with the lawyer who was absolutely wearing an itsy-bitsy polka-dot bikini.

I bulled about the riverbank yelling at the troops to get their shit together and they responded like frightened rabbits. I saved my best roar for the lawyer.

"Miss Collins, get some fucking clothes on!" She immediately began to respond but then stopped herself and bridled with indignation.

"You can't speak to me like that, I outrank you! Is that how infantry officers like to behave towards women?" The snotty bitch had me on a technicality because professionally qualified lawyers received immediate seniority as a lieutenant on joining the army. But Odin was siding with me that day.

"Bullshit, I'm the patrol commander and you are out of order. Now please put some uniform on." She accepted my point and waded out of the river. Despite my anger, I had to force myself not to stare at her shapely legs, tight waist and pert tits as she prowled towards me like a predatory water nymph.

Once the sun had gone down and I had checked on the sentries, I felt bad that I had succumbed to anger so easily and berated everyone with such vehemence. I found some spare shorts and a t-shirt in my bergen and took them to the room in the customs post that Heather Collins was occupying for the night.

"Heather, I'm sorry if I..." my apology stalled as I walked in and found her naked from the waist up. It had not occurred to me to knock before entering and I could not help but glance at her slender form. Heather started instinctively but then relaxed and actually made little attempt to cover up. I wallowed in more confusion.

I had joined the army hoping to avoid trouble with girls, I had come to Belize expecting to avoid trouble with girls and I had gone on patrol in the jungle certain that I would avoid trouble with girls and yet I was now stuck on the Guatemalan border with a near naked woman and the Devil urging me on. I swallowed hard and turned away from Heather towards the wall.

"I brought these," I said offering the clothes to her behind my back. "Perhaps you could wear them for swimming." I made to leave and Heather called after me.

"Thank you."

Next morning we packed up and continued with the programme, cruising back along the river, stopping to talk to villagers, leave useful items such as soap, matches and tinned food and simply demonstrate a presence. Having a woman in the team helped soften the attitude of folk that we met and casual conversation between village women and Heather elicited much more information than I did from talking with the elders.

The patrol was running smoothly until late afternoon as we were speeding back north along the Atlantic coast to our next overnight stop. The sea started to swell in a strengthening onshore wind. Sgt Gurung waved at me from one of the other boats and pointed to the shore. A storm was brewing and the shallow boats were in danger of flooding; Rigid Raiders were not built for heavy seas. We turned obliquely to run in to the shore so that the increasingly large waves would not capsize us.

We were too late. Heather's boat was dashed with a massive wave. It stayed upright but the engine cut out and it bobbed like flotsam in the angry sea. Suddenly, everything went tits up. We herded the boats together and transferred kit and soldiers from the swamped boat. Heather trembled as I helped her across the gunwales as the boats rolled on the waves. Then a second boat was swamped and the remaining craft had to ferry everyone and everything to the shore.

"Fellahs, take all your kit off, tie the weapons and bergens to the boat." I was yelling above the roaring wind, frantic to lighten the troops in case one was washed overboard. No one panicked and eventually we got everyone back to the shore: wet, cold and a bit spooked, but safe. The engineers dragged the boats out of the water, my soldiers secured all the kit and weapons and one even tried to make a brew.

Heather stood motionless and shivering. She had been scared much more than the soldiers who were now laughing and teasing each other for a lack of balls. I dragged her between some mangrove bushes away from the troops and rigged a windbreak with my poncho. I looked for her dry uniform but girls cannot pack a bergen properly and all her kit was soaked.

I sacrificed my only set of spare uniform and stripped Heather to her underwear. She stood pliant and sobbing as I redressed her and pulled her down onto her knees beside the poncho. Then I just held her while she howled like the wind that raged around us. When she was calmed I wrapped her in a foil blanket and laid her down on a roll mat.

I checked around the impromptu patrol harbour and was gratified that everything was in good order. The soldiers were either busy or asleep, they had organised a STAG[12] system, and all our kit was stashed under bushes. I returned to Heather and found her sleeping peacefully. There was no room on the mat and the sand was wet so I sat by her feet and leant against a palm tree with my rifle over my lap.

When I awoke a few hours later I saw Heather curled up like she was having a Sunday morning lie-in. She was watching me.

"You all right?" I queried.

"Yes, thanks," she nodded with a rueful smile, "bit stiff."

Tell me about it, I'm piss wet through because you're wearing my dry kit and I slept leaning against a tree!

I smiled too, lay my rifle across my feet, dug a little hole in the sand, chucked in two solid fuel blocks and brewed some coffee. With the leftover water I made us both some porridge. I scoffed mine quickly, stowed away the rubbish and quickly cleaned and oiled my rifle whilst drinking the coffee. Heather was still wrapped in her foil blanket like the Sunday roast.

"Don't you ever put it down?" she asked.

"What?"

"Your rifle, you never put it down."

I looked at it with surprise.

"It would get dirty."

Heather nodded slowly, a smile teasing her lips, and I sensed that our relationship had developed somehow. It would have been nice to chat but we had been static for too long. I went to coerce my soldiers into action:

"Come on ladies, let's rock and roll!"

The rest of the patrol ran like a training serial. There were no more problems and Heather was a different

---

[12] Standing Armed Guard - sentry.

person. She laughed with the soldiers but maintained a professional distance, she spoke easily with the local people, and she made copious notes, helping me to write the patrol report.

"Do you see any indications of drug smuggling?" I asked some US expats who had set up home on the coast in an idyllic cove of turquoise water and silver sand.

"Not at all," responded the husband, nervously glancing at his wife. She avoided his gaze. Heather was chatting quietly with her, offering coffee and sugar.

"Anything else you need?" Heather asked casually. The wife paused to consider what she might decently ask for.

"Some first aid items would be useful, plasters and antiseptic cream." Heather nodded and then addressed the patrol medic.

"Swanny, please see what we can spare from our kit. Could you get some steretabs[13] as well?" We gave the family the essential items that were not available in their version of paradise.

"Could I put your location in my report as a stopover for future patrols?" I asked the couple.

"Yes, of course," said the wife, immediately sensing an opportunity, "it would be good to have folk around occasionally."

I nodded, taking the hint.

"I'll recommend they bring extra supplies."

The pregnant pause became a little uncomfortable.

"We do sometimes hear small planes overhead," the husband admitted quietly.

"Yes," said the wife with much less caution, "and we also hear a loud splash out in the sea. It's followed by the sound of motor boats." She looked between

---

[13] Water sterilising tablets.

Heather and me to reinforce the sense of what she was saying and the risk that such a confession might have for them. I did not write anything down; I could do that later.

Working together allowed Heather and me some détente. One morning we sat drinking coffee in the early sunshine whilst watching the mermaids[14] play in a small fishing harbour. It was like being on holiday.

"You haven't hit on me, Billy," she remarked casually. "All the other officers have tried their luck." I was not sure if this was praise for my professional manner or chastisement for ignoring her womanly charms; I suppose she meant to be ambiguous.

"I'm leading my soldiers." She nodded slightly, clearly not convinced. I looked her in the eye. "And I didn't think you'd be interested." She laughed gently. Women like honesty in a bloke, apparently.

"No, I wouldn't," she smiled. "Not then." More ambiguity. Why can women not say what they mean? Her words were unclear but as she spoke she had that *I need a good seeing to* look on her face that was supposed to say what she actually meant but which I never understood.

As we docked the boats back at camp Heather turned to me.

"Do you fancy a drink in the bar later?" She looked at me directly and her meaning was very clear. This was temptation beyond reason and I realised immediately that I was not even going to attempt to resist.

Oh yes I do, Honey, and then I am going to undress you slowly, kissing every inch of delicate skin, before I lay you down and ride you like a Harley Davidson and

---

[14] Manatee.

43

show you exactly how infantry officers like to behave towards women.

"Yes, thanks, that would be nice." I smiled and she climbed on to the transport. I was surprised. We had developed some rapport on patrol but I had not expected it to become a personal relationship.

I walked into Company HQ like the proverbial dog with two dicks.

"Billy, good to see you," applauded the Company Commander with suspicious gusto. "I need you to lead another patrol. Actually, I need you to command the OP at Cadenas." I shrugged. I had been up there during the boat patrol and it looked like an easy option.

"Okay, Sir, when's kick-off?"

"There's a chopper inbound," he said casually, "be about thirty minutes."

Are you fucking kidding me!

"I just got in, sir, my kit's all dirty, I've no rations!" I bleated every excuse I could think of apart from telling my boss that I could not do a patrol because I was on a promise. Besides, the bastard had an answer to everything so I climbed into the helo with a bag of rations and new uniform and sat looking through the door as we rose above the trees. On the ground I saw Heather come running out of the mess attap[15] and as I became a speck against the clouds, she raised a hand and waved.

I learned later that there was an impromptu party in the mess that night and Heather was taken care of by another officer. In some respects, I was glad. I had avoided trouble and my relationship with Emily Fisher was safe. I was also a bit gutted. I had conducted the ultimate seduction, casually charming an archetypal ice maiden in austere conditions and a miserable base-rat

---

[15] Hut thatched with palm leaves that served as a bar.

had reaped the rewards; girls are so fickle.

Apparently, she did go like a Harley as well.

5

"Hi, I don't think we've met."

I looked up to see a dark haired woman and was immediately spell bound by her bright smile, warm brown eyes and glowing radiance.

"I'm Vivienne."

I reached out to shake hands, feeling conspicuously dirty.

"Hanson, Billy Hanson." She smiled at me again.

After another two months in the jungle, we had moved to the permanent Garrison near Belize City and had a break from the rigours of patrolling. It was like being back in civilisation: real food, regular showers, proper beds, and new people. Vivienne was a teacher in the garrison primary school.

She exuded passion and every young buck in the Officers' Mess had courted her favours but she had apparently spurned them all. I had heard of her beauty long before we met and I resolved myself to resist, not wanting to be labelled in the same way as my slavering colleagues.

But, when you have been living in the jungle for several months, a freshly washed woman with a fulsome bosom and a generous smile is more than any man can resist.

We first met in the Mess garden. I had just finished training with my soldiers and was soaked in sweat and covered in dirt. I was trying to remove my boots when Vivienne suddenly eclipsed my whole world.

The garden was full of garrison staff officers who were soft from easy living. Most of them had never ventured into the jungle. They had primacy of position but I was Odin's protégé and Viv held a smile for me that was conspiratorial and promising. I said nothing but held her gaze while she looked at me over the rim

46

of her glass.

"You're not supposed to bring weapons into the mess." One of the captains, a dandy, glared at me. He was right of course but I cared little and just held the rifle out of sight between my legs.

"Beer, please, Johno." I winked at the barman. He hid a smile and slid a bottle of Budweiser over the bar to me.

"Welcome back, sir."

I lifted the bottle and took long pulls at it, savouring the cool, refreshing liquid. It was finished with satisfying ease. Johno slid another bottle across the bar.

"Your manners are appalling, Mr Hanson." The Captain surpassed even his own pomposity but he was right and my calculated boorishness was close to impertinence.

"I am sorry, sir," my gentle tone did little to mask my arrogance, "but I was thirsty."

I picked up my rifle and the second beer and made to leave.

"Excuse me, gentlemen, I must attend to my soldiers." The dandies stirred in their seats, angry but impotent. I ignored them and turned to the dark haired lady who would soon be my lover.

"Ma'am." I nodded at her as I past. Vivienne smiled slightly.

Stuck in the middle of Central America, the Officers' Mess was the social focus and parties were common. At one such affair I sat alone drinking bottled American lager. Actually, I was trying not to stare at Vivienne who was dressed in a low cut frock that did little to hide her tanned cleavage. Presumably, it was not meant to.

"Hey, Hanson, why are you hiding in the corner?" Vivienne had sought me out. I smiled at her, flattered that she should want to leave the revelry in order to speak to me. I was also amused by her use of my surname; it inferred an intimacy that I found appealing.

"Just enjoying some civilisation, for once."

"Are you in more tolerable mood?" she asked with a mocking smile. The scent of her made me dizzy.

"For you I am, my lady." I held her gaze again and swam in the delicious torment of her dark eyes.

"Don't you want to join the party?" she asked, settling onto a bar stool beside me.

"I'm fine. I don't really have much in common with these people." I waved a hand vaguely in the direction of the party.

"No, it gets a bit tedious after a while." We shared a conspiratorial smile.

"Don't you get lonely out here?" I asked.

Vivienne shrugged gently and I tried not to stare at the reverberations.

"Not really, I'm not short of company."

"You certainly seem to be the centre of attention."

Viv looked rather wistful.

"To be honest, I get rather tired of being hit on. You guys get all horny out here and seem to think that any available woman is fair totty. But I came here to teach children, not provide lonely soldiers with casual distraction." I was pleased that she had taken me into her confidence, although I was rather disappointed that she seemed to have become the sort of friend that you cannot shag.

Viv went to join the party and I resumed my solitary beer drinking. Occasionally, she came and made me dance and I enjoyed the movement of her body under the thin dress but I suppressed the urge to seduce her. As the evening waned and the slow music started, I watched Viv deftly avoid the clutching hands of drunken officers eager for sympathetic company. She arrived next to me and gently laid a hand on my thigh.

She smiled and I thought the sun had risen early.

The trouble with girls is that you never know what they are thinking. Vivienne was especially full of female contradictions. She had clearly given me a brush off but then flirted with me all evening. Perhaps she was just lonely and wanted some male company without having sex. That seemed like a girly way to behave, although a man can never be sure. I decided that the best thing to do was to do nothing and let her lead me where she wanted.

"Walk me to my room?" she asked eventually in a voice that offered as much warning as invitation.

"I'd be delighted."

"How charming you are, Billy," she said and I silently thanked my humble Grandfather for his noble legacy.

When we were outside her room Vivienne embraced me gently but firmly.

"I quite like you, Billy Hanson." She was warm and sensuous and her bosom was heavy against my chest. As I looked down at her I could see the swell of her cleavage, dark and inviting. I wanted her so badly it hurt.

I was gently perspiring in the humid night and Vivienne reached a hand to my temple and wiped it gently. This lady had considerable natural charms and, being a permanent resident in the garrison, she also had an air-conditioned room; truly, she could take me to heaven.

I smiled slowly and was moved to say something.

"Vivienne, you were the most beautiful woman there tonight."

"I know," she said with startling confidence, "but if you want to shag me it will take considerably more than some cheap flattery." She looked at me with a challenge in her eyes so I snogged her as I imagined

Errol Flynn would have down. I let her go and she slapped me, hard enough to hurt, but not hard enough to put me off.

"And don't try any more of those cheap tactics." I snogged her again, almost bursting with lust. She responded aggressively by rubbing her hips against me and crushing her tits into my chest, creasing my shirt. Then she pushed me away and closed the door.

"Bitch," I called after her gently and with a great deal of affection. She opened the door again and stood there naked, gently rubbing her left breast.

"Goodnight, Billy," she said and then she shut the door.

Seduction is like a business deal, each party bringing something the other wants, but at a price. Vivienne drove a hard bargain. She was a playful woman and led me along for a week, flirting with me outrageously in private but in public she was rather aloof, only treating me to a rare smile when no-one else could see.

Resources were limited in the Mess and so men and women shared a bathroom; a torment at the best of times but impossibly frustrating when Viv dropped her towel in front of me, smiled and went into the shower cubicle next to mine. She sang softly.

I was not sure how long I could endure this torment. I walked past her room at night knowing that she was in there, waiting. I wanted to burst in, take her wordlessly and consummate my lust. Perhaps that was what she wanted; to feel so desirable that she could incite a man into such wanton disregard for social mores that he would risk reputation and rejection in order to sate his need for her.

But I did not want to be a mouse to this cat. I was also concerned that I was misreading the situation, so I allowed my conservative nature to take the lead.

Instinctively, I knew that it would happen eventually.

It was worth the wait. It happened in the classroom where she taught. During lunch breaks I had been reading to her pupils. Even though their Fathers were all in the Army or RAF, the children seemed fascinated by my uniform. They would gather around my feet gazing up at me as I read the stories, Vivienne in the background, smiling.

One of the children, a small girl with blond hair in bunches, sat so close to me that she could rest her chin on my boot when my legs were crossed. She would sit looking up at me as I read stories of fierce bears in dark woods and damsels in distress and brave knights who came to rescue them.

"The end!" I said one day and closed the book with a snap as I had seen countless readers on Jackanory do as I, myself, had been growing up. The children jumped up, excited about the weekend but the little blonde girl stayed close to me and held my hand.

"Thank you for reading us such a nice story, Billy." She looked at me with unblinking eyes.

Then all the little people went and there was just Vivienne and I left in the classroom.

"They like you," she said quietly. Ironically, it seemed that it was the children's endorsement of me that had finally persuaded Vivienne that I was worthy of the Forbidden Fruit.

She smiled and began to drop the blinds over the windows. When we were stood in the semi darkness she undid the straps of her summer dress and let it fall to the floor. The contrast of her nakedness with the obscure paintings of butterflies and dinosaurs that adorned the walls made it an unusual place to have sex but it was Viv's environment, a place of her choosing, and it put her very much in control.

I was unsure of myself and hesitated, waiting for

permission to move. Eventually, she beckoned me with a smile and we made love on a table; a passionate coupling, made more so by the waiting. Afterwards, as we lay naked on the table, Vivienne turned to me and smiled.

"B plus for effort, Billy." She smiled once more and I was deeply moved: so moved that I did it again.

Our affair ran on for a while. She was demanding and in control, I was ardent and appreciative and forgot all my hypocrisy about resisting trouble with girls. It was nice to be with a woman, to have regular sex, to share comfort in austere surroundings but, really, we knew that this was not to be. We both had partners elsewhere, the name Vivienne Hanson just did not sound right, and most importantly, the Army Bitch was jealous. She sent me away to go play by myself.

6

The black robed priest beside me clutched his rosary with disconcerting fervour; as if he knew something I didn't.

"God be with you, my Son," he offered, making me feel worse.

"And with you, Father." I was unsure if that was the correct response. Still, I was not sure if his blessing was for future protection or passed misdemeanours.

Then the small plane suddenly jerked forward and began to taxi along the short runway. The sea sparkled ahead of us, looking remarkably close as we trundled towards it. Just as I thought I should ask the priest for absolution, the small plane shuddered into the air and we climbed slowly upwards. The priest exhaled and smiled, although he still hung onto the rosary.

As a result of our extended labours in the bush, the Commanding Officer granted all the jungle warfare instructors a week's additional leave.

Four of us flew in a small airplane to Ambergris Caye, an idyllic island in the shallows of the Caribbean that was apparently made slightly famous by the Madonna song *Last night I dreamt of San Pedro*. We stayed in a cheap, wooden hotel, drank beer in the starlight and walked barefoot through the sand all day. It was the sort of week that makes an adventure.

The island's population was a kaleidoscope: local folk who lived in harmony with their environment; small numbers of tourists who stayed in the expensive US run hotels or, like us, in cheap local establishments; and an assortment of eccentrics who, through design or misadventure, found themselves living on a tropical island like a bemused Robinson Crusoe.

"Fancy a drink, Old Boy?" One of the eccentrics barked at me in a posh accent as I was mooching along the beach with a hangover.

"Well, it's a little early for me, sir." There was no actual reason for me to call him sir but he looked like the sort of bloke that a very junior officer should address that way. He was certainly comfortable with it.

"Nonsense," he chided, "never *too* early." He pulled me by my elbow into a bar. The smiling barman already had two bottles waiting and so I sat sipping beer with a complete stranger of late middle age and upper class credentials. He never asked my name, why I was on the island or why I thought drinking beer with a stranger before breakfast was weird. Belize was like that.

We drank until the beer overcame my need for coffee and food and the stranger was pissed.

"Alcohol," he declared with a waving hand, "like death and nudity, makes us equal." Then he fell off his stool.

"Fuck!" He struggled to get up. Another middle class twit type of bloke emerged from nowhere and helped the old guy to his feet; perhaps he was the boyfriend.

"Mr Ambassador, we should go now," urged the aide casting me a pleading look.

"Not a word," I agreed[16] and they staggered out into the sun.

I enjoyed the theatre of the island. I sat on the veranda of my hotel, enjoying the cool of the evening, cold beer in hand and taking slow, satisfying sips from the bottle whilst watching brightly painted sail boats glide into the bay like shadows in a dream. Reggae music rose up from a nearby beach bar and I sat listening to the sound of merriment, feeling deeply

---

[16] Until now, of course.

contented.

It was a beautiful week made a little sad by the lack of a soul mate. I missed Emily a lot; her smile, her sense of fun and her cool skin close to mine. I was due to go home in a few weeks and the nearness of it made me miss her even more.

Rather than wallow, I decided to spend the week learning to SCUBA dive. I paid an American instructor to teach me, as the military training establishment was so slow. It was more expensive than I could afford but it was something that had excited me since I had been a boy watching Jacques Cousteau's pioneering television series *The Undersea World*. Children should be encouraged to nurture their dreams into adulthood, for not all children's dreams are childish.

There is no better place to learn how to dive than the warm, clear waters of Belize. The sea teems with life and vitality. Darting shoals of silver fish contrast with the brooding presence of reef sharks and the stately passage of manta rays. Belize was not crowded with tourists like many of the world's dive sites and diving there retained a strong sense of adventure.

As a complete novice, I was supposed to practice in the shallow water on the beach but Carl, my instructor, was already busy teaching an American girl and I just joined in with her. He needed the cash and I only had a week to learn so my first dive experience was at twenty metres in the open sea. I was both nervous and excited.

Carl introduced me to the girl who was to be my dive partner.

"Hi, how're you doing?" she asked in that over-enthusiastic American way. She also gave me an appraising look and I was dismayed for I did not want any trouble with girls. Still, as we shook hands, I noticed her wedding ring and I relaxed.

"Billy, Billy Hanson."

"Doris," she said giving me a mock grimace. "My grandparents were East European immigrants and were obsessed with American culture, particularly Doris Day." I was charmed by her openness. I was also reassured that Doris Hanson was such an incongruous name as to preclude any association between ourselves: that and her being married.

Doris was quite good fun. Shared adventure naturally brought us together and I felt comfortable in the platonic nature of our relationship. She told me about her family and job and, from the way that she talked, I presumed that she was on a trip with girlfriends, apart from her husband.

In a mature way, she was rather attractive but she had a sense of sadness about her that I found disquieting. I tried not worry about that, this was a transient relationship and, despite mutual interest, we were not destined for each other's Christmas card lists.

At the end of the week we had to do a night dive and as we were waiting for the boat to pick us up, she started to tell me of her frustration with marriage.

"We married at nineteen. I have never slept with anyone other than my husband." She looked at me expecting a reaction. I nodded. "Duncan does not worry about it," she continued, "but I feel as if I have missed out on something. We get on great," she added. "He's very attentive in bed, I just want to know what it's like with some-one else."

Doris looked at me again.

"I bet you've had lots of women, Billy."

I shifted, not comfortable being her confidant about marital discord.

"Well, yes, but casual sex is not always that great." I was not sure what I was trying to say. Probably I was trying to reveal some of the loneliness I often felt after the more anonymous bouts of sex that had punctuated my life.

Whatever I meant to say was unconvincing because Doris just carried on.

"I often feel that I should have an affair, just so that I can say to myself that I had done it."

I sensed her need to discus this although I was unsure where to tread.

"But what if you did it and liked the other guy better? Even if you could just move on, you'd have to live with the sense of betrayal forever?"

I was speaking from the heart, from past experience and present attempts to avert a seduction.

"I suppose so," Doris said, "but if I don't I fear that my frustration will drive us apart."

Carl, arriving with the boat, saved me. He had the air of a man not concerned with the stresses of modern living. He did, however, sense something between Doris and me for he withdrew from his normal verbosity and quietly checked the dive gear in the stern.

We set off towards the reef, the small powerboat rising and plunging more than normal due to the offshore breeze raising the crests of the waves. It was getting dark but the air was still warm. Doris' nervousness made her talkative and rather annoying, particularly as my own anticipation rendered me quiet and reserved.

When we stopped Carl interrupted our reflections.

"Hey, Billy. Can you go in first? I need to help Doris into the water." I felt a ridiculous sense of pride.

I sat on the gunwale to steady my breathing and then flicked backwards over the side of the boat. In the dark, the initial splash in to the water was very disorienting and I sank slowly upside down. I turned turtle naturally and hovered in the black water with steady strokes of legs and arms.

I switched on my torch and gasped as it lit the

57

multicoloured splendour of the reef. Lobsters and crabs were held captive in the shaft of torchlight and the fronds of coral had an ethereal tinge of colour to them. Fish swam in their multitudes, even more than during the day, and regal manta rays glided around me like massive black birds.

I hung motionless in the water, enjoying the absolute seclusion of the darkness. I watched like a voyeur as the circle of torch light picked out snapshots of action on the reef: octopus peered out from dark caves; conger eels waved slowly in the gentle current; and a green turtle swam slowly by. I bit the hard rubber of my regulator as I tried to calm my breathing.

I was startled by Doris' entry into the water. She panicked at the unfamiliarity of her surroundings and I could see her eyes, large with excitement, through her mask. She saw my torch beam and swam over to me, reaching out for support so that the warm skin of her legs rubbed against me.

Carl splashed into our world and we began our tour of the reef. I had agreed to swim at the rear while Carl led, leaving Doris in the comforting middle position. As we swam, Doris' naked legs moved rhythmically in front of me and my torch beam carved a weirdly erotic view of her tight bum in the darkness.

As we explored the wild animation that unfolded below us, I checked my pressure gauge regularly, conscious that I was breathing more urgently than normal. I tried to contain it but I had not been so excited since I was a boy waiting for Santa and that made my breathing increase: that and Doris' bum cheeks.

Eventually, Carl stopped to check air gauges. Mine was low, beyond normal safety practice. I was concerned that my heavy breathing was prematurely curtailing the dive but Doris was visibly relieved that it was over. Her eyes poured gratitude through her mask and we rose slowly up to the surface.

On the way back to shore the sea was quite rough so we had to sit together in the centre of the small boat to give it some ballast. It was also cold but, even so, I thought Doris sat unnecessarily close to me. She held onto my leg and the beast of my libido reared its ugly head. I began to understand the meaning of her story about having an affair but determined myself to resist. I was going home soon.

The boat dropped us off at the dock near Doris' hotel and we walked along the jetty to the beach house. Doris was all energy and excitement.

"That was so exciting. Thank you for swimming at the rear, Billy, you were so brave." As well as my libido, Doris was stroking my ego and I was succumbing like an addict in rehab.

"No worries, it was fun."

"You are so cool," said Doris with a big smile.

We stopped at an outside shower. I just wore shorts and rinsed off quickly but Doris was wearing a light neoprene jacket that contained her curves in an impatient embrace. She rinsed her thick hair like a vision from a shampoo advert whilst smiling at me with excitement. I tried to not to stare but the trouble with girls is that you cannot resist them.

"Billy," she called gently and slowly pulled the zip on her jacket. She wore nothing underneath and her breasts tumbled into view, forcing the issue. I reached out to feel her softness and warmth and she wound around me in near tortured ecstasy. We had incredible, explosive sex, made more passionate by the exhilaration of the dive.

In the doldrums after our passion, I became very uncertain. I had never been involved in an adulterous affair but the real cause of my uncertainty was the realisation that I had fallen for the enigmatic and seemingly naive Doris. She, however, was elated and continued on the upward spiral started by the dive.

"Wow, that was fantastic!" Whether she meant shagging me specifically or simply sex with another man was unclear. We collected out kit and walked along the beach.

Then we met her husband.

"Hi, Darling!" Doris draped her arms around the man's neck and smiled at me. "This is Duncan." She had not re-fastened her jacket and the implications were obvious. I wondered if I would have to fight with Duncan although I was feeling so guilty I probably would have just let him hit me.

"Good to meet you," he said. "Thank you for looking after my lady, she's very special to me."

I was not sure if his gratitude was laced with innuendo or challenge. I shook hands with reticence because the evidence of his wife's betrayal was still wet on my hand.

"Not at all. It was fun."

He nodded.

"I can imagine."

They walked off together and left me alone on the beach feeling very confused: why did I get into so much trouble with girls?

Part 2 – The Fall from Grace

"I get slandered, libel, I hear words I never heard in the Bible..." Keep the Customer Satisfied – Simon and Garfunkel 1969.

7

I grew up in a chaste working class environment in Yorkshire where fidelity was a symbol of male honour. Quite why trouble with girls was so inevitable for me, was therefore unclear.

"We mustn't, Billy," said my teenage sweetheart every time I tried to get her knickers off.

"Why not?"

"The Bible says not."

"The Bible also says that Noah got two of every creature in the Ark; including mosquitoes."

"Don't mock my faith, Billy."

I endured the relationship for two years but, in truth, I knew that it was not manly resolve that kept me out of trouble so much as a lack of temptation. It was not until I went to university that I discovered the truth.

"Hi, Billy, buy me a drink?" Melanie had the relaxed confidence of all the middle-class folk from the South. Initially, I felt uncomfortable with the sophisticated university women. They seemed so grown up and cosmopolitan, most of them having spent a gap year somewhere exotic. I went straight from school to university.

Melanie approached me early in the first term but I felt unthreatened because we were friends. I grew up believing that there were girlfriends you could shag and friends who were girls who you could not shag.

"How are you settling in?" I asked, mainly because I was not.

"Fine." Melanie looked at me over the rim of her wine glass. "It's really cool being independent, having friends around whenever you like."

"Sure."

"I'm moving, actually. I'm getting a single room."

"That's nice."

"In fact," said Melanie lowering her voice, "I could make good use of your strong body this evening." She placed her elegant fingers on my thigh and smiled.

I relaxed then because being a young Northern chap, I assumed that the good lady needed a hand to move her boxes and furniture.

"Should I get a couple of the rugby lads to help?" Melanie hurried off.

My next disaster occurred whilst playing squash. Annie was also from the Home Counties and she was much better at squash but my inability did little to dampen her ardour and she manipulated me around the court, causing me to bump into her.

After a particularly clever shot I flattened her against the sidewall and was too knackered to move. I leant against her cool, smooth skin for a second, panting and dripping sweat on her.

"I'm sorry."

"No problem, Billy. You can press me up against the wall anytime."

I looked at her uncertainly.

"It's your serve."

It was inevitable that eventually a more persistent girl would break through my idiocy and that is how I first got together with Emily Fisher.

She was tall and sweet and the most fancied girl in the university. Quite why she should favour me was a complete mystery: but she did and I responded with customary clumsiness.

"Why are you sat here on your own?" she asked me one evening.

"I'm having a beer," I replied cautiously wondering why she had come to talk to me specifically. She looked at the empty barstool next to me.

"Might I join you?" I was about to say that my drinking buddy was sat there but Emily's lithesome figure promised the sort of delights that men fight each other for and some deep instinct held my tongue. I nodded dumbly and Emily sat down, her hair shrouding her face giving her an innocently horny look.

"I'm Emily." Her dainty fingers burned like a firebrand.

"Billy," I said, conscious that my paw was very sweaty, "Billy Hanson."

"Billy?" Emily rolled her tongue around my name, "that's a fun name."

I nodded again.

"More fun than William." Emily giggled.

Dan Harley, my roommate, returned from the bar but walked away discreetly. Emily stayed to chat and slowly I relaxed. She was uncomplicated and unchallenging and she seemed to accept me for the clumsy Northern oaf that I was.

When the bar closed Emily led me by the hand to the bike racks. I was a little hesitant.

"What's the matter, Billy?" she asked, large eyes beseeching. "Don't you want to come home with me?"

"Well, I never had a bike when I was a kid. I'm not sure I can keep up with you."

Emily smiled.

"Perhaps you need some encouragement." She removed her knickers and handed them to me. To Emily this was an act of deliberate eroticism, designed to celebrate her independence and wild spirit but I had to resist the urge to put them on my head. Emily wore a short summer dress and I pedalled like a steam train in pursuit of the soft white peach of her bum.

We got to her house panting and sweating through exertion or anticipation. Emily threw her bike down in the garden and pulled me inside by the hand. She pushed me against the kitchen wall and kissed me deeply, a hand in my hair and a leg wrapped around my own.

I lifted her easily and she wound both legs around my waist and pressed her breasts against me.

"Let me take my shirt off."

Emily dropped to the floor and took half a step back, holding my gaze.

"I'm sorry, I've creased it." She smoothed her hands over my chest and then ripped the shirt off.

Her breathing steadied. Slowly, she raised the hem of her dress above her head and dropped it to the floor. She stood naked before me and reached for my hands.

"Take me, Billy," she asked or demanded. I lifted her on to the table and we built a slow rhythm. "Faster, Billy! Do me harder!" The table started to rock violently so I turned her over and took her from behind. She clung on to the table for a while before breaking away from me. Suddenly, she looked very serious. She pushed me down onto a chair and rode me like a horse.

In the morning we went for coffee and croissants. Emily was sweet and mild, the intensity of the night belonging to a very different girl. We actually held hands.

"Where are you from?" asked Emily as she spread jam on my croissant. She wore a permanent smile.

"Yorkshire," I replied with a mouth full of crumbs, "you?"

"Kent," she said in an equally crumbly manner and we both giggled, looking around the café to see who was watching.

Nobody was, of course, the intimacy we had recently shared was exactly that and there was a sense of closeness between us that I had never experienced before.

"What are you studying?" asked Emily.

"Politics, you?"

"Biology," she said with a smutty giggle and as we

got to know each other it did not occur to either of us that such introductions were a little late in our relationship.

Emily and I got on well and I would have preferred to cruise along with her for the rest of my university career but I could never resist the temptation that was so readily offered to me. I joined in enthusiastically because it seemed like the done thing rather than a desire for any particular girl. Besides, when you're nineteen and full of hormones, you tend not to ask too many questions.

One girl even chose me to be her first lover. Carla and I had been friends for some time before it happened but I came to realize that you could shag your friends, as long as you asked nicely. She was gorgeous: shiny black hair, big girly lumps, and a dark-skinned, smouldering sensuality that she had not yet learned how to harness. Her Asian sophistication was in stark contrast to my blundering Yorkshire ways.

I had given up hope of exploring her pants but discovered that she was as intellectually stimulating as she was physically alluring: I had made friends with a girl.

I saw her while walking my dog that had come to stay whilst my parents were on holiday. He was a big, affectionate, old mutt.

"Nice doggie," Carla said. "What's his name?"

"Deefor."

"Deefor?"

"D for dog. I got him when I was a kid." Carla rubbed Deefor's ears.

"Is he friendly?"

"He's very friendly," I replied trying to restrain him from jumping up at her, "but he's also a bit rough and quite dirty."

Carla smiled.

"That's just how I like my boys, Billy."

She invited me round for supper and when I got there her flatmates were out. I had taken with me a bottle of cheap Lambrusco but Carla had two bottles of Claret breathing on the table. She did not drink much but I was nervous and drank most of the three bottles. I could not drive home.

"Stay here?" Carla suggested with an easy smile and I naively assumed I would sleep on the sofa. I went to get Deefor from my car and when I returned I could not find Carla in the lounge. Deefor found her, lying naked and beautiful on her bed, all the promise of India yet to be explored. I finally realised that I had been seduced. I was enthusiastic to respond but my panting dog spoilt the magic of the moment.

Carla clutched the sheet but looked even more naked.

"I wasn't expecting the dog to come in."

"Love me, love my dog." Obviously, I didn't mean that as it sounded. "Out!" I nudged Deefor with my foot and for once he obeyed me. I looked at her. She looked at me and slowly lowered the sheet.

It was a gentle, sympathetic coupling, which grew into a satisfying crescendo that matched the Vivaldi opera that Carla insisted on playing.

I asked her later why she chose me for the task.

"It was time for me to have sex," she said, "and I thought you might do it well."

At first, I was flattered but, on reflection, I felt like a hired hand. A more grown up man would have seen the tenderness of her behaviour and, in fact, our affair lasted for some time.

"Billy," she once said to me, "you're an easy man to fall in love with but you're impossible to love."

Having been initiated into easy promiscuity, I expected all relationships to be relaxed, but I slowly realized that the professed sexual independence of most undergraduate girls was a charade. This lead to constant friction and I hid behind a façade of drunken caddishness. My friends were unable to reconcile the two sides of Billy Hanson.

"You're incorrigible," a jilted girl once told me.

"Thank you," I replied cheerfully because I did not know what she meant.

Even the blokes seemed uncomfortable.

"Why do you shag so many girls, Billy?" One of the rugby team asked me after a lot of beer but I was not sure if his question was a reflection of admiration or condemnation. I shrugged.

"Because I can?"

But what I really wanted was a girlfriend; that one person that popular myth leads us to believe is waiting for us somewhere. That instinctive desire to meet the future Mrs Hanson was reinforced by childhood experience.

My paternal grandfather passed away when I was on the verge of adolescence and especially impressionable. A wizened great uncle cornered me with whisky soaked breath at the wake.

"Naw then, Billy lad," he said in heavy Yorkshire tones, "has tha got a girlfriend yet?"

"No, Uncle, I'm only twelve." This was not strictly true but I sensed that holding hands with Michelle Brown in the playground did not really count.

"Well, tha needs get a girl and start. You are the last Hanson."

"But girls are so difficult, Uncle." He looked at me with sympathy.

"Aye, lad, worse than driving a car. Basic principles are simple enough but negotiating the road is complicated. And't more beautiful the car is, the more difficult it is to drive."

Perhaps my trouble with girls was caused by single-sex schooling. I had floundered in the state education system, lacking the personal drive to succeed, so my parents made hard sacrifices to pay for private schooling. I excelled at sport and academics but learned little about girls other than that they had long hair, lumps in their jumpers and did not know anything about rugby.

My first real encounter with a girl was in sixth form Economics. Emma Briggs was a statuesque blonde girl and there were times in later life when I would have crawled across a field of broken glass just to sit next to her, but at school she was a different entity.

She climbed, naked and uninvited, into bed with me at a drunken teenage sleepover party. She said nothing but slid her soft tongue into my mouth. It was a wonderful sensation, enhanced by the feel of her womanly breasts pressed against me.

I was terrified.

"What are you doing?"

Emma was surprised at my reaction.

"I just wanted to get into bed with you."

"Well, it's only a single, there's not enough room for two."

I woke later to find Emma on her hands and knees, being taken from behind by a lad from the upper sixth. He bulled her with masterful strokes that I feared I would never be able to emulate. Her elegant rear rose gratefully to receive his attentions and her slender thighs flexed like a thoroughbred with each manly thrust, her fulsome bosom swinging daringly in the half-light. I shall be forever haunted by the memory of her pretty young face tormented with ecstasy as she was rhythmically shoved into the pillow.

But I had found women difficult as a young child so perhaps the boys' grammar school that I eventually attended was a respite from, rather than the cause of, my trouble with girls. I took the suburban security of my early childhood for granted. Our fathers were all at work and for some reason I was driven to mischief to express my frustration at matriarchal dominance.

The lady next door to us was a paragon of working class values and she hung her white laundry out on the washing line with depressing regularity. Our compost heap was right next to the garden fence.

"Billy!" scolded my mother one day with uncharacteristic vehemence, "why are you throwing tea bags at Aunty Margaret's washing?" I looked about me for inspiration or somewhere to hide but there was neither and I was dragged around to apologise. It was temporarily humiliating but there was little actual retribution. In fact, both women seemed rather amused.

My Grandmothers provided further confusion. One sought to affect my behaviour with sweets and trinkets whilst the other chastised and berated me for my mischief. I was misled into believing that, at least where women are concerned, the main issue in life is not right or wrong but influence.

I also had trouble at my primary school. Our class once ran a puppet production of *Winnie the Pooh*. I had the part of *Tigger* and my Mom made the most wonderful glove puppet out of an old sock and acrylic fur. It was orange with brown stripes and button-eyes and a red tongue. It was easily the best puppet in the class. At least it looked like a puppet, rather than a sock.

"Wow, Billy, look at your Tigger, it's brilliant!" said Charlie Crest who was in the football team and praise from him was better than sweets.

"I wish my Mom made me a puppet," whined Graham Adams who was Top-of-the-Class and I smiled, reflecting in unfamiliar adoration.

71

It was short lived. The middle-aged dragon-teacher cruelly smashed my expectation of praise.

"What have you learned by getting your mother to make it for you?" She was unnecessarily vehement, presumably because I had stolen the spotlight from her, and I replied with the unabashed malevolence that only a seven year old can muster.

"I learned that I don't come to school to sew."

8

Snow flurried about us and the cheer of dawn's first light remained a vague hope out to the East. I stood shivering with the other cadets waiting for someone to take us for a run.

I started jogging loosely.

"Come on, let's go."

"Do you think we should?" asked one of the other cadets.

"Well, I don't think we should stay here any longer." I ran ahead. There was uncertainty in the group and they remained huddled together in the dark.

"Sod this, I'm going with the big fellah." One of the girls broke out of the group and ran after me. The others followed and I led them slowly along the road, not wanting people to strain cold muscles or slip on patches of ice.

It was early November and a snowstorm was raging in the Yorkshire Moors. We had been ordered to wear only military issue shorts and T-shirts and we were ill equipped for the conditions so we ran gently for twenty minutes before I led the group back to camp. The spotty second lieutenant who was supposed to conduct the training turned up as we were running back to the accommodation block.

"Where the fuck have you lot been?" he yelled. He stank of booze, clearly having just emerged from his scratcher[19]. "Who told you to set off without me?"

"No-one did but we were freezing and you were late." I was fairly calm, thinking this was simply a case of different perspectives.

"You have acted out with the sphere of your

---

[19] Bed.

responsibility," he said. I considered twatting him.

"Fuck off, you were late!"

"I am going to report you for insubordination."

"Don't be a wanker." I ran inside. The others followed.

My first weekend with the University Officer Training Corps (OTC) was not going well. There were better things I could do with my time but I was sponsored at university through an army bursary and had to attend OTC as part of that commitment. At nineteen, I had a prestigious long-term career planned out. It had seemed laudable at school but it was an anathema to the supposed free spirit of most undergrads and this added to my social isolation.

The experience got worse during drill lessons.

"Get your fucking act together, don't you know how to march properly?" a diminutive sergeant major yelled in my ear with such angst you might have thought I had killed his dog.

"No, I don't."

"Don't what?" I was not sure if he was stupid or I was missing something

"Don't know how to march." Actually, I was missing something.

"Don't know how to march, sir," he reprimanded with accompanying spittle.

I had expected army people to have stature but the only impressive thing about this bloke was his moustache, which made him look like a cross between Freddie Mercury and a walrus. I joined the OTC not long after the Falklands War and the sense of machismo was so strong you could almost smell it. Masculinity was measured by the shortness of hair and the thickness of a moustache. In any other environment, army guys would have looked like misfits from The

Village People.[17]

The following weekend, I rose at dawn with an elephant sized hangover and woke my roommate by audible cursing about going to OTC.

"Don't go then."

"What do you mean?" I was incredulous, how could I simply not go.

"If going to OTC is so bad, then don't go," he said with parental condescension. I was tormented by indecision: not going to OTC was not simply "not going", it was fundamentally questioning everything that I had been told to believe as I was growing up.

I got back into bed with the Sword of Damocles swinging above my head and waited for the disciplinary summons. Eventually, the grown ups came to get me and I resigned from the army with enthusiasm. I had decided something for myself and that simple act of "not going" liberated me from my upbringing.

But liberated people are often the authors of their own downfall and I began to get into all sorts of trouble; missing lectures, drinking heavily and dancing with Eve and all her friends. I lived in the present, not realising that Peter Pan is a parody not a celebration of male youth.

My roommate did not help. Dan Harley was the most unlikely friend for a man like me. He had long hair and wore jeans whereas I had short hair and wore a tie. We were thrust together by the alphabetical process of the university accommodation office and initially we treated each other with mutual distrust, like two dogs sniffing bums.

---

[17] A 1970's pop group whose trademark was camp costumes and handlebar moustaches.

"What do you suppose we do now?" I asked him after we had both unpacked. I thought we might go the library or check out the gym.

"Let's go for a beer," he said. So we sat leaning against the bar getting the measure of each other.

"I saw your rugby boots as you were unpacking. What position are you?"

"Backrow. You?"

"I'm a hooker." Dan finished his beer in one impressive gulp. We became synonymous and our youthful hedonism was almost my undoing.

In the final year of University, I realised that I had not done any studying. That was not unusual, but the manner of my salvation was very disconcerting. One of my tutors had been replaced by an academic that I did not know and I rang her at home for help with an essay that contributed to the final marking of my degree.

"Hello, Dr Foster."

"Dr Foster, my name is Billy Hanson, I was a student under Dr Claridge." I paused, not sure how to develop the conversation.

"Hello Mr Hanson," replied the disarmingly sweet voice, "how can I help?"

"I was hoping for some academic advice."

"Sure, in what way?"

"Well, I've got badly behind with my essays and I need some focussed reading material."

"Okay, I'll be in college all day tomorrow, why don't you call in during the afternoon?"

The following afternoon I hovered like a naughty schoolboy outside her office. I knocked, expecting to meet an austere and dusty academic.

"Come in." I stepped into a cosy little office and stopped in surprise. Dr Foster was beautiful, tall and shapely with a warm smile and engaging eyes.

"I'm Billy Hanson," I said hesitantly.

"Hello," she replied extending a hand, "please take a seat." She gestured to an armchair. I sat, nervously waiting for the inevitable moment when I would have to justify myself and persuade her to help.

"How's it going, then?" Dr Foster immediately corrected herself. "Silly question, since you're here." She smiled at me again and I relaxed a little.

"What is it you're working on then?" Dr Foster sat in the armchair opposite me and curled a leg under her self as if she was watching a Sunday afternoon movie. She was not actually much older than me but she moved and spoke with an assuredness that was both engaging and disarming.

"I am doing an essay on the impact of industrialisation on Japanese culture and politics in the 18th century." I delivered my rehearsed line with as much authority as I could. The doctor mused for a while and then replied gently.

"That might be a little difficult," she said. "Industrialisation in Japan didn't really take effect until later in the 19th century. When is the essay due?" I shifted uneasily.

"Yesterday." Dr Foster hid a smile behind her coffee. She nodded at her mug.

"Excuse me, Mr Hanson, I've not offered you coffee." She gave me a quizzical look and raised her mug.

"Yes, please," I said relieved that she hadn't laughed out loud.

"Milk? Sugar?"

"No thank you, just black." She looked at me again with that gentle challenge.

"This coffee is very strong, Mr Hanson."

"So am I, Dr Foster."

I faltered immediately, worried that I had now alienated her, but her face broadened into a warm smile.

"I'm sure you are, Mr Hanson," she said, passing me the coffee as she sat down again. From then on the emphasis of our relationship seemed to change subtly, although the academic doctor remained in the ascendant.

"So what has so distracted you from academic study?" It was an odd thing to ask since I doubted that she really wanted to know. I wanted to tell her, to tell someone, that I had lost myself and become a drunken seducer but I sensed she knew that already.

"I'm captain of rugby."

Dr Foster nodded slowly, as if she understood.

"What's the basis of this essay, then, what's your underlying perspective?" Her change of direction caught me offside.

"I thought I'd focus on the capitalistic influence from the West and the corresponding effect on the ancient systems of civic power..." my words trailed off but Dr Foster was sympathetic enough not to dig further, realising how shallow my underlying perspective actually was.

"Right," she said slowly. "I would need to have a look at some texts and see what I have available." Then she held my gaze for a long while as if she was considering me directly. "In order to give you any meaningful direction at this late stage," she said with carefully measured words, "I would have to help you more than I technically should. I hope you understand the implications of that."

"Yes, of course," I replied rather taken aback that she was so willing to help. At that moment another tutor knocked on Dr Foster's door and stuck his head in to the office.

"Hi, Alice I was wondering if you were free for lunch tomorrow." His demeanour was artificially casual; like a man trying to arrange a date.

"Probably," replied Dr Foster, "can I get back to you?" She looked towards me.

"Oh, I am sorry," gushed the interloper a little too vehemently, "I didn't realise you were busy." Dr Foster smiled at him.

"We were discussing some work," she said and the other tutor withdrew. I was surprised but encouraged that she had not simply dismissed me to the other tutor as a struggling student.

Dr Foster looked directly at me again.

"I'll do a little research and photocopy some material that would be useful to you. Why don't you give me a call at home later this evening?" My interview was clearly over so I stood up to leave.

"Thank you Dr Foster," I said quietly and she smiled at me as I left her office. I closed the door behind me and walked slowly away, entirely bemused as to what had happened. Clearly I was grateful for some help but I was also full of uncertainty about what to expect next.

I called Dr foster early in the evening hoping to be told that she had a small pile of academic material that I could work on through the night.

"Mr Hanson, hello. I found some papers that should help you. I had to bring them home with me. Do you have a car?" She gave me her address with instructions to call round about eight o'clock.

"Have you eaten yet?" she added conversationally.

"No."

"Good, I'm making pasta."

A woman making supper for a bloke seemed natural enough but Dr Foster was a tutor and she surely would not want any personal involvement with a wayward student. But recent experience and instinct said otherwise.

My trepidation grew more pronounced when she opened the door. She wore tight jeans, a loose shirt and a very generous smile. She led me into her kitchen that was new and functional and stylish.

"Did you find the house alright?" she asked whilst peering into a pan of something that smelled delicious.

"Yes, straight away," I replied although in truth I had been driving around for twenty minutes nervously trying to find it.

I offered the wine.

"Merlot!" exclaimed Dr Foster, "thank you, it goes well with pasta. Is it a favourite of yours?"

"One of many," I replied, "I think it goes go well with pasta as well. It's fairly light." She looked at me seriously.

"Do you know much about wine?" I was about to bluff her but thought better of it; I had learned that lesson from Carla.

"Not really, I rang my Dad." Dr Foster smiled slowly.

"Your honesty is refreshing."

She served up two dishes of pasta and glugged the wine into two large glasses. We went through to her lounge where we ate whilst sat on the big comfy sofa. At some point in the meal she became Alice and our legs began to touch.

"More wine?" she asked me after the food was eaten. I looked at my glass with surprise not having noticed that it was nearly empty.

"Well, I have to drive home."

"Oh, yes," replied Alice uncertainly. "What 's your car then?"

"Austin Maxi," I said a little defensively. Alice nodded gently.

"I'd have thought you'd be more a Triumph Spitfire kind of guy," she mused with her gentle challenge.

"It's okay," I replied, "I can squeeze half the rugby team in it."

"That sounds like fun."

"It's certainly useful," I parried, "I used to drive my Mother's Mini Metro." That was a bit lame but I was struggling to keep up with her teasing.

"I used to have one of those. I suppose it was less useful, not being so big."

"Big enough. I had sex in it once." Alice's subtlety was beyond me and I instinctively reverted to schoolboy smut.

She seemed to drift off into a private reverie.

"I once had sex on the bonnet of mine," she breathed.

"Weren't you cold?" Alice smiled at me with sweet triumph.

"No, the engine was warm underneath me, which was nice because it was raining at the time."

I gulped like a cartoon character.

"Didn't you dent the bonnet?"

"No, Honey," she said with a sweetness that would have driven Odysseus mad with lust, "but I did scratch the paint with my heels."

She rose like the Queen of Sheba from her throne and filled my glass with wine.

"I have to drive." My protest had much less conviction. Alice took my glass in her elegant fingers and set it aside on the table. Then she knelt across the sofa, placed a soft hand on the back of my neck and pulled me forward. She kissed me with a soft determination that left me breathless.

"Don't worry about that," she whispered.

I left in the morning in a state of confusion. I was exhilarated for we had enjoyed good sex (at least I had) but I was also concerned. My naïve logic suggested it was okay for me to have a crush on her because she was a tutor but I assumed that she was not supposed to have a relationship with a student.

I did not tell anyone of the affair, it was simply assumed.

"That'll be twenty quid, please," said Stig Mason to another member of the rugby team. Olly Duell handed over the cash.

"Christ, Billy, is there no woman you haven't biffed?" I felt like Spartacus, the sporting amenity of the ruling caste. I slept with Dr Foster because I did not know how to avoid the situation; at least that's how I excused myself. The Tree of Knowledge bears such bitter fruit.

9

"Billy, I want you to start knocking this interior wall down so we can put in an extra door frame." John, one the builders I was working for, was casual with his instructions. I lifted the sledgehammer.

"How far back do you want me to take it?" John sighed.

"Don't worry about it, Billy, start at this end of the wall and work inwards. I'll be back before you get very far." He shook his head a little and went off to do something else. "College kids," I heard him muttering. I did not work with him often so he had not seen me with a hammer or shovel. To him I was just a college kid who spent all day in the library.

I swung the sledgehammer. There was a satisfying thump as it hit the wall but there no discernible impact. I swung again into the same place and was rewarded with crumbling masonry and a dislodged brick. I enjoyed this type of work and I swung the big mallet as if it was Thor's battle hammer.

"Billy, why the fuck are you sat on your arse? Why aren't you knocking the wall down?" yelled John when he came back half an hour later.

"I did! And after I'd cleaned up there was nothing else to do." John glowered his dislike of me.

"Well where's the hole in the wall that you're supposed to be making?" he growled, looking at the external building wall.

"It was here," I replied indicating the line of bricks in the floor where the internal wall had stood.

"But you've knocked the whole fucking wall down," he gasped. I realised then that I had perhaps got a bit carried away with the hammer.

"Well, you said keep going until you told me to stop."

"Aye, Billy, I did," John said sadly, as if the wall had been important to him personally, "but did you not think that since we're supposed to be fitting a doorway, you should have left enough wall to hold the door?" He was right, I suppose, but he could have been more specific and less demeaning.

"Well, I hit it a couple of times and it sort of crumbled."

"Crumbled?"

"Yes, like Jericho."

"Jericho?"

"Yes, Jericho. In the Bible, Joshua led his followers around the city blowing their trumpets and the walls came tumbling down." John's smile reduced from a bemused grin into a frustrated grimace.

"Billy," he said with forced patience like an irate father, "shut the fuck up, go back to the yard and get four pallets of bricks and some cement." He gave me the keys to the pick-up and I left quickly.

"Fucking Jericho," I heard him mutter.

Initially it had been a relief to leave university to work as a builder's labourer back in my Northern homeland and the male exclusivity that had been the Eden of my youth. I even managed to conduct a near normal relationship with Emily Fisher and for a short time it appeared that I too would lead a comfortable, innocent life.

I had worked for a building firm during the university holidays and it was easy to move back into it. I focused on playing rugby but, eventually, even I had to admit that I was not going to progress beyond the Second XV. Having resigned from the army whilst exploiting the hedonism of university, I also started to lament my lack of career prospects. Having a degree did not guarantee entry to the Promised Land and, as my erstwhile university colleagues started lucrative jobs wearing a suit, I mixed concrete and humped bricks about. The enigma of my job quickly tarnished in the bad weather.

Even the builders' tolerance of my idiosyncrasies began to wane. That was ironic considering my working class roots but private schooling and a university degree meant that I drifted into a cultural twilight zone, still thought of as a Northern oaf by my university friends but considered a pompous wanker by the builders with whom I worked.

Then Emily Fisher dumped me. Quite why was never explained.

"It's just doesn't feel right, Billy," she whispered to me one morning when I went to visit. She seemed genuinely sad, if a little rehearsed.

"How can you say that, we haven't seen each other for months, you've only just got back from Greece?" Emily had been working abroad and I had waited at home and so, quite apart from sadness at the demise of our relationship, I felt used.

"I know," she cried, taking hold of my hand, "and I was so looking forward to seeing you but it just doesn't feel right." The implication that there had been another bloke was strong but I did not find out about it for a long time. As Emily crapped all over me her soft hazel eyes seemed quite hard. For the first time since we had met I sensed she had no sympathy or compassion for me and certainly no love.

I went running across the moors of my Yorkshire refuge. I was very fit and during the long, lonely miles I contemplated my future, reaching the obvious but awful conclusion that I needed a proper job.

The first interview I went to was for a job as a transport manager for a brewery. The personnel manager who interviewed me was sympathetic.

"Billy, you seem very capable of the job but don't

appear committed to idea. I get no sense that you've always dreamt of being a transport manager." I was not sure how to reply; does anyone ever dream of being a transport manager? It was a good job in terms of pay and prospects but its main selling points were that it was a male dominated environment in Yorkshire.

I prepared myself better for the next interview and went with greater confidence. However, my enthusiasm waned as I walked into the room and saw an angry looking woman with close-cropped hair. She glared at me and introduced herself as the MD.

"Why do you want to work in media?"

"Well," I muttered without even convincing myself, "I want to be able to use some of the analytical skills that I learned at university." The MD cast a dismissive glance at my CV.

"Politics?" Her cohorts around the table all looked at me for a response but whether their attitudes were of challenge or desperate pity was not clear.

"Yes, I wanted to learn about the dynamics of society. I thought it would be more pertinent than history."

The MD continued to glare at me. I thought she might start beating her chest before walking around the table on her knuckles. Instead she started smoking a large foul smelling cigar so that she looked like a female Churchill.

So I went back to the university careers office to see if they could offer some ideas about where the future might take me.

"You look a bit nervous, Billy", the careers lady said to me as I sat down to the inquisition.

"I am."

"Why's that?"

"Well, most of my friends have left here wanting to be accountants."

"Don't you want to be an accountant?"

"No."

"Oh. What do you see yourself as then?"

"Ernest Hemmingway."

She did not laugh right away.

"Do you have the right qualifications," she asked gently.

"What qualifications do you need?"

"A rich Father."

"Oh."

"Do you have one?"

"No."

"Perhaps you should consider being an accountant."

A career in the army became increasingly inevitable and I went on a familiarisation visit to a regiment to see if they would accept me into their ranks. It was like an extended interview but scrutiny of social skills was as rigorous as those for intellectual and physical abilities. I had successfully been through the mill as a teenager but, having subsequently resigned, I had to do it all over again.

I entered the officers' mess of a potential sponsor regiment with a strong sense of being an impostor. It was a dark, austere building, with leather armchairs and dusty books and solemn portraits of whiskery old men in uniform. There were even some dead animals on the wall that supposedly demonstrated the skill and vigour of former officers but to me they just reflected the anachronistic nature of the place.

"Welcome Old Boy," said a caricature of a figure from a Dickensian novel as he shook my hand. He was a large bloke who dominated the group of younger officers with a mix of physical presence, acute awareness of his rank as a major and crap humour that everyone else seemed to find highly amusing. We had pre dinner drinks in the bar and then moved into the dining room in strict order of rank priority. It was 1990 and the formality of it was ridiculous, almost comical.

Fortunately, I sat at the end of the table next to another chap from the North.

"What do you miss most about being in the army?" I asked hoping for a glimpse of normality. I expected him to mention a girlfriend or a dog or something sane.

"Chip butties," he replied enthusiastically. "I just love chip butties but we can't have them in the Mess."

"That's a shame."

He shook his head happily.

"It's okay. I have invented the *Officers' Mess Chip Butty*. What you do is take a big bite of bread and then immediately follow it with a couple of chips; the taste is the same." He looked at me for approbation.

"That's novel," I offered, hoping not to offend the sad bastard.

"But!" he continued with scary enthusiasm, "they don't serve bread with the main meal so you have to save it from the soup course." He proudly indicated the bread roll he had kept from being cleared by the staff. I smiled, hoping that *chip butties* was a euphemism for strict behavioural codes in the mess. But then I realised he was not smart enough for that. I went back to the building site whilst I tried to decide what to do with my life.

Ironically, it was one of the builders with whom I had shared a difficult relationship that helped me to resolve my uncertainty.

"What will you do with your life, Billy?" he unexpectedly asked me one day. I shrugged.

"I'm thinking of re-joining the army." He looked at me thoughtfully for a minute.

"Do it," he said. "Or else you'll end up like me; a wife you don't love, kids you can't afford and a grotty council house that you despise even though it is your only shelter."

He was not a man gifted with eloquence and so his words offered a particularly salient philosophy. I left home once more to join the army, which was the grown up version of running away to join the circus, although when I joined, there were more clowns in the army.

Part 3 – The Army Bitch

"How could I be so blind to this addiction?" Toy
Soldiers - Martika 1989

10

"If you need sympathy, sir, you'll find it in the dictionary between shit and syphilis." My platoon Colour Sergeant glowered at me, pointing to my boots with his pace stick[18] as if they were an affront to civilisation. His glower was like a parody of Windsor Davies[19].

He had asked me why my boots were not done up tightly.

"Because I have some bad blisters, Colour Sergeant," I replied innocently.

"Do you expect me to be sympathetic, Mr Hanson?"

"No, Colour Sergeant."

"Then why are you telling me about your blisters, Mr Hanson?"

"Because you asked me about my boots, Colour Sergeant."

"Are you trying to be funny, Mr Hanson?"

"No, Colour Sergeant."

"Good," he glowered again with his army-issued glower, "because you'll never be funny as long as you've got a hole in your arse." Then he stomped off to the next officer cadet in line to find something to criticise him about.

I stood rigidly to attention outside my room listening to the rehearsed randomness of his rants. This scene was played out every morning in the first few weeks of officer training and it always left me rather bemused. I could see little merit in spending an hour at six o'clock on a Saturday morning standing still whilst

---

[18] The iconic wooden stick of a British Army SNCO: It is used to measure the pace that a marching soldier should take.

[19] Windsor Davies starred as the Scowling Sergeant-Major in the BBC 1970s SITCOM "It Aint half Hot Mum".

being criticised for not having tied my boots in a regulation manner. After eight weeks of military training at the Royal Military Academy, Sandhurst, I still could not read a map.

But I actually quite enjoyed army training; it was exciting, demanding and better than humping bricks or selling photocopiers, which had seemingly been my employment alternatives. Moreover, being a young army officer was quite glamorous so, whilst I constantly toyed with the idea of leaving the army, I felt compelled to stay.

My initial army experience was free from trouble and my shirts were very well ironed. I actually enjoyed some aspects of basic training, especially the physical side, which I found quite easy although this was another area of confused military priorities.

"Mr Hanson, your fitness levels have actually dropped whilst you've been at Sandhurst," queried my platoon commander during my first assessment interview. "That's unheard of?" I was not quite sure how to respond.

"Well, Sir, we don't do much phys," was the best I could manage. Captain Adams looked at me uncertainly.

"There's at least an hour of physical training every day."

"Aye, sir," I responded carefully, trying not to be sarcastic, "but before I joined I worked on a building site all day and trained for two hours every night. I also took a month off before coming here and trained five hours a day." The captain looked at me in disbelief and then referred back to his notes.

"Well, the training regime seems to be enough for most people. Officer Cadet Cavendish has improved his performance by a hundred percent."

"Yes, sir," I agreed, "but Fatty Cavendish can still

only do 20 press ups and I can do 80."

"Oh, really, how many could you do then?" asked the captain as if he had proved his point.

"At least a hundred."

"Well, try not let your standards slip any further," he said with pointless rhetoric before focusing on more important things such as my loosely tied boots. Army life was underwhelming. I had expected praise for my fitness and criticism for map reading but I clearly misunderstood Sandhurst priorities. Still, I only joined because Emily Fisher had dumped me and perhaps I lacked commitment to the idea.

The reputation of the Military Academy was foreboding but the physical appearance of it was totally daunting; I suffered significant culture shock. Sandhurst is not a place so much as a province, occupying several thousand acres of prime land near London. At its heart is a collection of old and modern buildings that stand authoritatively amongst playing fields, manicured lawns and a boating lake. Its civilised façade completely belies its function.

The army is well practised at training people to good effect but my personal experiences at the Academy were disconcerting. As captain of the university rugby team I had regularly organised fifty blokes into training sessions, matches and social events and I joined the army with that same confidence. A year's military training, however, left me unsure about making the most innocuous decisions.

"Can't we use wet wipes and a battery razor to shave with?" I naively asked the Colour Sergeant on our first field exercise. He glowered.

"No, Mr Hanson, not until you have passed the first five weeks of basic training. Until then you must wash and shave in your mess tin[20]." I looked at the sludge in my mess tin after I had scraped off two days of dirt and stubble, and shuddered at the thought of cooking food in it.

Our first night of field training had a freezing chill and I gratefully climbed into my newly issued sleeping bag to try and grab four hours kip. Then I realised that a six foot bloke does not fit into a size small maggot[21]. I lay awake shivering.

"If you don't have a sense of humour, you shouldn't have joined, Mr Hanson," smiled the Colour Sergeant when I told him in the early morning. I smiled grimly and carried on with the task of filling in the trenches we had dug.

"Anyone want a hand?" the Colour Sergeant asked as we toiled away. No-one seemed willing to accept his offer in case he was not serious but I could not resist the temptation.

"You could help me, Colour Sergeant, it won't take you long." He looked at me, critically.

"Why, what are you doing Mr Hanson?"

"I am filling in the shit-pit!"

"Are you trying to be funny Mr Hanson?"

"No, Colour Sergeant, you said I couldn't be funny." I waited for retribution but, for once, the Colour Sergeant seemed unconcerned by my frivolity.

Later in the exercise we lay in a night ambush in a wooded area of a local training ground. There were a few civilians walking about since the Armed Forces use huge tracts of land to which the public are allowed access.

A night ambush is difficult to execute, requiring

---

[20] An eight-inch cooking pan for small camping stoves.
[21] Army issued sleeping bag; so called because its tapered end makes the user look like a maggot.

discipline and training. On this particular evening we had done it quite well so, as we lay in the dark, listening for signs of the approaching troops who were acting as the enemy, I felt gratified to be part of a developing and increasingly effective team.

Eventually, we could hear footsteps approaching along the track in the wood that we occupied. The atmosphere became tense as we waited for the signal to open fire. There was quiet for a moment as the enemy seemingly stopped. Perhaps they had seen or heard us. Maybe they would open fire on us. It was dark; we could not see or hear what was happening.

Then the first trip flare went off and there was an immediate and massive sound of training ammunition blasting out in the night. It was an impressive, frightening experience and as the glowing trip flares illuminated the track we realised that our quarry was not the intended enemy but an unlucky civilian who was walking his dog, which was then traumatised and running with its tail between its legs into the distance.

As well as crashing my hopes for a satisfying career, Sandhurst was also the first place where I realised that I was not the over achiever that I had assumed myself to be. Attending a small private school had given me the wrong impression. I was cross-country champion and rugby captain, positions I carried to university. At Sandhurst, however, I did not even make the first team.

Above the portico of Sandhurst's iconic Old College is a statue of Mars and Minerva. The Roman God of War and Goddess of Wisdom supposedly reflect the attributes that a British army officer should portray.

Both quickly shunned me in deference to Venus[22].

The perfume of womanhood was as powerful at Sandhurst as it was elsewhere. When I joined, the army was still an odd place for a girl. There were prissy eighteen year olds from the Home Counties, highly competent graduates looking for more excitement than Marks and Spencers, and girls who had served with distinction in the ranks. There were also some girls who seemed to have joined in order to get laid or married. I resisted for a while, mainly because I had a girlfriend when I first went to Sandhurst.

Our relationship was largely comprised of compromise since we actually had little in common but Jane was a selfless, attractive, intelligent and sexually enthusiastic woman, so it worked for a while.

"Good morning, sleepyhead," she said on the Sunday of my first weekend break from Sandhurst. "Sleep well?" She gave me a coffee. I sat up in bed, trying to drag myself from a deep sleep. I was so knackered that I had fallen asleep over dinner.

"Yes, thanks. What time is it?"

"Nearly lunchtime."

"Damn!" I started to get up in panic. "I have to wash and iron all my kit."

"I've done it all, Sweety." Jane gave me a big bacon roll. When I finished it she took the plate, smiled at me, and dropped her bathrobe to the floor.

"We've got all day to ourselves."

Only Billy Hanson could find fault but Jane wanted to be Mrs Hanson. She wanted to be Mrs Anybody really and, despite her very obvious charms, I found such presumption difficult and I was surprised when

---

[22] Despite my Christian upbringing , I leaned to the Norse Gods due to my perceived Viking heritage, but I was expedient enough to accept patronage from whichever deity had primacy at the time.

our easy going, highly sexed relationship turned into a domestic drudge of rows and accusations.

Jane was the first woman to buy me a copy of "Men are from Mars but Women are from Venus"[23] since we had a communication problem, apparently. In reality, the problem was that Jane wanted to communicate and I did not: *Jane Hanson* sounded okay, but it was a bit dull.

My first trouble with army girls was with Tania. She was tall, attractive and confident and I had subconsciously labelled her as the sort of friend that you cannot shag. We were study partners in military history.

"Not interested?" I asked her during a lesson on the Israeli tactics of the 1973 Yom Kippur War. She shrugged.

"I did not join the Army to spend all day in a classroom."

"Why did you join?"

"To get some action."

"Me too," I replied, dreaming of winning gallantry medals in conflicts all over the world.

"I thought that with all these men around I would get plenty of action," she said, "but I'm not getting any."

"Don't worry Tania, I'm a man." It was an instinctive response not meant to cause trouble. She looked at me seriously for a moment.

As I left the dinner table that evening, Tania invited me into the bar for a drink. Her smile was warm and innocent and I was naive and weak. We spent all evening on a sofa in the bar and Tania's dress revealed a deep and promising cleavage that seduced me all by

---

[23] John Gray, Harper Element, 1993.

itself.

The accommodation corridors in the Academy were single sex but that did not perturb Tania. In fact, she was positively excited by it.

"This is so exciting." She kissed me deeply with a hand held firmly against my cheek. I undid the remaining buttons of her thin cotton dress and let it glide to the floor. She smiled and kissed me again.

Then, naked but for a wicked smile, she sauntered arrogantly along the corridor to my bunk, high heels clicking impatiently on the tiled floor. I watched her gazelle like haunches disappear into my bunk. I followed her in and she pushed me down onto the floor, using me with some urgency.

Next morning the Colour Sergeant took us on a bastard of an endurance run; I was sucking in air from Kuala Lumpur.

"Still got plenty of energy, Mr Hanson?" How he knew about Tania was a mystery. Why it concerned him so much was even more uncertain but I was not going to let the fucker beat me.

"Aye, Colour Sergeant, why d'you ask?"

"Because we'll do fireman's lift now," he grinned. "You pair up with Mr Cavendish." Fatty Cavendish smiled at me apologetically. He had lost a lot of weight but was still big enough to stress any fireman. I hefted him onto my shoulder and ran up the hill.

"Too slow!" yelled the Colour Sergeant as I lumbered back towards him. "Go up again!" He made me do three more laps whilst the rest of the platoon watched like a scene from *Officer and a Gentlemen*. I ran until I puked down my front.

"How's it going, Billy?" asked a dark haired girl with a soft Welsh lilt. I looked up at her slowly, trying to make sense of the diverse images in my mind.

Eventually, I realised it was Laura, recognising her from some of the lectures we had shared through the year. I also remembered that she had been Tania's accomplice in my first bout of trouble.

"Okay," I responded quietly, worried that too much movement might upset the balance of alcohol in my stomach. Laura stroked my cheek like a nurse with a sick patient.

"Take a deep breath," she ordered, "it'll make you feel better." I was unsure that anything short of death would help me feel better. Laura gave me a bottle of water and sat on the wall next to me.

"Are you enjoying the party?"

"I was, but over did the beer a little." She nodded.

"I think everyone did."

We had completed our basic officer training with a field exercise in the Dordogne Mountains in France. It was a great improvement from training in the damp Welsh mountains and at the end of the exercise we celebrated in traditional army fashion with a BBQ. In the warm French moonlight, the atmosphere was fuelled by a strong sense of comradeship forged through shared achievement: and excessive alcohol, of course.

One morning we practiced river crossings in a deep limestone gorge. It was a beautiful location; a lethargic river winding its way through a pine covered valley with the sun rising slowly in the background. We paddled our boats across the river, climbed onto the bank and waited for the kick-off.

The steep sided gorge hugely amplified the explosions that simulated artillery fire and the valley was filled with a deafening noise. We stormed through the bushes, firing our weapons and charged through the middle of a French student orgy.

There were 2CVs, empty wine bottles and sleeping

bags full of naked people who ran about in confusion and panic. I was keen to stop and administer some military aid to the civil community but the Colour Sergeant was equally keen that I did not.

"Where are you going, Mr Hanson?" he yelled above the din of mock battle. I pointed towards two naked French girls clutching each other in terror. He shook his head. "Just for once, Mr Hanson, keep your cock in your pants and press on with the attack!" Some people have no sense of priorities.

"Eat this." Laura gave me a burger and interrupted my reverie. "It'll help to sober you up." Laura stroked my cheek again, her hand running to the nape of my neck as she pulled me forward slightly. She covered my mouth softly with hers and kissed me tentatively. I responded equally gently and let my tongue caress her lips. Her reaction was instinctive and urgent.

Eventually she stood up but held my jaw with her fingers.

"Why me?" I asked wondering why any girl would want to play with a drunk and sweaty bloke like me. Laura smiled at me with a gentle confidence that overcame all the limitations of alcohol.

"Tania said you're a sure thing."

"Isn't every bloke?"

"You'd be surprised," Laura scoffed but I was a little uncertain then, being a sure thing was not that flattering, really.

But Laura was determined, slowly undoing the buttons at the front of her dress. She wore nothing underneath and reached for my hands to place them on her breasts, ensuring that it was my libido not my ego that was calling the shots. I stroked her smooth skin and kissed her neck and breasts and she sighed with each ardent lick.

Then she pulled my head away from her tits by my

hair.

"Go get your roll-mat[24] and meet me in the ruin in the copse behind camp." Laura stood and walked without looking back towards the copse. I hurried to my bivvy and grabbed my roll-mat, ignoring the inquisitive glances from my platoon. As I approached the small collection of trees I found Laura's dress hanging on a branch.

I forced my way through the bushes into the copse to find a place of surreal beauty. The moonlight was strong, illuminating the ruin with a soft glow and reflecting off Laura's naked skin with an intoxicating effect. The thick bushes surrounding the copse provided a complete screen so we could act with brazen confidence.

Laura stood waiting, dark hair contrasting with pale nakedness. She watched as I moved closer and her silent appraisal was utterly compelling. She stepped forward and took the roll-mat from my hand and laid it on the ground. Then she undid my shorts and blew my mind.

She pulled me down onto the mat and rode me magnificently, heavy breasts swaying in the moonlight as she sought her pleasure from me in the French countryside.[25] I awoke alone the next morning in the middle of a bush, painfully sober and butt-naked, being eaten by mosquitoes.

Laura was nowhere to be seen and I presumed that was the end of our affair although once we had returned to Sandhurst she suddenly appeared in my bunk one night. She became a regular visitor, coming to my bunk

---

[24] Polystyrene mat for sleeping on that rolls up tightly.

[25] Clearly, there was a pattern emerging here about army girls wanting to be on top.

in the evening and doing my ironing whilst I was out having a beer or running. When I got back she would love me and leave me to sleep; it was almost a perfect relationship.

Inevitably, however, she wanted more than I could give.

"Haven't you got any friends that might join in?" Laura once asked me in post-coital daze.

"Join in what?"

"With us." I had never considered a threesome before but once it was out of the box, the notion had some potential.

"Get a life you fucking pervert!" was the standard response when I explored it with my cadet colleagues and so I had to meet Laura's demands on my own.

My adventure with Laura was intensely exciting but the unnerving thought of being a sure thing persisted, reflecting the notion that, despite joining the army, I still had no control over my libido or ego.

But we had finished our training by then and the focus of our lives was the final parade. It was a big deal with hundreds of people on parade and thousands, including royalty, in the audience. I was still uncertain about army priorities; my boots were intensely shiny and I could march in good order but I still could not read a map. I was not actually certain that I wanted to be an army officer. I had only joined because Emily Fisher had abandoned me but she had written recently, implying that she wanted us to get back together.

I was confused, but I had completed nearly a year of officer training and I had no other career options. So, for want of something better to do, I marched onto parade with the bands playing and flags flying: It was impossible to resist. The Army Bitch had already made us addicts and it really was like having sex with a beautiful but manipulative woman; you know you shouldn't, but can't stop yourself.

My confusion was not helped when the guy next to me on parade, a whimsical Jock of great character, whispered in my ear:

"Billy, are you sure you want to do this?"

"No, but it's a bit late now."

"Shit," he said a bit too loudly, "I only joined for a bet." I stifled a grin.

"I know what you mean, I only joined to get away from trouble with girls." The jock had a silent laugh then, as much as you can whilst stood to attention in front of the King of Spain.

"Well you didn't do very well, Billy, at least I won my bet."

11

"You seem like a nice boy," smiled Mary.

"Thank you." I swirled her round and held her more closely. "You seem like a nice girl." She responded naturally, folding herself into my arms, so I chanced it a little and slid my hand lower. Mary gave her consent with a coy smile and we danced together a while longer.

I had gone to the wedding straight from Sandhurst and was having a thoroughly good time. I had seen Mary in the church watching the brand new officers in our smart new uniforms. She was gorgeous and caught me staring at her, smiling at me in admonishment.

"Cheeky boy," she scolded as she walked past me under our swords as we formed a Guard of Honour on the church steps. Then she came to speak to me in the reception.

"You look a bit lonely, soldier, so I came to rescue you. I'm Mary." I was enchanted: she was warm, bright and very pretty. I also found her confidence alluring.

"Billy," I responded, taking her hand and kissing it lightly. That was a bit pretentious but it seemed like the thing to do and I was still not sure how army officers were supposed to act. Mary seemed to accept it.

"Why are you all alone?" she asked, "no girlfriend to play with?"

"No, I'm solo, but you could be my girlfriend."

"You're not shy, are you Billy?"

"Well, I'm the strong silent type." Mary laughed.

"I bet you are but I have to go do family stuff." She turned to walk away but then stopped and came back. "Ask me nicely later," she whispered, "and I'll consider your proposition." Then she clicked off on high heels into the throng.

And now we were dancing together. We danced to

everything, jazz, pop, swing; we even had a waltz with the oldies.

"You're quite an old charmer for a young bloke," said Mary as we whirled around quite fluently. I grimaced a little.

"My father made me have lessons when I was a kid."

"Good for him," smiled Mary as I held her firmly against me. I was pleased. Most of my brothers-in-arms had girlfriends to take to the wedding and I had felt very lonely at first. Every man has his limits, however.

"I am not doing the *Birdy Song*," I told Mary as I led her away from the dance floor. She laughed.

"You wouldn't do the Conga, either."

"No, it's not cool." We sipped more champagne and Mary looked at me over the rim of her glass.

"So, what would you like to do, Billy?"

I was not sure but it seemed like an invitation; something about the way she said it, I suppose, or perhaps it was just the way her eyes held mine for that eternal moment.

"I would like to do you, Sweetheart." Then we danced to another wedding cliché, *Careless Whisper*[26]. I dropped one hand to the small of her back and raised the other to the nape of her neck and leant forward to kiss her.

Mary responded gently but passionately and we embraced for most of the song.

"Is this you switching modes from old charmer to young seducer?" Mary teased when we eventually parted. I was not really sure what mode I was in; that's the trouble with girls, sometimes you just cannot tell.

"I don't think I'm switching anything. I am just responding; you're leading this dance, aren't you?"

---

[26] George Michael 1984.

Mary smiled a laughing acknowledgement as if it was obvious and I was a bit thick.

"Does the army not do subtle?"

"No, I'm used to taking orders." Mary took my hand and led me away from the dance floor.

"Well, I order you to take me upstairs."

Mary continued to lead the dance in my hotel room. She was ardent, almost urgent, as she undressed me whilst snogging me and running her fingers over my skin. Every time I tried to explore her body she evaded my hands.

"Be patient, soldier boy, I'm in charge."

When I was naked, Mary leant forward to kiss me. She allowed me a little latitude and I gratefully stroked her skin with fingers and kisses as I slowly undressed her. I sat her on the edge of the bed and knelt down to burrow my head under her skirt. Mary gasped and pushed me away.

"I was wrong!" she said. "You're not a nice boy at all, you're bad." I tried to look chastised.

"Sorry, Mary, I'm very bad." Then I forced my way back under her skirt and was very bad until she gushed all over my face. Mary fell back on the bed looking flushed and very inviting. I stood up to press my advantage but Mary stared at me with a look of guilt spreading over her face.

"Billy, I can't do this. I'm engaged." Her admission took a little while to register.

"It's a bit late for fidelity now, isn't?"

She nodded whilst hurriedly trying to dress.

"I'm sorry but my problem is that I wasn't sure I could be faithful to one man for ever. I had to test myself." She was almost in tears and I was actually beginning to feel sorry for her although I still felt a bit used.

"Well, what about my problem," I demanded. Mary

looked at my groin.

"Yes, that's quite a problem, but I'm sure you'll think of something." Then she left.

"Bitch." I was confused and not sure what to do. Still, a man with an erection is in no need of advice[27] so I got dressed, rather awkwardly, and went back to the wedding.

Shortly afterwards, I ended up in bed with the bride's sister. Quite how is not clear but it did not cause too much trouble as it is acceptable at middle class weddings, apparently.

"No-one wants to be alone at a wedding," Vicky said in the morning. That was fine by me, still not very flattering but at least she had been honest. However, I did not go in to meet her father when I dropped her off at home.

Before reporting for duty at my new regiment I had a couple more days of leave and I planned to spend them with a girlfriend (the sort you could not shag) in London. As I drove up the motorway it started to rain so I picked up a hitchhiker. I had assumed it was a bloke but once inside the car I realised it was a pretty young girl with short hair and denims.

"Excellent," I thought at first but then I was concerned that a seventeen year old girl was hitch-hiking alone at night on the A303 in Wiltshire.

"Where are you going?" She turned to look at me before replying.

"Home to London." She paused briefly. "I'm holidaying with my mother in Devon," she said. "Father's still at home working."

"I used to go to Devon with my parents for

---

[27] Samuel Pepys , 17th Century.

holidays," I said, "In fact, I went a couple of years ago with some University friends, we had quite a hoot." I was not sure whether I was reflecting on past holidays or the fact that I had been to university. Either way, she was not much interested.

"What do you do now?" she asked, more out of politeness than interest. It was my turn to look at her and consider my options before replying. This was my opportunity to reveal that I was an army officer, which apparently impresses some girls, but it seemed rather pretentious, especially after the clumsy reference to university.

"I'm a soldier." She nodded slightly, seeming rather more interested.

"So, what's your name, soldier?" I smiled. I liked her.

"Billy. You?"

"Charlotte, Charlie."

We stopped for a coffee and as we sat dunking biscuits we talked about ourselves, our futures and other intimate detail that I would not normally divulge to a girl that I had just met. Charlie, however, was easy-going and we seemed to have a lot in common.

Perhaps that was why I asked her if we could see each other later on. She seemed uncomfortable with the idea and her reaction surprised me. We had chatted easily enough and having supper together seemed natural. We travelled along in silence and I drove Charlie home to North London, even though my friend lived in Wimbledon, but it was raining more heavily and it was very late by then. She got out of my car and leaned in through the window.

"I quite like you, Billy," she said, "but I don't think we'd get on."

"That's a shame." She smiled at me, making me feel worse, and walked off into her home.

I drove away and it occurred to me that I knew more about Charlie and her background than I did about the last three girls that I had slept with. This was a sad indictment of the character I had become and how much I had changed from the nice boy I had been as a kid.

"Mommy, when I get a girlfriend should I have sex with her before we get married?" I did not actually know what sex was when I asked the question but references to it were emerging in the playgrounds and tree houses of my childhood environment. My mother was caught off balance by the question, we had never really had the birds and bees chat.

"Well," she mused, "it is better to wait until you're married, then it's more special." That made sense at the time but that was before I had been seduced by Eve, and as I chewed the idea over all the way to Wimbledon, I decided that the best way to make marital sex special was to get in loads of practice beforehand.

I arrived in Wimbledon later than planned and Fiona was already well acquainted with a bottle of wine.

"Billy," she smiled from the window, "hurry up, you've kept me waiting long enough." I ran up the stairs to her flat and we exchanged hugs. Fiona had been the girlfriend of a university rugby player and we had become friends after we had both left college. I had always managed to resist temptation with Fiona, mainly because that was how she wanted it, but also because I strongly believed that men should not usurp each other.

I proffered my standard bottle of Merlot and we sat down to gossip. It was pleasant to be able to confide and share intimacies with a girl without the oppressive expectation of an inbound seduction on either part. We both had an eye for the other and we flirted comfortably but the rules of this game had been clearly

111

stipulated some time earlier.

But the trouble with girls is that they cannot be trusted. After we had finished most of the wine Fiona stood up and smiled at me.

"I have a surprise for you," she said. "Wait there." Fiona disappeared having assumed the look that girls get when seduction is anticipated. I began to get a little weary, our friendship was strictly platonic, I thought, but I was getting confused about that and would not have been surprised if she had come back wearing a French maid's outfit. I started to prepare myself for any possibility.

But, the one possibility I had not imagined was the sudden appearance of Emily Fisher.

You bitch; I joined the fucking army because of you!

Actually I was bereft of words. Later, I was brimming with devastatingly witty remarks that would have reflected the fact that I considered her to be unworthy of my concern and that it was all her loss because I had a plethora of beautiful young women competing for my affections.

"Hello."

Emily smiled hesitantly.

"Hello," she almost whispered. We were like strangers, which was odd because we had once been so intimate.

We talked awkwardly through dinner. I was torn between indignation that a girl who had rent my heart so badly should contrive such a meeting, and an ardent desire to bend her over the table. Ego and libido again rubbing up against each other with the added complication of lost affection; perhaps even love.

It was impossible to tell quite how Emily felt. She had written implying a re-match but I knew she was seeing a bloke so I steeled myself to accept disappointment. Perhaps it was for the best, being commissioned as an infantry officer had given me a degree of resolve and I realised that me and Emily together would be a very retrograde step. *Emily Hanson* just did not sound right.

The awkward atmosphere was made even more difficult by Fiona who sat relishing every stifled exchange between Emily and me. Still, she had brokered the meeting and probably felt she was entitled to enjoy the drama.

"How is the army, then Billy?" Emily asked me.

"Good, I am enjoying it," I lied.

"I enjoyed the graduation ball," chipped in Fiona sweetly, trying a little female subterfuge. It worked.

"Where was my invite?" asked Emily in mock anger but she was way off target.

"Well, I hadn't heard from you for a year," I said a little too vehemently. Fiona took that moment to excuse herself and left Emily and me looking at each other across the table.

We sat amidst the silence of a thousand shared memories, wondering what to do next.

"I missed you, Billy." Emily ventured the first move. I remained silent, struggling to respond. Working class Northern boys do not really do emotional. I wanted to say it. I wanted to cross the dreadful space between us and join us together again. I nodded, hoping that said enough.

"I am sorry," Emily sighed. "I was away, busy," her voice trailed off a little. Then she found some resolve. "And I was hurt. We broke up in such a bad way."

"We didn't break up, Emily," I interrupted her, "you dumped me. You broke my heart." She looked up at me with a mixture of pain and defiance.

"Well you did a good enough job on mine when you shagged somebody else!"

"Well, you were hardly Snow White!" I countered

"and we were on a break." Emily looked at me and slowly shook her head.

"No, Billy. We weren't exclusive but we were never on a break. Why did you think that?" But I had no answer, at least not one I could explain because the real trouble with girls for me was that I was easily suffocated.

So we sat once more silently waiting for détente. Eventually, I accepted that too much time and pain had passed for us to resolve our problems. Besides, Emily was with another man. I said good night and retired, dignity intact, to bed.

I lay awake feeling like a fool because I could not push my ego aside and find a way to repair the relationship that had once been the making of me. But a while later Emily came in looking tall, slim and resplendent with flaming hair and nothing much on apart from bright lipstick and some very small pants.

She knew me well, despite our year apart. She knew how to tease me, gently sliding her smooth white legs across mine, her luscious red mouth provocative beyond restraint. Emily knew how to repair our relationship.

It was good to be with her again, to be with some one that I knew and cared for and the months of separation melted and we were one again. An embrace is generally more passionate if the participants are familiar with each other. They know what is to come and that makes the anticipation all the more thrilling.

Emily Hanson? Sounded okay, actually.

12

I stood in front of the twenty-four soldiers trying not to look nervous. They stood in three ranks, looking straight ahead without moving. I was their new platoon commander on my first day after joining the regiment. I was terrified. There was an awkward pause until I realised I should speak. My first words needed to be concise, firm and authoritative.

"Good morning, boys," I said in the way I thought Montgomery would have done.

"Men, sir." One of the soldiers in the front rank interrupted me.

"Pardon?"

"We're not *boys*, sir, we're men, soldiers." His tone was that of a weary parent and I wondered how many new platoon commanders he'd had to break in during his military service.

I faltered badly, my moment of glory having been crushed on a point of reference. Not only had I managed to collectively insult my soldiers, I had also been thrown completely off balance. As the saying goes, you never get a second chance to make a first impression. I could see them all thinking, "WANKER". Tiny, my platoon sergeant, was stood at the back with a grave face. If I failed this test his job was going to be difficult.

It was an aspect of my new profession that had been ignored throughout my training. There had been no mention of what to do when you first meet the guys that you inherit as a new platoon commander. One of the more amenable and professional young officers in the mess had offered me some advice.

"Keep it simple," he said. "As long as you are fitter than them, smarter than them and punctual, you'll be okay."

On my first day I was late. I felt like Daniel about to enter the lions' den because, although the troops were ostensibly parading for me to inspect them, they would view me much more critically and any impressions that I made at this moment would be enduring ones.

I tried to recapture the initiative quickly.

"So, you think you're all men do you?" I asked, trying to sound amused and unthreatened but actually sounding like a pompous wanker. He looked me in the eye, thinking *WANKER* to himself, but he smiled slightly.

"Yes, sir, I do." Tiny's face had gone puce. Shit, shit, SHIT! I was uncertain what to do but suddenly realised that what I needed to do was back off; after all, the guy did have a point.

"Okay, I am sorry. Hello, men, it's good to meet you."

There were wry smiles all round; even Tiny relaxed. In the strange way of soldiers I had done all right and my concerns about not living up to their expectations of me proved unfounded, principally, I realised later, because they did not have any expectations of me.

Joining the Officers Mess was equally daunting and even less successful for me. The Officers' Mess is the place where the young officers live and it is the social and cultural focus of a regiment's officer corps. It is reputed as a place of great companionship and professional excellence but it was far from that when I first joined at the end of the last century.

As a teenager I read the memoirs of Billy Beaumont, Captain and revivalist of the England Rugby Team in the early 1980s. In his book *Thanks to Rugby*, Beaumont writes about his early reception into the England squad, describing the environment as reactionary, aimed more at preventing upstarts from usurping the places of established players on the team than promoting a sporting and positive attitude.

When I first joined my regiment, the Officers' Mess was like that, especially for a graduate officer like myself who received seniority in rank, and therefore higher pay, by virtue of having attended university. I also had a working class background, which added to the prejudice against me.

I soon realised that much of the professed gentility of the Mess was a veneer that would peel at the slightest provocation and certainly one that was easily dissolved by alcohol. My first social event in the mess began as a civilised wine tasting evening but it quickly deteriorated.

We had all been encouraged to invite a girlfriend along and, since Emily Fisher lived way up North, I asked Fiona to attend with me.

"This is a ladies' night," I told Fiona, as she was getting ready, "so there will be lots of other girls here." I led her in to the bar and immediately noticed the total dearth of other women.

"Hello, welcome to the mess!" said the senior officer there, extending a hand. He was a pompous old major whom I found difficult to like. He was at least trying to be friendly, though; most of the other officers were looking at Fiona like slavering dogs.

"Have you been dating long?" asked a young captain who, up until then, had largely ignored me.

"No, Billy and are just friends," said Fiona.

"Oh, I see," said the captain, deliberately standing between Fiona and me.

People were drunk before supper and after the meal they seemed to regress even further. Fiona suffered behaviour so indelicate that it would have made an Italian blush. My new comrades in arms made lewd suggestions, they made direct and vulgar propositions and they squeezed her bum by the fistful.

"Thanks for the evening, Billy," Fiona said as she was leaving in the morning. "It's interesting here." She never came to the Mess again.

My most dreadful memory of my initiation into the Officers' Mess was, however, our "Dining In": a formal dinner wearing our brand new scarlet dinner jackets and black jodhpurs. As I did my bow tie and observed myself in uniform, I felt a surge of pride that, in becoming an Infantry Officer, I had achieved something positive.

In less ostentatious societies, being "Dined-In" would be called an initiation ceremony but such things are rather vulgar and not the sort of thing one did in the officers' mess, or at least admitted to. The evening began by being forced to drink a vitriolic concoction of spirits, quadruple whiskies and pints of lager before we sat down to dinner. *Good form* dictated that you did not refuse a drink when offered.

There were three of us being *Dined In* that night and the celebrations were conducted with an intense spite because I was a graduate and the other two had both previously been corporals in other regiments and we were not deemed to harbour the necessary social acumen to be in the Officers' Mess.

Before we went in to dinner a bugler in a red tunic and white helmet gave a five-minute warning.

"Where are you going, Mr Hanson?" one of the senior subalterns asked like the troll in charge of the bridge. I was a little confused.

"To the toilet, sir," I said, "before dinner."

"I don't think so," he frowned. "I think you should have another pint instead." He pushed a silver goblet of cold lager into my hand. "In one, d'you think, Charles?" he asked a captain stood nearby. The captain pretended to think for a minute.

"Be fair, Simon, young chap's not been dined in yet.

Let him have two gulps!" The pair of them carried on like a charade from *Tom Brown's Schooldays* and physically prevented me from going to the toilet. Nothing short of a good punch from me was going to convince them what a pair of wankers they were and I sensed that sort of thing was not done in the mess.

Once at the dining table, it was considered extremely bad form to go to the lavatory before the meal had been cleared and the toasts made so I sat suffering from bad bladder pain. The Mess Sergeant saw my problem.

"Try this, sir," he whispered in my ear and passed me an empty champagne bottle under the table. I suffered the ignominy of getting my dick out under the table and trying to piss in the bottle. I could not do it so I sat in severe pain for the next three hours.

During dinner, inductees were sent scribbled messages demanding that they crawl under the table and try to remove a senior officer's spurs from his boots. Everyone else would then do their best to land a good kick on the unfortunate under the table. Head injuries requiring stitches were not uncommon.

After the meal the inductee was given three glasses of Drambuie, which was ignited and drunk whilst still alight, the Mess Sergeant stood close by holding wet towels in case some one set fire to themselves. Present at our *Dining In* was an Italian Catholic Priest who was visiting the regiment and my last conscious memory of the evening was of the totally horrified look on his face as the Mess Sergeant extinguished the flames leaping from the head of one of my young colleagues.

"No!" roared the Commanding Officer after I had drunk my flamers without incident. "Do it again!" I looked down and saw a flicker of flame in the glass of my third Drambuie because I had left a tiny amount of liquid in the glass. I had to "show again" with three

119

more shots. Even the captains looked sympathetic.

After dinner we were dragged half-conscious to the Commanding Officer to request his permission to join the Regiment. Afterwards, I was able to claw my way unaided to bed but the other inductees had to be carried upstairs where one of them was sodomised with a shampoo bottle. I slept until late the next afternoon and I continued to vomit the residue of that evening for two days afterwards.

My Grandfather was not a wealthy man and did not hold any civic authority, but when he died nearly the whole of the village where he had lived his gentle life turned out to wish him farewell. I was deeply moved by this, by the fact that a man who had never had much interest in accumulating wealth or social position could evoke such a unanimous demonstration of support simply by being a gentleman.

It was the only time that I ever saw my own father cry.

"Your Grandfather always had time for you."

"He was the kindest man I ever met."

"He was a true gentleman." And that was the greatest praise I could imagine, for that was my Grandfather's own mantra.

"Follow the wisdom of Solomon[28], my Son," he said to me as I was growing up, "and you'll always behave as a gentleman should."

So, having been received into the Officers' Mess where talk of *gentlemanly conduct* was common, I was devastated to realise that talk of such things was as close as most of the officers in my new Regiment would ever get.

---

[28] Widely believed by clerics to be the Book of Proverbs.

13

The rain came down in sheets, relentless and depressing. We always manoeuvred at night so as well as being wet, I was permanently knackered. This was infantry officer training and it merely confirmed my view that the Army Bitch and me were not destined for a long and fruitful marriage.

Initially, I had been glad to leave my Regiment after two weeks in order to go on the course. It was supposed to teach us how to command our troops but we seemed to spend most of our time digging trenches or tabbing about in the dark. I did learn how to keep going when I was miserable, lacking in motivation and completely uninterested. The technical phrase for this is *Monging*.

We had some Floppies[29] on the course and they really suffered, often being dragged away from semi-tropical homes and forced to trog[30] about Wiltshire or Wales in the rain in November. There were some experienced soldiers amongst their number and some of the African officers, whose nations had been torn by conflict, had seen combat at close quarters and fared reasonably well, despite the conditions. Some even retained that universal soldier trait of humour.

"This is ridiculous," said Nkome, an African officer in my syndicate, as we trogged across Salisbury Plain in a downpour. "In my country, if there was this much mud we would build a village." You had to feel sorry for them but they did make us feel better.

The most soul destroying aspect of Salisbury Plain is that it is surrounded by warm, cosy pubs and often it

---

[29] Foreign student from a warm country: It is a term of affectionate abuse since they reputedly lack backbone and "flop" over.

[30] Mindlessly tabbing about in the dark.

was possible to see people spending an evening of warmth and good cheer whilst we were cold, wet and tired. On very still nights we would be able to hear people talking in the car park, occasionally a couple snogging; we hated them.

"I can't wait to finish this course so that things get better," said one of the young officers. Another officer who had previously served as a corporal smiled benignly.

"It doesn't get better," he said wisely, "you just get used to it."

A further frustration was that, having reconciled with Emily Fisher, I was now stuck in rural Wiltshire. At the weekend, the guys with London based girlfriends disappeared but Emily Fisher lived far away in the North, leaving me feeling quite lonely.

Still, I had joined the army to escape the turmoil that women caused and so I tried to make the best of the situation. At the weekend those of us still in camp would take part in a sad male ritual called a "Score or Die" mission: if you did not score with a girl in town, you would die whilst walking the thirty miles back to camp; or pay for a taxi.

I rarely participated as one night stands were not my thing and I could not afford the cost of a taxi across Wiltshire so it was with customary incompetence that on the one night that I did go to Bath I managed to both score and die at the same time. It was late on a Saturday night in a particularly seedy nightclub and I had begun to contemplate the lonely trip back to camp. I had even made financial provision for it and was actually looking forward to leaving the dark, noisy hole of a nightclub.

"Hi," said a girl, quite suddenly standing next to me. She was a big girl and not pretty. I smiled in drunken politeness. "You not managed to pull anyone?" she asked. I shrugged.

"I'm not very good at chat ups. I never know what to say."

"Me neither," she said. "So let's just go together?"

I was not expecting that. I have never understood why women are prepared to face the social stigma and physical risks associated with one night stands simply not be on their own the next morning.

I went home with her. Perhaps I did want to get laid, even with this unlovely stranger, and my libido was calling the moves. Perhaps I was just drunk: The fruit with which Eve tempted Adam must surely have been well fermented.

There was no romance, seduction, or even much foreplay. In fact, there was very little mutual interest but the act of copulation was necessary to justify our being together.

Whilst getting dressed back in camp, I assumed that I would be coming home alone on a cold November night. Consequently, I found myself in a strange flat with a strange girl trying to undress with some dignity by removing my trousers and my army long johns in one go. Perhaps I was trying to maintain the mystique of the moment.

Never before, or since, have I had such a loveless coupling, bereft of compassion or even sympathy. It got worse when I squeezed one of her breasts a little too firmly. She grunted manfully.

"I'm sorry," I said.

"It's okay," she replied, "I quite like it."

"What?"

"I like it rough."

I felt the Devil's hand on my shoulder. I slapped her. She moaned and tried to hit me back but I restrained her whilst slapping her again with my other hand. Then ensued an episode that shames me still, my slaps and her groans increasing with corresponding vehemence.

Early next morning I sneaked out of her flat wearing my shame like an old overcoat. My quest to be a better person lay in shreds on the ground. And in the hasty tangle of my departure, I forgot my long johns.

Back at camp, I was unable to share in the macho jocularity of the previous evening's reminisces. My reticence was chastised gleefully.

"Jeez, Billy, you got yourself a real lady last night," said one.

"Venus she wasn't," said another.

"More like Medusa," said a third.

"Why did you do it, Billy?" asked one of the more sympathetic young officers. I survived his scrutiny for a while before looking away.

"I don't know," I said, "I really don't."

The final exercise of the course was in Wales. We tabbed through the rain into the hills as night approached, bergens heavy on our backs, but minds far away. I longed for the warmth of Emily's embrace.

It rained so much that we were pulled off the hills for the last night in order to dry off and get proper rest before we conducted the final stage of training with live ammunition.

"Mooooo." Phil Staples' cynical humour was very apt. A hundred of us were herded into a barn, dripping wet and completely dispirited. He had already served for a year with his regiment before attending the course and his stoic good nature was a crutch for those of us who, like me, had come straight from the officer factory[31]. His disregard for the establishment, however,

---

[31] The Royal Military Academy.

did not suit the instructors.

"Ye may well jest, sir," said an angry little Scottish colour sergeant, "but yous young officers do look like a herd of coos." Phil smiled at him.

"Nah, Colour, cows are treated better than us."

I cleared the straw from the barn floor and made a little bonfire with solid fuel blocks to dry out my sleeping bag. I had a hot meal. It felt like Christmas.

"Hey fellahs, I've found some chocolate powder in my bergen. Anyone want it?" Phil held a packet of ration box drinking chocolate in he air. It actually tasted crappy but after two cold and wet weeks in the Welsh hills it would be lovely. I had long since drunk all mine.

"How much?"

"I'll give you two quid."

"Five!" The bidding went beyond reality, driven by humour as much as desire for hot chocolate.

"Twenty quid!" The final offer came from a rich Guards officer. Phil Staples hesitated.

"Nah, I'm gonna have it myself".

Next morning we were herded back out into the rain. I had slept well and was warm and dry for the first time in days: perhaps the Army Bitch was not so bad, after all.

"Sir, you cannot wear your waterproof jacket whilst on patrol." One of the Colour Sergeants immediately sort to spoil things.

"It's pissing down, Colour."

"The enemy will hear you moving."

"Surely the thundering rain will make more noise."

"It's not good practice."

"I wouldn't have thought that it was good practice to get piss wet through, either."

"Take it off, sir." I immediately got wet.

Eventually, it ended. We went home. I ran back to the ravishing charms of Emily Fisher. I was very pleased to see her. My ardour was ardent. In fact, I was so ardent that her underpants became a very real obstruction and I had to rip them off. Afterwards, she complained, but not too vehemently. I told her it was her own fault.

"Why is it my fault?" asked Emily.

"You should realise that sex occurs at twenty two hundred hours and be undressed accordingly. That's ten p.m. for civilians"

"You're becoming a military bore," she said. Indeed, I was but I was trying to become a better person. Anyway, later that evening she came and stood to attention in front of me.

"What's up?" I asked

"Emily Fisher reporting for sex, sir." It was twenty two hundred hours and her pants had been removed for inspection. I feared, though, that such behaviour did not make me a better person. This did not seem to trouble Miss Fisher.

"You were much better," she said.

Next morning I had to drive her back up to London to catch a train. Her ardour was still harder than mine and she fumbled with my flies as we drove along the A12. She stroked me gently with her leather gloves still on. I was sweating like a pervert on the beach. I could not change gear, the engine screamed in protest. Then a police car arrived and began to tail me. Eventually, the blue light came on and I pulled over, pulled Miss Fisher off and pulled my zip up.

Why do policemen take so long to walk from their cars?

"Is there a reason why you are not wearing your seatbelt, sir?"

Seat belt!

I was worried about being charged with dangerous driving, indecent exposure or even possession of an offensive weapon, but not failing to wear a seat belt.

"I forgot."

"You forgot!" said the policeman incredulously. That puzzled me. If I had given some outrageously implausible excuse, I could have understood his scepticism. I wonder what he would have said if I'd told the truth:

"Well, actually Officer, I wasn't wearing my seatbelt because I was getting a hand job at the time."

14

The next year began right after Christmas. It was spent in the jungle and, initially, the year seemed like a very long road indeed. The word *jungle* conjured up all sorts of daunting images in my mind: torrential tropical rain, enormous insects, snakes, leeches and prolonged isolation from Emily Fisher were all regular features of my nightmares.

For the uninitiated, the jungle is a nightmare. It is strangely dark under the trees and moving along the ground is slow, hard work. The branches of low trees and fronds of giant plants all seem to have cruel thorns on them that reach out and grab your clothes or skin and are reluctant to let go. Sweat runs like tears and your clothes are constantly soaked.

It is physically difficult to drink and absorb enough water to allow your body to function. During our first days of acclimatisation we drank 10 litres a day and often that was not enough. Dehydration became a constant companion so that our feet swelled up in our boots leading to agonizing blisters and the palate in our mouths ached so much it seemed like it would crack.

Escaping the dark prison of the trees into a clearing or plantation provided only temporary relief since the burning sun soon desiccated already parched beings and then the rain would fall like vengeful insects stinging exposed skin and suddenly making us feel cold and weak. The real insects were just there for comedy value.

"Ah, fuck, fuck, fuck!" I yelled one night as I flopped exhausted onto the only patch of dry ground I could find; it was an anthill.

"Keep the noise down," hissed one of the instructors, "you'll give your position away."

`"Fuck off," I hissed back with such vehemence that

the instructor melted back into the trees accepting that discretion sometimes is the better part of valour.

We had inserted a patrol by river into a mature mangrove swamp. The engines had droned wearily as they struggled to push the heavily laden boats through the brown, glutinous water. Once beached, we climbed out onto the exposed roots of the mangrove plants and hefted our 80lb bergens onto our shoulders.

Then we clambered painfully through the forest of massive mangroves, balancing precariously on the thick roots. We lumbered all day, top heavy with our radios and ammunition. The thick roots that protruded through the mire were slippy and treacherous and a misplaced foot resulted in your leg crashing through the roots until your groin cracked against the root bar. It was impossible to pull yourself free unaided. Progress was slow. By nightfall, we had only gone eight hundred metres.

"Water patrol," ordered the team commander to one of the corporals and me. We collected a water bottle from every man and crawled through the roots trying to find water that was not spoiled with turpentine from rotting mangrove.

"Is that it?" gasped Corporal Williams when we eventually found a pool of water. It was brown and filled with leaves and other debris.

"Looks like it, Willy" I said, lacking the enthusiasm to comment further.

"Surely we can't be expected to drink that; how will we strain it?" I was desperate; the five litres of water that I carried in my personal kit were long since exhausted.

"Let's use this," I said holding up my last dry sock. We perched on roots and spent an hour filtering stagnant water through a sock before sterilising it with chlorine. When we got back to the patrol base I strung my basha and hammock from some sturdy mangrove branches. Pathetically, it looked really cosy and I crawled into the desperate sanctuary of the mosquito net and lay like a corpse in the hammock, feeling sleep rush through me like a drug. I was wakened an hour later to go do STAG.

Getting used to the jungle took time. I was a novice soldier and I struggled a lot with specialist first aid, jungle tactics and communications, relying heavily on the support of more experienced colleagues to show me things that had not been taught in basic training.

"Put your bergens in the chopper," ordered one of the instructors, "but keep your webbing on[32]." I was acting as the platoon commander for a phase of the exercise and had to take the section commanders to recce[33] a site for a defensive position.

"Were do we sit, sergeant?" I asked the instructor since our four bergens completely filled the interior of the small Wasp helicopter. He smiled at me pleasantly, as if he was offering me a cup of tea.

"You stand on the skids, sir, and perch your bum on the edge of the cabin. Make sure you clip into the harness, though, we don't want you falling out." His smiling condescension was almost malevolent. I clipped in and braced myself against the skids, my heart starting to beat faster, nervous sweat almost gushing out of my pores.

The engine began to whine as the pilot revved it up and the frame of the small helicopter began to shudder, shaking us about like dolls. The engine's pitch

---

[32] Personal equipment needed for immediate use, such as ammunition, water and compass and binoculars, worn around the waist on a heavy belt with shoulder straps.

[33] Reconnaissance.

increased as the chopper tried to lift its burden and then with a sudden lurch it broke free of its lethargy and launched vertically upwards into the swollen sky.

Once clear of the treetops the little chopper titled and then charged forward just a few metres above the jungle canopy. I thought I might shit myself. I had been in helicopters before in basic training but I had always been safely inside, not hanging on the skid like a loose part. The trees rushed under my feet, menacingly close as if I might catch my foot, and the air buffeted my face making it difficult to breathe.

I managed to squint through half closed eyes and look forward to see low, dark clouds that hung ominously in our path. The pilot leant back and tried to shout something that was unintelligible above the wind and screaming engine. I got his meaning when the rain stung like pellets as he cheerfully flew through a tropical storm. When the ride was over I staggered away from the chopper on weak legs like a drunk. Then we had to dig trenches.

Eventually, as our collective machismo drove us on, we learned to adapt and even to enjoy the jungle. I also relished the all-male environment and the mutual support that came with it. At last I felt a sense of belonging.

It was still lonely, however, and when the mail drop eventually found me in the jungle, I was ecstatic. I received a card from Emily Fisher and realised that St Valentine's Day had slipped past unnoticed; other than night or day, time had lost meaning for us.

In the card was a pair of lacy black knickers and Emily described how she slipped them off under her work desk and put them in the envelope to remind me of her. I put them on my head and breathed deeply but the 8000 miles between us had robbed them of their perfume. The soldiers cheered.

"Hey, Boss, read us the sports page."

"She says that she misses me."

"Oh, bollocks, they're all the same, women. She'll be getting it from some big fellah named Winston."

Not everyone had an Emily Fisher to write them seductive letters and they drew comfort in different ways. Perhaps they did not actually need comfort, as such, but considered their actions to be excusable because they were a long way from home. At least that is how some of the blokes explained their self-indulgences with the lady boys

Lady boys start life as male but gradually seem to move into a transient gender somewhere between transvestite and transsexual. They proffered their favours towards us, it seemed, because sexual conduct with a heterosexual man confirmed their arrival in the new gender.

They hung around the back of camp, teasing us through the wire.

"They're disgusting," said Matt Fuller, a young officer who was full of bravado.

"Aye, you'd have to be fair desperate to do that," agreed Sergeant Cleary and we collectively turned our backs on them.

But the lady boys persisted and attitudes began to change as the troops became lonely or sexually frustrated. One night after a drunken BBQ, Matt Fuller slipped away to the back fence.

"Just want to see what they're like," he said. We watched him chat with them for a while until he suddenly dropped his trousers, thrust his hips against the fence and hung on, moaning with pleasure. The taboo was broken and a strange mating ritual developed whereby a soldier clung to the wire fence so that a lucky lady boy could perform fellatio on him.

"Oh Lonny, you so big, I lurve you long time." I

witnessed one old sweat lumbering over to the fence muttering:

"Ah, fuck it, you're only gay if you take it up the shitter."

My Yorkshire naivety was rudely exposed but the social degeneration got worse during the only weekend leave period of the course. British troops in Brunei are the guests of the Sultan and are duty bound to respect the Islamic culture so a few of us spent our weekend leave across the border in Malaysia, in a place called Miri.

Humanity is not a precious commodity in Malaysia, oil and mineral deposits taking precedence. Things are cheap, especially women and part of my military initiation was "to bed a whore". I was reticent at first but it all seemed to be part of the big adventure so I went along with the plan. The place to conduct such liaisons in Malaysia is at the barbers.

Being the most junior officer, I had to go first. It was a sweaty, seedy place and as soon as we arrived the barber gave us all a can of beer. I sat in the chair and watched in the mirror as an enormous Momma came lurching towards me with a massive bosom and an equally dangerous pair of scissors.

"You want girl?" The shop owner paraded a line of girls in front of us like a Holiday Camp Beauty Pageant. They wore swimsuits with numbers on their wrists. My Brothers-in-Arms drank beer and organised themselves girls for the night. Then they left for the bar and I had to chase after them, stopping briefly to order myself number 14 from the line.

We spent the day getting drunk and then went to wait in our hotel but the girls did not come. I was sharing a room with Simon and we both tried to remain nonchalant.

"Do you think it's okay to do this?" he asked me

while we waited.

"Not without a girl," I said.

"I'm not sure. Maybe it's wrong."

"Well, if no-one gets hurt, surely it's fine."

"But what if they don't want to do it?" he asked earnestly. It was a fair question and I took some time in answering.

"They are getting paid, they're not gonna do it for love."

"But what if they are being forced into it by their father or something?"

"If they don't get the money they might get beaten," I said. "It's probably better for them to sell themselves than not, on balance."

"Yes, but if they weren't so poor they would not be in this position in the first place." Simon continued to argue and I was not sure whether he believed it or just needed reassuring that he was not an evil person.

"Yes, but that's not your fault. You're as trapped as they are into it. There's nothing you can do about it so you may as well get laid and if you really want to help the girl, give her a tip."

It was surprising that a simple act of financially recompensed sex could evoke such profundity but Simon had a point. I was so keen to pursue the adventure that I had not really thought about the moral aspects of it. Still, we had no girls yet so it was a moot point.

I rang the hotel porter.

"Hello, this is Second Lieutenant Hanson in room 24."

"Yes, Sah."

"Erm..........have there been any visitors for us?"

"No, Sah."

"You sure?"

"Yes, Sah." I looked at Simon, "Perhaps we got it

all wrong, wrong hotel, or something."

"Ring Mark," he suggested. "See if his girl has arrived." I dialled the number for Mark's room.

"Fuck off, I'm busy."

"Mark's lady has arrived," I told Simon.

We waited a while longer. Eventually, I rang reception.

"It's Mr Hanson again. We're still waiting for some visitors."

"No-one here, Sah." I put the phone down and sat on the bed. We drank gin and melancholia, our adventure seemingly at an end.

Then the phone rang.

"Hello, Mr Hanson, this is the Duty Manager." He sounded very formal and I could not help negative thoughts racing through my mind; perhaps the girls had arrived and there was a hotel policy on whores or something. He might have the police with him. I decided to brazen it out.

"Hello."

"Were you expecting some visitors?"

"Yes," I replied excitedly making *pwhoar* faces at Simon. "Have they arrived?"

"No," he said triumphantly.

"Oh." There was a long pause.

"Do you want me to get some for you?" he asked suddenly.

"Err, yes please, that would be very kind. Actually we'd like two please."

We waited nervously for their arrival, Simon still trying to resolve his moral dilemma over the issue. Eventually they arrived, escorted by the hotel manager who would presumably add some commission for having brokered the deal.

One of the girls was petite, almost elfin, with smiling features and a cool reassurance that was immediately alluring. The other was less attractive to parochial European eyes. She was squat, less pretty and very young but it was her discomfort that was most off putting.

Whilst I made the financial arrangements, Simon managed to over come his moral dilemma and dragged the prettier of the two into his lair like a hungry bear. I was left with the child-like girl who was shaking like an unlovely flower. I did not know her name and she spoke no English, though why these problems held any importance for me I do not know. It was not as if I had to conduct any seduction, my dollars and her poverty had already taken care of that.

Besides, this relationship was not about attraction, or even sex. For me it was a man thing, adventure, something. For her it was about poverty, exploitation and desperation. For a brief, shameful moment her vulnerability held some attraction for me.

Neither of us knew what to do. She ran a bath and gently washed me. Then she lay down on the bed like a corpse.

I could not do it. I felt an enormous sense of irony that my incompetence with women should extend even to this perfunctory relationship but, as she lay there waiting to be violated, the enormity of my exploitation was too much. What right did I have to penetrate her fragile body? Perhaps the money that I had paid, that she needed, afforded me that privilege but at what price do you buy another person's humanity?

She lay motionless on the bed, her presence illustrating my failure in the military passage of manhood and I resented her for it. I wanted to send her away but thought of the little Match Girl that my Grandfather told me about and I worried that if I dismissed her she would be made to go out and sell herself again.

I made her get dressed and gave her what cash I had left in my wallet. I made a bed for her on the couch. Simon slept little, his bed squeaking with rhythmic satisfaction through most of the night. I could not decide whether I was pleased or sad that he had overcome his concerns.

In the morning when the whores had all gone, we gathered for breakfast.

"What a night!" said Matt Fuller. "I gave my bitch a real hard time." Another captain, Tom Dantry, nodded.

"I felt like I was getting my own back on every girl who's ever dumped me."

"What really got me going," said another captain, "was that the girl had no choice but lie still and take it."

I sat quietly, trying not to be noticed, but Matt would not allow that.

"Hey, Billy, did you enjoy yourself? You a man now?"

I shook my head.

"I couldn't do it." I expected a tirade of abuse but the guys were not interested. Instead they picked on another silent figure who was sat at the edge of the group.

"Johno, what about you?" Matt prodded. Toby Johnson shifted uncomfortably and tried to avoid the question. "Come on, tell us," Matt persisted.

"My girl offered me some blue pills. She said they'd make me hard." There was sudden interest; Viagra was new on the market.

"What happened?"

"Did they work?"

"I fell asleep," said Johno. "She took everything, wallet, camera, contents of the mini-bar. She also made a load of international phone calls which I had to pay for." There was a brief sympathetic silence.

"You stupid bastard."

"Why d'you do that?"

"What a bitch!" The irony of the last comment was missed.

I was appalled at the attitude of some of my colleagues and my own sense of failure became one of triumph. I had shared the same intentions as everyone else but I had seen the depravity of my actions and it had scared me. Maybe, just maybe, I could become a better person.

Then we went back into jungle for the final exercise. We crammed apprehensively into the Bell Huey helicopters, anticipating two weeks in the bush with no respite. The choppers hummed slowly and then started to vibrate as they lifted us up into the air, tilting forward to fly over the trees. I felt nervous about the challenges ahead: the desperately hard work, the physical privations and the haunting twilight of the jungle. But I also felt elation that in the trees I could hide from my shame.

Part 4 – Valhalla

"It's closer to the truth to say you can't get enough..."
Addicted to Love - Robert Palmer 1986.

15

The ancient oak wood creaked under each delicate step. Scowling generals looked down with impotent anger from their portraits on the dining room wall. Lights from the corridor cast gentle shadows on Emily's pale skin as she moved gracefully along the full length of the table. Each time she reached the end of her stage, she turned with elegant precision like a ballerina in Swan Lake.

Or perhaps she was a dancer in the Moulin Rouge, for behind her poise was an intensity that threatened to overwhelm me. Each step was accompanied by the release of a button or strap as Emily removed the barriers to my desire. First her blouse, then her skirt, then her knickers until she performed in only stockings and camisole, like Emma Hamilton dancing for Nelson.

With her business suit on the floor like discarded morals, Emily came to the centre of the table and slid her camisole, the last remnant of virtue, from her shoulders, letting it gather, unwanted, around her ankles.

She stepped out of the silky restraint and stood towering above me with her long, black-stockinged legs leading inevitably upwards. She knelt down and ran her long fingers through my hair to the back of my head, then pulled me slowly but inexorably forward. I did her bidding as she shuddered and sighed, holding onto my head for support.

Then Emily lay down on the smoothly polished dining table and moaned as we became entwined.

"Billy," she sighed as her stockinged legs wrapped around my back and shoulders so that she could pull me closer, deeper. "Fuck me, Billy, fuck me hard." Emily urged me to greater effort until her back arched upwards whilst the eyes of the old painted generals watched and despaired from the wall.

"Yes," she moaned at last and then relaxed back on to the table with a slow, languorous, exhalation of contentment. "I've missed you, Billy."

"I've missed you, Sweety."

She raised herself up on one elbow and studied my face. Then she smiled and relaxed back onto the table, lying naked and intolerably sexy on the hard, uncompromising wood.

"I'm glad you're back," she said dreamily with her eyes closed and a hand stroking herself idly between her legs.

"So am I."

It was good to be back home, especially since I had unexpectedly been posted to the recruit-training centre outside York. My departure from Belize had been hastened by a month because of the misdemeanours of one of my fellow officers.

"Mr Hanson, I am sending you to Strensall," said the Commanding Officer from behind his desk. He was a tall, lean man, the typical infantry officer, and he had the thoughtful crossed brow of all senior officers. I had been summoned to his office in Belize and assumed I had dropped a bollock somewhere so this news was very welcome.

"Thank you, sir," I replied but perhaps with a little uncertainty for the CO raised an eyebrow. I presumed that was my invitation to speak. "I thought Max Wrench was going there, sir?"

"Well, he was but he was found in the Rose Garden[34]." The CO sat down and let a wry smile escape his lips. "In fact, he was escorted out of the place twice by the RMP[35] and then arrested on the third occasion."

---

[34] Raul's Rose Garden: The infamous Belizean brothel, which was out of bounds to officers.

[35] Royal Military Police.

"Anyway, Billy," he said, "you've done quite well in your first year and have made a good impression so you deserve an opportunity like this." He handed me my annual appraisal, which was distinctly average. I read it and looked up at him, clearly unimpressed. "I don't believe in giving excellent reports[36] to first year subalterns," he said.

The CO dismissed me and sent me to my company commander.

"Congratulations, Billy," he said, "you'll have a great time. We'll miss you, though, you've been a great addition to the team in B Company.

"Thank you, sir," I smiled thinking of all the long-range patrols I had led on the border and the training exercises that I had been part of.

"Yes, indeed," he continued like Captain Mainwaring, "I was most impressed that night you dressed up as a chef and volunteered to do the Mess BBQ when the staff were on night off."

Are you fucking serious?

As a completely inexperienced officer I had led border patrols, done a population census, unearthed evidence of drug smuggling, illegal deforestation and Belizean Police corruption leading to murder. My patrol reports had been used by the CO as a model for all other patrol commanders and the Brigade HQ had used them as the basis for intelligence analysis that reshaped the entire patrol programme.

But the CO did not think second lieutenants should get excellent reports and Major Fuckwit, my Company Commander, had been impressed because I did a BBQ one night. The Army Bitch was a mad cow; at least my

---

[36] Appraisal reports used to be graded "good, very good or excellent".

regiment was, and I was glad to be able to walk away from it.

Emily met me at the airport.

"Hi, Billy," she called loudly as I emerged through the arrivals' hall. Her delight at seeing me was palpable and people looked over to see who was lucky enough to be met by this delightful young woman. Those first moments of reunion were utterly blissful. We embraced, Emily cried a bit and I felt I had come home.

I dumped my bags on a trolley and Emily sat on them, facing me, a stockinged leg curved from under her coat, the promise of things to come. Once in the car park, she rose from the trolley and gently unfastened her coat. She wore only a scarf, suspenders and high heels and her slender beauty was luminescent in the glow of the car park lights. Emily had a rare gift of being sweet, sophisticated and sexy all at once. I was enveloped in her warmth and passion.

The next day I had to drive North into God's Country to report for duty at my new unit. Yorkshire still clung to the last vestiges of autumn, the trees had a beautiful brown, red and gold tinge and as I drove through the county of my upbringing, I was at peace. The Army Bitch seemed to favour me. The regular posting cycle in the army means that you get to make a fresh start every couple of years and I began my new posting with optimism.

It was dark when I entered the officers' mess which was to be my home for the next eighteen months. Remembering my last induction into a mess, I was apprehensive about arriving and establishing my relative position in the pecking order, but as I entered the bar, the young officers all stood, hands outstretched.

"Hi, you must be Billy."

"Welcome home."

"We've delayed supper, Chef's special, steak and

chips. No need to change, we're going out straight after scoff."

"I'll put your bags in your room, you have a beer."

This was how I imagined life in the officers' mess would be and I indeed felt I was home at last.

We sat down to a noisy meal and promptly departed for the drinkeries of York. I immediately got into trouble; with a nurse in a pub.

"You look brown for this time of year," she said.

"I just got back form Central America."

"What's a nice chap like you doing in Central America?"

"I'm a jungle warfare instructor."

That was all it took. We chatted. I made her laugh and she made me feel wanted. That should not have been sufficient temptation because I was already wanted; Emily Fisher had made that very clear. But I was beginning to realise, though unable to admit, that it was a dominant libido and weak ego that made me so vulnerable to temptation.

In the morning I ran out into the cold, lost, uncertain and already tarnished. I had an expensive taxi ride back to camp followed by a painfully long coach ride to London with a terrible hangover because I had been picked to play rugby, even before I had arrived. The other chaps were impressed in the pointless way that young men are impressed by promiscuity and I managed to delude myself that it was a forgivable act of drunken irresponsibility.

Indeed, my relationship with Emily Fisher blossomed. We saw each other a lot, exploring the city, discovering new restaurants, museums, and hidden adventures amongst the ancient walls and walkways of York. Just holding hands walking along the Shambles was a delight and even shopping could be an amorous adventure.

146

"I couldn't decide what to get you for Christmas," I told Emily one Saturday morning. "So we need to go shopping." Emily looked a little disappointed, although not altogether surprised. "I have some ideas, though." She smiled a little and I tried to make the whole day out together part of my gift.

We started the day in ye olde tea shoppe, one of Emily's cute eccentricities.

"I'll have a large espresso and a bacon sandwich, please," I asked the old lady who came to take our order. She looked at me as if I had asked for a line of coke.

"We don't serve espresso."

"Black coffee, then, please."

"I'll have Earl Grey breakfast blend with toasted fruit teacakes," smiled Emily like a connoisseur. The old lady beamed at her and then glanced at me with a *what's a nice girl like you doing with an oik like him* type of grimace.

"Where are we going shopping, Billy?" Emily asked with her eyes bright and I began to worry that my ideas might be a little underwhelming.

I lead her by the hand to Coppergate. "This is Bruno." I introduced Emily to a huge brown teddy bear in a toyshop.

"He's lovely," gushed Emily although I could not tell if she was genuine. She did look very sexy hugging Bruno like that. Next we went to a large department store that had an infinite supply of exotic lingerie. Emily almost ran in with excitement.

"This is what I had in mind," I said showing Emily some sumptuous lace French knickers and camisole. I had spent an almost orgasmic couple of hours in the store choosing a selection for her.

"Mmm, nice," Emily enthused in husky undertones and held the ensemble against herself in front of the mirror. The effect was exactly as I had anticipated and I wanted to jump her right there, but I bought Emily a lot of underwear so the gift was not that special.

I took Emily to see some matching luggage, a holdall and suit carrier.

"You're always using mine," I said and the fact that I had chosen something that Emily specifically needed, made it seem like a highly personal gift, although a bloke can rarely tell.

"That's nice." Emily picked it up and smiled but without the gushing: Perhaps sometimes a bloke can tell. Next we went across town to one of those middle class semi-country clothes shops that York seems to specialise in.

"I saw these and thought they would suit you," I explained holding up a pair of cropped cord jodhpurs, a simple but elegant white blouse and very cute sheepskin waistcoat. I was quite hesitant as this was my last shot at impressing her.

"I like those," Emily said slowly, reaching out to touch the waistcoat. She rubbed the sheepskin gently between thumb and forefinger and then she finally took the clothes from me. "Can I try them on?"

We went into a changing room and I locked the door. For Emily, taking her clothes off was necessary to try on new outfits, but for me the simple elegance of her actions was irresistible.

"These are nice, Billy, thank you," she smiled and began to undress again. I stepped forward to embrace her. If she was surprised by my determination she quickly overcame it and responded naturally by opening her arms and legs to me as I entered her. She wound around me tightly and breathed in my ear. "Merry Christmas, darling."

It was good to be back with Emily Fisher.

16

It was also good to be training recruits. The training was programmed and well organised so everything ran smoothly, in stark contrast to the chaotic nature of operations in the jungle. I led a training team that was fully staffed with experienced and motivated NCOs and so life with the Army Bitch was as I imagined it would be.

Inevitably there were some frustrations.

"Keep going fellahs!" shouted Monty, the platoon sergeant, during the first run with my first training platoon. A recruit who looked like he had not started shaving yet flopped at his feet.

"I can't go on, sergeant," he groaned pitifully.

"You've only run a mile and a half," Monty said with exasperation.

"I didn't think it would be this hard," whinged the recruit. I thought Monty might have a stroke as he struggled to contain his angst.

"You joined the army, you Muppet, what did you expect." The recruit looked so pathetic I almost felt sorry for him.

"My father said I had to."

The new platoon formed up with 44 recruits. We lost 25% immediately after the first detailed medical inspection.

"Collins is to be MD[37] because he has been on anti depressants since he was 12. Jones is due to have an operation on his back and the doc says Williams is not getting enough calories to sustain the training regime." Monty read out the list of medical complaints to amused grins in the platoon office.

---

[37] Medically Discharged.

"Why doesn't he eat more scoff, then?" suggested Chalky, one of the corporals, "there's enough available." Monty shrugged.

"Apparently he can't absorb real food. He was brought up on Pot Noodles and stuff."

Army recruitment and training seemed designed to accommodate and hide failure. There was no holistic management of the process and the effect was that the recruiters brought people into the system who were wholly inappropriate for the army, the training regime was under pressure to keep as many of those recruits as it could, and the public perception seemed to be that youngsters who failed to get a "proper" job could always join the army. Still, that was what I had done so I was not in a position to be too critical.

At least the recruits we were left with had joined the army for positive reasons, to be part of something fulfilling and to leave behind the failings of the societies from which they came.

"I wanted some discipline and structure in my life," said one surprisingly erudite young recruit when I first interviewed him.

"I didn't want to be part of the drug and petty crime scene in my area," declared another with some feeling.

Helping young blokes achieve something inspired me although I had reservations about the training regime that put me at odds with the rest of the staff; a position I was quickly getting used to in the army. Military educational specialists wrote the training theory and programme but its implementation was left to junior officers and NCOs such as myself.

There was an ethos of shouting at people and forcing them to make mistakes. In theory of course, supervising the training was my job but I had only been out of training myself for less than a year.[38]

"Hold the rabbit like this," explained Chang, one of the corporals, during the first field exercise. He held the rabbit in one hand with two fingers behind its ears, its legs scrabbling piteously in the air. "Then you flick your hand like a whip!" Chang used such force that the rabbit's neck snapped instantly. It hung lifeless in his hand. "You must do it sharply," he added with a sick grin, "so that bunny does not feel any pain."

Corporal Chang was a big bloke with wrists and forearms like a grizzly bear but most of the recruits were puny and could not flick a three-kilo bunny with enough force to make it a quick kill. The result was sickening.

"I bet you didn't know that rabbits squeal, sir," smirked Chang as I looked around at recruits trying to chop rabbits' heads off with penknives or break their necks with shovels. One young recruit, desperate to prove his manhood, had hold of a rabbit by its hind legs and was ineffectually swinging its head against a tree.

An older recruit who had been a trainee butcher before he signed up had killed, skinned and filleted a couple of rabbits with remarkable efficiency. As they were roasting on a fire, two of his friends were holding a rabbit skin puppet show.

"I don't think we're achieving much with some of the training practices," I suggested to the team in my next planning meeting. There was general consent and we took a different approach from then.

"You gotta admit that the rabbit skin puppet show was funny, though," said Chang.

Despite these concerns, it was rewarding to see

---

[38] Military training has improved immeasurably since I was a young officer. It is supervised closely by
the military establishment and external organisations such as
Ofsted.

young blokes, who were often from difficult backgrounds, develop into capable soldiers who had some spirit about themselves and pride in what they were doing. Not all were like that.

"Thanks, Boss," said a forlorn yet strangely confident looking recruit whose discharge papers I had just signed. We had tried to keep him from being discharged but he just was not up to it. I had taught him how to swim to show him that he could achieve things but that was all he had achieved in eight weeks.

I looked up from my desk.

"I am sorry I couldn't manage to keep you on, Haile."

"That's not what I meant," he said quietly and with more strength than he had shown during training. "I knew you wouldn't be able to keep me. I just meant thanks for trying."

"No worries." I felt inadequate. He looked at me very directly, something else that he had not previously done.

"No-one ever tried to do anything for me before. No-one ever stood up for me." He looked me in the eye a while longer and then walked away. Out of a total of 44 recruits on day one, my first platoon only passed 14 out of training.

I also enjoyed Strensall because of the social life. We drank heavily, starting with Friday and Saturday night forays into the city. Then we began a Thursday night black tie dinner club in the mess that was aimed at bringing in guests but this invariably failed since most normal people work on Fridays and do not want a steaming hangover. The result was a dozen overdressed blokes all sat together with no totty in sight.

I occasionally managed to persuade a few nurses to come along but they suffered an onslaught of drunken young officers and rarely came twice. It was called the YODA, York Officers Dining Association, and at the time we deluded ourselves that it was a Byronesque gentlemen's club but, in retrospect, it probably just looked like an upmarket Blue Oyster Club[39].

The weekend was extended to Sunday night and quickly brought forward to Wednesday night after we had been playing rugby or football and in the end, Monday and Tuesday were the only chance to recover and sleep normally.

Under such distraction, my relationship with Emily Fisher could not last. I became increasingly detached, lacking the maturity to commit to the relationship any more. We had shared interests, went horse riding, watched rugby, got drunk and had great sex but the elephant in the room was that the paths of our lives were never going to converge. Emily was looking ahead whereas I rarely looked beyond the weekend.

Despite its inevitability, the manner in which our relationship ended was sad; Emily deserved better than that. Actually, she deserved better than me and I was at least man enough to recognise that.

Things came to a head in the street. I had kept her waiting whilst I got drunk.

"Where have you been?" Why do women ask such obvious questions?

"In the pub."

"All evening?"

"All day, actually."

"You were supposed to be meeting me." As well as being angry, Emily was hurt. My guilt made me defensive.

"I was busy."

---

[39] The now iconic gay bar in the 1984 film Police Academy.

"You're so selfish."

"You don't own my life, Emily."

"You bastard." She slapped me hard across the face. It was actually very satisfying. No woman had ever slapped me seriously before. Emily was the only one who cared enough to bother.

"I never wanted to own your life," she sobbed, "I just wanted to share it with you." As she walked away from me I realized that I had truly and irretrievably fucked up this time.

I went back to the pub.

"I thought you went to fetch Emily," slurred, Riley, one of the colluders in my loss.

"I did but she's not coming." He was too drunk to notice.

"Later then?" When I slowly shook my head he finally got the message. "Oh, shame," he whispered with genuine feeling, Emily had been a regular visitor to the mess for a year and she was very popular.

"Why so miserable?" mumbled another friend.

"Billy just broke up with Emily," declared Riley to the general audience of heavily boozed army officers. There was some immediate concern from my brothers-in-arms, but not much.

"Double whisky for the loser in the corner," yelled Riley and he bade me drink it in one.

I had another. Then another but it did not lessen my sense of failure and I sat slugging whisky, cogitating on the depth to which my hedonism had taken me. I was uncertain what to do.

As I was growing up my Father always said that when you are not sure what to do in life, you should do what you are good at. I do not think he meant drunken philandering but that was what I was good at. In fact, apart from physical endeavour, boozing and fornicating seemed like the only thing I was good at.

154

It seemed to be more than coincidence that at church parade with the recruits the following Sunday the Padre preached from The Book of Ecclesiastes: A life of vanity is empty and that vanity and evil lurk in the darkness[40].

The Temptation of Adam always seemed confusing, if not contradictory, to me. If Adam were without sin until he ate the fruit from the Tree of Knowledge, then he would not have yielded to Eve's persuasion in the first place. There must be a more fundamental instinct that supersedes the conscious notion of good and evil. Clearly, the blinding temptation of naked totty, as Eve is always depicted in renaissance European art, was that force.

In York I succumbed to that force willingly and what happened there was sordid or splendid, depending on your perspective: Oliver Reed might have been proud of me but my Grandfather would certainly not.

---

[40] There is some debate about the meaning of "vanity" in this context but the implication for me was that my life had become empty and would get worse.

17

I stood on the deck of the quaint old steamboat sipping my champagne and watching the pantomime around me. We chugged over a calm Lake Windermere and the brooding mountains formed a picturesque backdrop to the perfect wedding reception. Even the omnipresent Lakeland clouds stacked high above added to the day's splendour.

I had gone to the Sunday wedding alone. In fact I had been at a wedding on the Saturday and got into trouble with another nurse and so the dash from York to Ambleside in time for this wedding had been chaotic and I was still suffering from a hangover.

Still, I had champagne in hand and a few promising dalliances in mind, so things were perking up quickly, so to speak. There were also some regimental colleagues, on leave from Northern Ireland, clustered in the stern like public schoolboys sneaking a drink in the dormitory.

It was good to see them, although I was on the periphery, not party to all the current chat about operations in the Province since I was still posted at the training depot. More importantly, I wanted to exploit the opportunities presented around me by Eve, not get mindlessly drunk.

"Thank you, miss," I smiled taking a glass of champagne from a waitress with a tray of bubbling flutes. She smiled back. I had noticed that her circuit of the top deck was taking a while. "Do you mind if I take another?" I whispered conspiratorially.

"Okay, but don't tell anyone," she replied coyly. I lifted another glass.

"You and I should get to know each other better." She giggled. I had not actually intended to flirt, I just wanted to ensure a ready supply of bubbly, but the smart blue tunics and swords we wore to weddings always seemed to have that effect.

Then I saw a girl of breathtaking loveliness. She was dark and slender, displaying an intense sensuality that petrified me. Surely, she was the Future Mrs Hanson: just add ring, pour on champagne, shag senseless and live happily ever after. I was immediately in love but the throng of the crowd kept us apart. I spent the rest of the day trying to get together with my Helen of Troy.

A bridesmaid interrupted me in my campaign. She was the bride's sister and she seemed less than pleased that she was still on her own. That was a fair premise I thought since she was quite lovely and fully on display in her plunging ivory gown.

"Let's dance," she ordered and I was happy with that, the bride's sister had been a rewarding seduction at a previous wedding.

"Are you having a good time," I asked as we whirled about.

"Sort of," she said, "but I am struggling to play in a supporting role." I was not quite sure what she meant and it was difficult to explore the sentiment above the din of the band. She thought so too.

"Let's go somewhere quieter. I'm Karen, by the way." Karen's notion of going somewhere quieter was quite different to mine, it appeared. I suppose she wanted to go somewhere to talk so we could get to know each other but she did not protest too much when I led her into the kitchen, which seemed to be the quietest place around.

"You're not shy, are you Billy?" she asked as I lifted her onto a table and began kissing her neck.

"Oh, sorry, am I being too forward?" I asked genuinely, never sure what women meant.

"Yes you are," grinned Karen, "but don't let it put

you off." So we enjoyed some intimacy as I ensured that Karen was the centre of attention, having realised by then what was troubling her. Our increasing passion was rudely interrupted when Karen's mom came looking for her.

"Quick in here." Karen dragged me into a walk in fridge. The wedding reception was in her parent's hotel so Karen knew her way around. The fridge was dimly lit with tiered shelves, heavy with different foods. It was a strange place for a tryst but, always happy to try something new, I pressed on.

"What's this?" I asked quietly, sticking my finger into a tub of chocolate.

"It's for cake dressing," replied Karen with frustration. I suppose she was wondering why I would let such trivia interrupt our flirtations. She was obviously not using her imagination. I ran the tip of my finger lightly across Karen's lips and she instinctively licked the chocolate away. I smiled and ran a thick smudge of chocolate across her lips.

"Bad, boy," she admonished with a smile and I kissed her slowly, savouring the delicious contrast of cool chocolate and hot passion. "You're a very bad boy," she scolded gently as I ran the chocolate down her neck into her cleavage.

"Stop!" She pushed me away. "You'll ruin the dress." It probably was not meant to be, but her exclamation seemed like an invitation, so I flicked the fastenings of her dress open and gently pulled the bodice away so that her breasts hung free with beautifully pointed nipples in the chill air. I ran four chocolate covered fingers over her chest and began gently licking it off.

"Karen, Karen, where are you? Time for more pictures." One of the other bridesmaids forced another interruption.

Damn.

I hastily wiped off the rest of the chocolate, although I could not resist a final lick of a chocolately nipple, and fastened Karen's dress. She stumbled, giggling out of the fridge. She turned back to wag a finger at me.

"Naughty boy, go to my room."

Being abandoned at a wedding just at the point of seduction was becoming a habit so, feeling suddenly lonely but irreversibly horny, I went back to the party. There I saw the FMH sitting alone at a table. I also saw my drunken regimental friends who were playing by themselves in a corner of the dance floor doing some strange acrobatics.

"Billy, come join the Tumbling Tumbleeroes," cajoled one. I looked at him and his flushed, sweaty friends and then I glanced over at the cool but smouldering young woman sat by herself.

"Later," I promised and went to ask the lady for a dance. She smiled broadly and rose slowly from the table to reveal an enormously bandaged leg.

"Don't worry," she laughed, "it's not permanent. I just fell off my motorbike."

"Oh dear," I said as her soft hand sent wild vibrations up my arm. We began an incongruously slow dance to some pop music with the lady's bandaged leg sticking out at an angle. At least the pedestrian nature of our dancing allowed us to talk. I had to lean in close to hear her soft voice.

"Do you ride a motorbike all the time?" I asked innocently, although the vision in my mind of a semi-naked, leather-clad biker babe straddling a beast of a machine was far from innocent.

"No," she smiled, leaning close to my ear, "I fell off a moped while on holiday." The song of her voice, the whisper of her sweet breath and the intoxication of her

159

scent were overpowering. She pressed against me and I enjoyed the feel of her tits creasing my shirt.

"I'm here with my mum. My dad's away on business," she said. Reality crashed back into my world: rampant seductions were out then. "I'm Susie," she said, making me realise how lost in a dream I was.

"Billy," I replied with a smile and there seemed no need to kiss or shake her hand since I already had my arms around her with a promise of future embraces. Susie relaxed against me and time stood still.

Susie's mother was hovering with cruel intent to split apart our nascent romance and I had to walk them home in the rain to another hotel. I had found an umbrella and held it over them whilst I got drenched and my gallantry seemed to naively assuage Susie's mother's suspicion of me.

It was a shame to leave Susie at her hotel but prising her from her mother's grasp had proved difficult. Still, I had her telephone number and sensed that this was a relationship with a shelf life of more than a few weeks: Susie was worth waiting for. Besides, a man does not pass up on chocolate covered bridesmaid without very good reason.

Shortly after the wedding I went to visit Susie and enjoyed the beginning of strange but wonderful relationship that oscillated from complete loving commitment to estranged periods of extra curricular activity, on both our parts. It began well enough.

"What a beautiful home," I said to Susie when I first arrived at her house. It was a large Victorian building over three floors and it was furnished with an eclectic mix of exotic furniture that her father had bought during his foreign business travels, and tasteful English décor that reflected her mother's more subtle taste.

"Thank you," smiled Susie with sweet sexuality, "I

love it here." She ran her fingers sensually over the dark polished mahogany of a carved dresser in the hall. "I particularly love this floor," she said stepping lightly over the deep brilliance of the oak flooring." I admired it too with genuine sentiment.

"I love flooring like this," I said. "In fact I have always wanted to make love on a floor like this." It was a genuine and instinctive comment that was not intended to be suggestive but, even as I spoke, I realised how boorish it must have sounded to the sweet and obviously well brought up Susie.

"Oh, I see," she whispered as I looked up at some of the paintings to try and hide my embarrassment.

"Nice pictures," I said but it was too late to recover the situation. Susie had assumed that my comment about the floor was a suggestion. Her reaction, however, was completely unexpected. I turned to find her stood in the hallway of her parents' home, innocently naked and devastatingly attractive. Her dress lay on the floor and her hands were raised up in invitation. I went to her with a passion that I had not experienced before.

Our relationship had moments of elation when Susie really seemed like the FMH, and moments of frustration when I realised that she was entirely too young and vivacious to be tied into an exclusive relationship. The irony of it was that Susie was just as I had been at university; exploring the world for the first time. In some respects our additional adventures added flavour, intensity, as if we were reclaiming each other by trying harder.

"You smell of preservatif," she giggled at me early one morning when she was back from France.

"That's French for condom!" I challenged. Susie looked at me, refusing to be sorry. So I pushed her back onto the bed and opened her legs. She responded

161

instinctively, raising her hips to meet me with a sneer on her face as if to say:.

"Go on, Billy, fuck me harder than the Frenchy."

Susie was working in France during her university holidays and went back there after my visit so I had to provide my own entertainment for the rest of the summer. I went on holiday to California with a couple of friends, driving up the Pacific Highway.

California is warm and sunny, has majestic mountain ranges, expansive pacific beaches and colourful, relaxed towns as well as seedy, dirty ones. People had always told me that Californian girls love Englishmen and if a bloke could not score there he must be gay.

Maybe we were gay then, although we tried hard enough to get laid (by women). We did meet some Irish girls in Caesar's Palace in Lake Tahoe but they were looking for some tall blond surfer dudes. That is another one of the strange things about girls: a bloke looks for surf bunnies at the beach, but the Irish girls were looking for surf dudes at a mountain resort a hundred miles inland.

Having failed to seduce an Irish woman, we went to see Donna Summer in concert, which did not do much to allay the sense that three blokes sharing a room on vacation in California was just a bit too comfortable. Then we drove up to San Francisco which was full so we had to stay across the bay in Oakland. We hailed a taxi and clambered in. The driver was a large black bloke with an easy laugh.

"Where to, dudes?" he asked once we were inside.

"Take us downtown Oakland," we replied in the manner of a local. The taxi driver coughed violently and turned around, eyes gleaming, to look at us.

"You don't want to go down there," he said

incredulously.

"Why, what's wrong with Downtown?" I asked.

"Man, that is one bad place, even niggers don't go down there." I was not sure if he was trying to be funny but then he opened the glove box and brought out a Smith and Wesson .38 handgun. "You're gonna need one of these if you go down there."

"Okay," said Mark, "Where should we go?"

"What you want to do?"

"Have a few drinks, maybe meet a few girls." The driver smiled.

"Man, I know just the place."

He took us to one of the seediest bordellos that I have ever frequented. I would not have had sex in there if the girls had paid me. It was not even tacky, it was just awful; still any establishment called the *Chicken Ranch* is unlikely to host the most genteel of clientele. We had one beer that cost about $20 and left.

We took another taxi that was driven by an old salty sea dog type of character wearing a battered black leather jacket with a woollen cap pulled down over his eyebrows. Popeye was impatient. He sped off down the road leaving John to hang on with the door still open. The cab was filled with acrid smoke from the driver's cigar that he smoked without the use of his hands. This would have been less remarkable if he had been using his hands to steer the cab.

"Where to, guys?" he asked eventually, by which time we must have been nearly there.

"A bar in San Francisco where we can get some food," said Mark. The driver nodded and, without a word, he heeled the cab down a side street with one hand and proceeded to launch the vehicle over San Francisco's notorious hilly avenues.

Eventually we screeched to a halt outside a restaurant by the harbour piers and we all slid onto the floor of the cab. The restaurant was not what we were after but no one dared admit it so we settled into a bar and began downing whisky. The three of us had established an uneasy balance to our friendship but we were badly in need of some external company.

What we really needed was some girls. I met a chap in the loo. Meeting a chap in the loo of a bar in San Francisco is not to be recommended. Fortunately, he was a Jock who took me over to a group of studenty back packer types from all over the world. This was odd as there were only a few girls amongst the group and men do not ordinarily bring in additional competition.

It seemed, however, that the Jock had fetched me over at the behest of Lisa. She was a Kiwi: dark and alluring, intelligent and urbane but with an air of innocence that was quite beguiling. We got on well although I do not remember why since I was well pissed by then. I do remember kissing her. In fact, we kissed deeply and quite passionately so that I began to have all sorts of ideas about fate and destiny.

"Where are you staying?" she demanded.

"We're in a hotel across the bay."

"That's too far," she said. "I'm sharing with six other people. She looked at her watch. "Oh, damn, we'll never get another hotel room at this time." She looked genuinely upset. I was quite flattered.

"Where are you going next?" I asked. She regarded me with casual and disarming confidence.

"Why?" she asked, "What have you got in mind?"

"Maybe we could meet up later, plan things better."
She nodded:

"Yes, lets. We're all going to Santa Barbara."

"Excellent," I almost yelled. "That's where we were going as well. I'll see you there."

"How will we meet?" Lisa seemed really concerned

164

but I was cool and masterful.

"It's not a big place, we'll just bump into each other," I said, demonstrating my stupidity, arrogance and inebriation. I would barely recognise her if we had arranged to meet somewhere specific so I had no hope of meeting her by chance. I suppose at that stage of the evening I did believe in fate, but the reality was that I spent a pathetically fruitless couple of days wandering around the bars and beaches of Santa Barbara looking for her.

Our adventure along the Pacific Highway then led us to Santa Monica where I met Tina who was from New York. Apart from that and a drunken memory of her pretty face, it was all a blur. It was our last night in California and as I was leaving the bar Tina handed me her business card. I returned to York rather disillusioned.

Towards the end of the summer I had the opportunity to go to Canada to lead walks in the Rocky Mountains. It was a legitimate military exercise although it was, perhaps, a little disingenuous of me to ask my company commander if he could spare me for a few weeks when he was very drunk at a party.

"Yes, of course, Billy," he slurred, "It'll do you good to broaden your experience. How long would you be gone?"

"Just into next month," I replied, which actually was near the end of October and it was then just early September but I had presaged my question by indulging him in a whisky tasting session in the Sergeants' Mess and, for all he knew, it could have been 1815. So, before he could sober up, I phoned the parent unit and was en route to the Rocky Mountains.

The campsite nestled against a glacial pond at the edge of a forest and the view from my tent each morning was of snow capped mountains shining in the bright sunshine of early autumn. We made fresh tracks in the snow over the tops and in the pine needles through the wooded valleys.

I planned my own walking routes, the only constraint being the distance we could walk in a day and the bears that roamed the forests. They were man-eating bears, apparently, and particularly dangerous at that time of year as they were bedding down for winter.

It was something that we paid little heed to until a report came in that a bear had killed and half chewed a couple at a remote campsite; the wife had survived with a limp but the husband had been dragged out of the tree for lunch. The rangers found the bear quickly and killed it, which seemed rather harsh but, apparently, once bears have eaten human flesh, berries and rodents just do not fill them up anymore. There was supposedly a bear living at the back of our campsite, although we never actually saw him.

When we were not walking over the low mountains we rode horses through the shady forests, hooves pounding through the snow and mud, over crystal streams and out over ridges with splendid views over the valleys below. It was akin to Belize, where we had ridden through the jungle with reckless enthusiasm on sturdy American ponies that ran with muscular energy in stark contrast to the controlled precision of the English horses I had ridden as a boy.

We also went white water rafting on heaving, tumultuous rivers that terrified me just to look at them. We rode a river with Grade 6 water which had not been commercially rafted before. The river guides figured that a bunch of soldiers would be a good trial run; it was not for civvies.

We loaded the rafts; large sturdy craft that tugged at the mooring lines like nervous horses. Then we were unleashed into the current, into immediate action, paddling to keep the raft facing downstream, the gnarly old oarsmen shouting instructions for more effort.

"Pull harder, pull harder!" he urged over the roar of the water, straining at his oars to keep us from being sucked into whirlpools and eddies. It was wild, unadulterated excitement. The strain on his face like a cartoon illustration, telling us that this was for real.

We heard the roaring crash of the first falls as we drew near.

"Hang on!" All our energy was focussed on riding the rapid, launching into the air with a sickening lurch and then crashing into the lee of the fall. "Now paddle!" he yelled. "Left side, left side!" The Herculean effort of straining on the paddles kept us from being sucked back into the plunge pool. There was no time for rest as we raced for the second rapid. The anticipation was worse since we knew what to expect.

The tense excitement was sustained through eight, nine rapids, I lost count and then suddenly, blissful calm as the river escaped its rocky canyons into a wide, grassy flood plain. The crashing water was a distant symphony as we idled into the slow, lethargic, sanctity of the lower reaches of the river. Exhausted salmon lay flapping moribund on the riverbanks waiting for the feasting bears to amble along and pick them up as if they lay on the fishmongers stall for fat, hairy women to collect.

We floated effortlessly down river to the bemused glances from the bears and one massive, magnificent moose which paused briefly from its drinking to stare at us impassively and whilst I sat in the boat, heart beating with adrenaline and exertion, I marvelled at both the beauty of mother nature and at the Army Bitch's cynical gloating as she offered me just enough of a glimpse of an ankle to ensure my continued commitment.

And whilst I was occupied by the adventure strewn, heavy drinking pattern of life, I was blind to the temptations of Eve, patiently waiting in the bars of Jasper[41]. The first girl to drag me off, almost literally, was Tracy. I was dancing with her quite casually when she jumped into my arms in a dark corner of a bar, snogging me furiously.

When she led me back to her room I found one of the corporals shagging her sister. He waved enthusiastically.

"Hey, Billy, when you've finished d'you fancy a swap-over?" he hollered with no sense of decorum[42]. The idea of swapping had a strong attraction to it but Corporal Woolf was a rather fat, sweaty Jock and so was his girlfriend, although she was not Scottish, so, on this occasion, I declined.

"I'll stick with Tracy," I replied sheepishly, worried that my reticence would spoil everyone's fun. We still had a very shabby night and, not wanting to miss an opportunity, Woolfy jumped on Tracy as soon as I got off. The only person who did not get all that she may have wanted was Tracy's sister although she seemed content; Woolfy had a surprising amount of energy for a fat bloke.

Early the next morning we caught a cab back to camp.

"That was fun, eh, Billy," enthused Woolfy wrapping his big arm around me. "Who'd a thought you and me would be spunk brothers?" I smiled at him nervously, not sure when he had last showered. It was not that I minded being *spunk brothers* as such, but I

---

[41] A tourist town in the Canadian Rocky Mountains.

[42] It is common to use first names whilst "Adventure Training".

was damn glad that I had gone first. The cab dropped us off and Woolfy went around the back of the campsite to avoid being seen coming back so late.

"What about the bear, Woolfy?" I asked. He shrugged.

"I'm mer afraid o' the Sarn't Major than some saggy ol' bear."

The second girl I met was Holly. We got chatting in a bar and it was inevitable that we had to consummate the nascent relationship physically because simple social intercourse was not sufficient, although neither of us could have explained that sentiment logically.

When I woke in morning I was concerned as to why I was so driven to pointless promiscuity. It was clearly not Holly's beguiling beauty and nor was it simply the lure of sex. Perhaps it was an addiction to sexual adventure. Perhaps it was just my ego, not my libido that needed to be stroked? But I had been in this place before and still could not accept that my ego was so fragile that it could be satisfied by sex with an unlovely stranger.

Furthermore, as the end of our period in Canada drew near, the RAF was too busy surging into the Balkans to fly us home and we were given two weeks unplanned leave. I rang Tina in New York. She was surprised that I got in touch, but then so was I.

I stayed with Holly for two days in Toronto, waiting for my flight, which was possibly one of the most cynical things I ever did but I had succumbed to devilment completely by then. We were so lacklustre together in every respect that I thought it was clear that we had no future together so I was surprised when she dropped me off at the airport.

"I'm coming to the UK next March, I'll be able to visit you," she said. I escaped into the terminal.

New York was fantastic. The flight approach over

Manhattan was exhilarating, sun shining on skyscrapers, Hudson River drifting idly past Liberty Statue, and a palpable excitement rising from the street even as we descended into JFK. I jumped into a yellow cab and rode across the Brooklyn bridge into the City: Billy's big adventure in Manhattan was about to begin.

Bizarrely, since I could barely remember her, I was really looking forward to seeing Tina. She was still at work when I arrived so I dumped my bag with her apartment building doorman and wandered down Broadway, staring up at the buildings, dodging the hurrying crowd, musing over how fate had brought me to NY City.

Tina had to work later than planned. I bought a large bouquet of pink roses and found myself in an Irish bar across the street from her building. A man sat at the bar immediately turned to me with gushing enthusiasm.

"Gee, you're from England." I became a minor celebrity and every newcomer to the bar was dragged over to meet me. "This guy's from England!" exclaimed my new buddy.

We drank a lot; even the roses began to wilt. By the time Tina arrived I could barely speak. This was the state in which she had first met me but, for some reason, she still seemed pleased to see me.

When I emerged from the sofa bed next morning, Tina was at work. For the next few days I saw the sights of Manhattan solo. I went to the Statue of Liberty, Battery Park, Central Park, the Natural History Museum, the Empire State Building, the Twin Towers, everything that New York had to offer. I fell in love with the place.

In between my sightseeing and Tina's work we developed a romance, leaving each other notes in her apartment arranging dates in the city, meeting across from her office in boutique coffee bars, having dinner in smart restaurants and doing river cruises together. The time we stole together in the evening really was special although pushed into a corner of my mind was the sense that I was enjoying the freedom of the daytime more.

Tina and I were actually ill suited as a couple but her cool city chic seemed well balanced by my basic approach to life and Tina seemed to find me amusing.

"Easy tiger," she laughed gently as I crashed into her apartment one afternoon. I had been running around Central Park enjoying the glorious sunshine. I was not expecting Tina to be home and I was sweating heavily.

"I ran up the stairs," I panted as Tina avoided my hugs, not wanting to spoil her linen suit.

"Why?" she asked simply, "There are 42 flights of stairs." But I did not know why, it just seemed like a good idea.

That night I was migrated from the sofa bed to a position of greater intimacy.

"That's nice, Billy," whispered Tina as I ever-so gently traced my fingers down her back in slow exploration as I undressed her for the first time. Then we rolled together in climactic unison and for a short while we were good together.

The "but" in our relationship was inevitable and unwelcome but we just never seemed to graduate from the energetic enthusiasm of initial attraction to a balanced, enduring relationship. Tina was looking to stabilise her life but I was dipping my toe in the water.

I was glad to go home. I had enjoyed getting into trouble in North America but walking away from it to the cool of a Yorkshire autumn was satisfying. Then I was hit by a sudden collision of interests, receiving a letter from the archaeologist from Belize asking if she could come visit, another one from Holly in Canada informing me that she had brought forward her trip to

171

England and a phone call from Tina inviting me back for New Year.

Then Susie wrote to say she was coming back from France. I had not committed to anyone but things said in drunken lust can be perceived differently and, as I was writing the letters of termination, I realised there was little justification for my behaviour.

In reality, I had little time or inclination for remorse. I returned to the depot and was launched straight back into training a new platoon of recruits and also a commitment to compete in multi-event endurance race. Life had carried on without me and I had to reassert myself in the pecking order; running in a race was the most effective way I had of doing that.

So I posted the letters and cynically stepped away from the trouble with girls and focussed all my attention on Susie. She came to our Christmas Ball in a tight fitting and elegantly sexy black dress. Her long, shiny black hair shimmered down her back and her shy smile enchanted everyone who saw it. Susie had an effortless sensuality that she exuded like a perfume and if I was ever uncertain that committing to her alone was a good call, the silent gasps of admiration from my brother officers was all the endorsement I needed.

18

I had to keep going. Just keep running for the next eight miles. But my Legs were stiff. I did not loosen off properly. I needed another mile or so to ease the muscles and get some adrenalin flowing. But it was starting to hurt already.

I could have done with a couple of minutes for some stretching but I could not afford the time. Two teams had a lead on me at that point. I passed the first pair easily enough; they were actually tabbing! Trying to compete in the race by just tabbing along, as if they were on a CFT[43]. Pointless, you had to run to have any impact.

As we ran past them they faltered, realising how ineffectual their efforts were going to be. But the leg leader was half a mile ahead, we only had seven miles to catch him. My running partner and I were loping along like good infanteers. He was one of my training team, running head up, loose limbed and breathing easily. We were not making much ground though; the leader was maintaining the distance.

I figured the hill towards the end of the race leg would stop him. He was a whippet. He would run along the escarpment where it was flat but after seven miles his legs would be weakened and the drop into the valley followed by a mile long hill would be too much for him. I knew we would take him there. But I had to keep going, not let him get away from me or the hill would not slow him enough. I just had to keep running.

I was starting to sweat then, which was good. It meant my body was beginning to work and would ease up soon. Endorphins would be flowing, muscles easing,

---

[43] Combat Fitness Test: Eight mile forced march carrying 30 pounds of kit done over two hours.

legs opening up and increasing the pace. Once I got into the zone I would close the gap and bear down on the leader. Keep pushing and wear him out.

He had not looked around at that point and did not know we would catch up. He was too relaxed. He had a half-mile start and ran ahead merrily not knowing we were behind him, coming after him as surely as a cat after a mouse. I needed him to glance back, to feel some pressure, to know that I was coming and would not stop.

I was through the initial pain and stiffness then and felt loose and steady. My breathing was even and not so heavy. But I was thirsty and needed a drink. I knew it would not help; my body was too stressed to absorb water at that point. I had learned that in the jungle. I just had to keep running.

That was all I could do. Run. I was a grunt from the North with no skills. There were many different disciplines in this race; cycling, canoeing, open water swimming, but I was not good enough at any of them to compete effectively. So I just had to keep running with my boots on and a bergen on my back. It was not much of an impediment, only 30 pounds.

"What's your race strategy?" one of the company commanders, a major, asked me before I set off on my leg of the race. I looked at him, not sure what he meant.

"I'm going to run a steady pace to keep as close to the leader as I can," I said pointing to the whippet who was disappearing around the first corner of the road. "Then get past him when he falters on the hill." The major looked at me incredulously.

"You're just going to run with a bergen on for eight miles?" He had a Special Forces background so why he was sceptical about my plan was unclear. Perhaps he did not believe I could do it.

"Yes, sir," I replied. "What else can I do?" The

major shook his head.

"Nothing," he mused although I noticed a wry smile slide across his mouth. When we first looked at the structure of the race the bergen run was the unsophisticated, hard graft and unglamorous option that nobody wanted to do. But it was all I could do and I ran it the first year and won, beating the other teams into submission. It sort of summed me up, became what I was most reputed for.

Years later when I was a company commander myself an old LE officer[44] with whom I had served in York was posted to my Regiment. The subalterns in the mess asked him what I had been like as a young officer.

"All I will say," counselled the old hand to the young bloods, "is that Billy was very fit and brought some stunning women back to the mess." It was not a bad reputation for a young army officer but there was something euphemistic about it that was not very flattering.

Still, success brings its own glory and this year I was a darling, expected to win and compensate for weakness in the team elsewhere. Besides, I did not have time to worry about it just then as the preceding leg runner came in and it was my turn to start running. Running with my bergen on. It was not heavy but it was enough to slow the whippet up that hill. At least I hoped so.

"Race the Sun": It was a grand titled race for all the minor units in Yorkshire to compete in. But I did not feel like a grand competitor. I was just legs, sweat and guts. No skills, no competences. Just running. Legs and balls, that's all I had. That was all I had ever had. I was captain of rugby at school and university, not because I

---

[44] Late Entry Officer: An officer commissioned from the ranks after full service.

175

was the best player, but because I was committed. Is that enough for a man to succeed? At times in my life it seemed that trying hard was insufficient compensation for a lack of talent.

When the Commanding Officer committed his unit to this competition I watched all the gifted and privileged officers volunteer for the skilled disciplines that they had learned at school; road cycling, mountain biking, orienteering, sculling, and a list of other sophisticated disciplines. I had nothing to offer but strong legs, a stubborn will and commitment. And fuck me I was committed now. I had to keep running.

I loved to run. I enjoyed the feeling of fluid movement I got once my blood was pumping and my legs were driving hard over the ground. It became all consuming, all-important. Nothing else mattered: frictions at work, trouble with girls, my sense of isolation in the mess were unimportant. Even the boots and bergen could not constrain the feeling of freedom I had when I ran.

But it was starting to hurt. In my stomach. In my lungs. In my back. That was okay, though, I could run through that. As long as my legs kept moving, I was okay. But the leader was not slowing much. I could not close the gap. He had seen me. He knew I was coming but he had not faltered. Arrogant bastard thought he could beat me.

I only had four miles to catch him at that point, but he was not slowing. I could not afford to increase the pace. I had to save some energy for the hill.

"Should I change tactic then? Do not try to close the gap? Keep with him but let him think he's winning? Yes, that's it. He does not know about the hill. He did not run last year. He does not know of the pain yet to come. I will catch him then. Poor bastard." My mind was running as much as my feet and I was rambling; a sign of dehydration.

And it did hurt, so perhaps I was fooling myself; perhaps I would not catch him. Was I losing my nerve? I was certainly drying out. Stiffening up after only five miles. I had got the race prep badly wrong.

"Odin, help me!" I called in my mind, "don't let my muscles cramp." I was begging him, getting desperate. I had to keep running. But I did want to stop. Want to rest.

Maybe I could just slow up a bit. Ease down slightly, just to rest the legs. No! Keep running! He'll notice. The leader will notice you're slowing and he'll be encouraged. Don't slack you fucker. Keep running."

"Keep going, Billy!" urged Charlie Gates, my running partner. He was a corporal but there was no rank in this shared adversity, just mutual reliance. He must have sensed that I was faltering slightly. "Come on, man yourself up!" His vehemence was hard, critical of my weakness.

But he was right. I could not allow myself the luxury of self-pity. When I was rugby captain at university we lost our annual grudge match against our arch opponents, Lancaster University. "The Roses" fixture was the clinch game of the season. We rarely won. They were a bigger university and a stronger team.

But we nearly won that year. When I was leading the team we were more committed, fitter and better organised. We did well, even though they were better. But, in the end, we lost. Despite our physical and emotional commitment, they won. I wanted to cry, to give up, but my father was watching; stern faced and angry. Not because we lost but because he knew I wanted to give up.

"It's not winning or losing that marks a man out, Billy," he said, "but how he deals with victory or defeat." I resented the lack of sympathy but then I understood the fundamental truth of it. I regarded my teammates who were dejected and miserable. They *looked* beaten. So I sucked it in, all that weakness, and shouted at them:

"Form the line!" They looked at me, picked themselves up and formed the line to congratulate the winners. We felt better about ourselves.

But that was not how I felt now. I was slowing down. I was weak. My feet hurt. My back was sore. Sweat was stinging my eyes.

But no-one gives a shit, Billy, they're expecting you to win. Nothing else will do. You've only got two miles to catch him. Don't be weak.

"Odin, help me!" My mind cried again. But Odin is not omnipotent. He is not God. Odin has no time for weaklings. And I was weak. I was dizzy, my vision obscuring, and I was stumbling. And I had not even got to the hill yet.

Keep running, Billy. Keep going.

Then I felt hands lift me and push me forward.

I'm flying. The Valkyries have taken me. Lifted me up to carry me from the battlefield. No they haven't, you soft fucker, you're delirious. But you're through the wall. Getting second wind. You're strong now. Invincible.

There was the hill. The leader had reached it. He was still going. FUCK! I had to keep going too. Keep moving up the hill. But it hurt badly then, my legs were beginning to weaken. I could not keep going.

At school I was the junior cross-country champion because of a big hill at the end of the race. I was not the fastest runner but I ran the hill at best pace, knowing I could break the others. At the top of the hill the race favourite faltered because I had broken him physically and mentally. He doubled up and puked his guts and I

178

ran on to the finish.

However, the following year, in seniors, the race route changed and the hill was at the beginning. This meant that I had to use the hill to break the more proficient runners at the start. I was a rugby player, heavily built and not used to distance running like the lean and long legged athletes from upper sixth.

But I had bigger nads[45] in my shorts and I beat them on the hill. Head down, arms pumping, driving up the hill at near full pace so that by the summit all they could see was my arse disappear into the horizon. When I came to run the second loop in the woods I was overtaking the middle runners as they came for their first circuit. At least I thought I was, but actually the second loop was not part of the circuit, it was only run twice for training and no-one had told me. I had only done the route once for practice and so I was beaten by my own stupidity.

I had never tasted such bitter defeat and struggled to deal with it.

"A moral victory," the sports master offered me in consolation. I nodded, trying to summon the spirit to speak.

"But not a real one."

"Billy," he said gently, "you ran a mile more than everyone else and still came 16th out of a hundred." I looked up at him through tears.

"But I didn't win." He looked away.

"Men don't cry, Billy."

And now I was determined not to taste defeat again. I would keep going. Then the leg leader stumbled on the hill. He was only half way up. Now I could take him and I felt like I was flying. The Valkyries really

---

[45] Gonads – testicles - balls!

179

had come for me, were lifting me up to Valhalla.

No, you soft fucker, you're having an adrenaline surge and it won't last long so you have to beat him now.

I moved forward more quickly, exploiting the adrenaline, and began to climb the hill. We were catching the leg leader. He was struggling. Then he fell. We would pass him and climb the hill to victory. But you do not leave a man down, even in a race like that; especially in a race like that which was about military endeavour, not shallow victory. We helped him up; he was hurting bad. We tried to carry on up the hill but we had lost momentum and we were hurting ourselves now. Our muscles ached, bodies dehydrated.

We could hear the crowd at the end of the race now. They were cheering loudly, seeing us take the lead.

"Billy! Charlie. Billy! Charlie!" The crowd were spilling down the hill chanting at us forcefully and I felt that I could truly hear the Valkyries singing to me now, urging me on. We kept going, each step a victory of determination. It hurt badly but we were still running, still moving forward.

We crested the hill and the roar of the crowd at the finish line pulled us forward. We began to sprint. Yearning for the finish, driving to win, to end the pain. Charlie pulled away from me and crossed the line a few metres ahead.

"Billy!" he turned and yelled, "come on!" I careered forward, stumbling over the line in a lunge and collapsed into the arms of supporters. They held me up while I gasped for air. Unseen hands pulled off my bergen and dragged me away from the road, dropping me into the grass where I sagged onto hands and knees and puked my guts up.

19

"You raped her!" The screaming harridan made her accusation with vicious, drunken spite. I looked around in mild amusement wondering which lucky chap deserved such attention. Then I realised she was yelling at me.

"What are you talking about, you daft cow?" I queried, assuming an immediately defensive posture.

"You! You bastard!" spat the vexed woman pointing to another girl nearby, "You raped her!" I looked over at the other girl in complete confusion. I did not recognise her at all. My friends in the queue for the nightclub all moved away from me, so much for male solidarity.

"What are you talking about?" I proclaimed, "I've never met her." I looked at the girl again, hoping for her absolution.

"Don't lie, you fucker! You took her home from this nightclub and raped her!" There was an amused crowd gathering and I was glad that no one seemed to be taking it too seriously. I studied the forlorn girl at the centre of this ruckus. She was mildly attractive with a kind look although her stress was evident in her frown.

Actually, she did have a vague familiarity and I had to hide a smile. It had been quite an exciting minor adventure although it was some weeks distant, before I had gone to Canada.

"I should report you to the police!" persisted the wife of Quasimodo.

"She was on top!" I maintained my innocence, more to convince the gathering crowd than either of my accusers.

"Well, you still forced her to do it!" she screamed.

"Actually," I scowled back at her, leaning forward into the attack, "your friend stopped the proceedings to smother me in baby oil and then rode me like Calamity fucking Jane." My riposte was delivered with a snarling distaste of this woman who continued to accuse me with a fag in her hand and no justification in mind other than some misguided sense that sex with a bloke is an admission of commitment and that a woman can trap a man simply by opening her legs.

"It was still rape!"

"Well, there's a police car," I snarled back at her waving at the patrol car. "Tell them!" The police stopped at the kerb side and opened the window but the women had already gone.

"Everything okay?" queried the police officer from within his safety zone. I nodded.

"She was making false accusations." He nodded too, but not with any sympathy.

"We heard. Maybe you should be more careful, then," he said carefully and drove away.

It was a shame that what had been frivolous and fun could turn so vitriolic and it was especially ironic that this should happen just as I was committing to one woman. The past does not always remain passive, however, and events that began in this particularly seedy club had a habit of developing in ways that I had not intended. Another liaison in the same club had also recently turned sour.

"Did we have sex last night?" asked the girl as I was driving her home at best pace next morning.

"No, you were too drunk."

"Thanks."

"For what?" She looked at me for a minute.

"For not taking advantage of me. Most blokes would have." All I could offer in response was a grim nod, not being inclined to lecture her that she should not put herself in such a position. I drove as quickly as I could, anxious to be free of this unwelcome situation and I suppose I should have listened to my own sanctimony and not put myself in such a position either.

We quickly gave up any pretence of small talk and accepted that this relationship was stillborn. A sentiment that was confirmed when the girl suddenly convulsed and barfed all over my dashboard.

"Sorry," she mumbled. I passed her my handkerchief. I pulled up outside her house with more enthusiasm than was fair; I had been very drunk myself.

"I don't suppose you want my 'phone number?" she said. I tried not to stare at her smudged make-up, torn tights and messed up hair, or at the festering pool of vomit on the floor of my car.

"I don't think we'd get on," I said and drove away.

In the midst of such trouble, I welcomed the news that I was to be posted early from the training depot to Northern Ireland as the Regimental Intelligence Officer. At the time, Northern Ireland represented the epitome of British Army capability. It was an enduring campaign supporting the police and was the only environment that represented any real threat; minor as that may have been.

The only downside was the almost inevitable demise of my developing relationship with Susie who was too beautiful and free-spirited to be constrained by an absent boyfriend. She needed loving too much so to consolidate our relationship and extend its shelf life, I took her to Greece for a week before I left for the Province.

We went in early June before the crowds arrived and the sun became too punitive so we had our choice of secluded beaches and quiet restaurants. We went exploring one day and climbed over cliffs and wandered through shady groves of pine trees until we came to a broad sweep of sand nestled between two protective rocky promontories.

"Wow, Billy, look, our very own beach!" Susie's enthusiasm was uninhibited. She peeled off her swimsuit and wandered with naked innocence across the beach. We splashed into the sleepy Mediterranean and the contrast of her warm body to the cool water made me delirious.

I built a little shack from driftwood, driving branches into the sand on which to rest a roof as I had in the jungle.

"Billy, you built me a house!"

It was on that beach in the secluded cove that I spent possibly the happiest day of my life. The sea shimmered deep blue in the thickening heat, the sky reflected its depth and peerless colour, and the sand was yellow like the presiding Sun God sitting high above us.

The other Gods were smiling too, nodding their ascent. I was part of the Odyssey, one of the Argonauts; there was Perseus standing guard at the bay's entrance, and Heracles, resolute on the cliff edge.

Susie emerged from the sea and walked towards me, naked and shining wet like Aphrodite, firm breasts casting shadows like the Parthenon over Athens. She was so impossibly beautiful she was almost menacing. She stood over me, sweeping back her flowing mane and ran her hands over her own voluptuous figure, mouth parted slightly, tongue licking her lips.

She was Andromeda, she was Europa, she was all things; a Nymph, a Goddess fit only to be worshipped. And worship her I did, moving slowly, Susie demanding greater reverence, always wanting more, subjugating me to her whim, her pleasure my only concern. Faster, faster we went until our passion surpassed that of the Deities. She screamed her demands; harder, harder she wanted it, all restraint gone now, total abandon reigned. I gripped her waist and forced myself into her as hard as I could, throwing back my head to praise the Gods.

"Thank you Zeus, thank you Zeus, THANK YOU ZEUS!"

Part 5 – Land of My Fathers

"...I keep on waiting, anticipating ..., for some tender arms, hold me tight..." You Can't Hurry Love - Phil Collins 1982.

20

We lined up in loose patrol formation behind the huge steel gates. The atmosphere was tense as we waited for the signal to bomb-burst out onto the street. I was uncomfortable in unaccustomed body armour and helmet, fidgeting nervously to get used to the heavy ECM[46] equipment on my back.

"Steady, fellahs," the patrol commander, a young sergeant, calmed his troops. I looked at the men around me: generally, they were youngsters, some still teenagers, and they were stiff and anxious. There were a few old hands who were more relaxed, almost casual, in their demeanour. They had done this many times and were familiar with the drills. Of the whole team, I was the patrol virgin, an initiate needing to be shown the ropes.

The soldier in the sangar[47] high above our heads raised his hand in warning, preparing us to get ready to move. There was a tense stirring amongst the troops as they waited for the moment of truth. Even the experienced soldiers grimaced. I shrugged my shoulders to adjust the ECM into a more stable position. My hands closed tightly around my rifle. My breathing quickened as the adrenaline began to flow like a drug. We were gladiators about to charge into the arena.

The sentry's hand dropped in emphatic gesture.

"Now!" yelled the patrol commander. The gates started to swing open leaving the forward troops exposed. The soldiers jostled each other as they tried to force their way through the slow moving gates so they

---

[46] Electronic Control Measure; equipment to disrupt remote controlled explosive devices.

[47] An elevated sentry position with wide fields of view and fire.

could get into less vulnerable positions out in the street. We ran, keeping low and moving quickly to reduce our target profile.

The soldiers moved efficiently, dropping behind cover as best they could; walls, cars, ditches, anything that could protect against a sniper or IED[48]. I stumbled about trying to keep low, maintaining my position in the centre of the group to provide cover from the ECM for everyone, and make myself less of a target. My thighs screamed at running in a crouch. My back ached from hefting the heavy kit and my sphincter was twitching like a bastard from nervous excitement.

I dashed to some stone steps inset into a high wall and dropped into a prone position. I relaxed a little and cast about me to get my bearings. I could see right up the street. I was loosely in the middle of the patrol. I had protection from sniper shots and blasts; it was a good position. In fact, it was such a good position that an IED bomber could have anticipated its use.

Shit!

I frantically began looking about me for signs of wires, disturbed bricks or anything that would indicate a device. There was nothing but my complacency was short lived.

"Excuse me." I whirled around, rifle to the fore, to face my first encounter with the enemy. I was breathing in harsh pants, eyes darting about nervously. An old lady burdened with shopping bags was stood at the bottom of the steps.

"I need to go up there," she said indicating the steps. "That's where I live." I suddenly felt very foolish. My instinct was to carry her bags up the steps. Instead I

---

[48] Improvised Explosive Device; a homemade bomb that would be anything but home made.

189

lowered my rifle and moved aside for her, mumbling an apology. She looked down at the ground, not wanting to seen as being friendly towards me, and pushed past.

I was hit by a wave of acute sadness: I was tooled up with body armour, helmet, rifle and ECM, ready to do battle on the streets of the UK. This was the country where I paid taxes and voted for government and where I was prepared for bombs and gunfire. It was Monday morning; people were going to work, to the shops, doing their daily business.

We moved through the busy streets, relaxing slightly amongst all the civilians where an attack was unlikely. We passed a school playground full of noisy children enjoying the morning break. I had been told that talking to children was good. Giving them sweets was even better, not just as a goodwill gesture, but because being surrounded by children protected you from being shot.

I moved passed the school gates and saw a young boy of about eight.

"Hi, how you doing?" I asked him cheerfully.

"Fuck off, bastard." He spat at me expertly and moved away. One of the soldiers moved past me as I stood looking at the viscous gob sliding down my combat smock.

"Natives are not so friendly around here, boss."

"Doesn't he realise that I don't want to be here either?" The soldier looked at me with a degree of sympathy.

"I don't suppose his parents mentioned that bit," he said whilst looking down his rifle sights into the distance.

We moved away from the City centre into the Bogside housing estates, site of the famous "Free Derry Wall". Republican murals were everywhere commemorating those killed on Bloody Sunday and denouncing British interference. This was a bit more like it. Londonderry was home to a good many Republicans and terrorist suspects, most notably Martin McGuinness and John Mitchell McLaughlin, and I felt less awkward plying my military trade in these areas.

"Brit bastard," said a local who then spat at my feet as I patrolled towards him. I stopped on the pavement in front of him. He was an unremarkable individual, overweight, unemployed and clearly a lump of life's flotsam but Republicanism lent him some purpose, allowed him to be defiant.

"That's hard," I remarked at his spittle on the pavement. "You struck a real blow against British imperialism there." I do not know quite why I was so antagonistic towards him, although being spat at does tend to rile you somewhat.

"Fuck off."

We stood toe to toe then, glaring at each other, all pretence at ideology, of Irish Republicanism and British democratic principle forgotten, just two blokes facing each other off, which perhaps offered some explanation as to the longevity of the conflict. I did not really know what to do next but the patrol commander, a big man from Lancaster, came to resolve the situation.

"What's your name?" Carter asked the Irishman.

"Aw, fuck off, you know damn well who I am." Evidently there was a degree of macho one-upmanship amongst the Republican fraternity that if the Brits knew your name, you must be a real hard sympathiser.

"Indeed, Mr McFail," said Sergeant Carter, his formal tone heavy with sarcasm. "Where are you off to today then?"

"That's none of your fucking business," said Mr McFail but it was not readily apparent whether his hostility was genuine or simply for the benefit of the

191

few passers-by.

"That's where you're wrong," said Sergeant Carter in a mock imitation of McFail's accent, "it's exactly my business," and he got out his patrol notebook.

"Well, now," he said, "it's not Tuesday so you can't be going to collect your dole. What will you do without British Social Security payments once there is a united Ireland, Mr McFail?"

"Fuck off."

"So, since it's nearly lunch time, you must be off to either the pub or the bookies or possibly both," said Carter in pensive tone. "No doubt having told the missus that you're going to a Sinn Fein meeting."

"You Brits are so fucking smart, aren't you?" snarled an impotent McFail.

Sergeant Carter's cool sense of authority was impressive. His troops watched in amusement, used to these confrontations. Amusing as it was, it was unlikely to further the cause of detente or reconciliation so we let McFail go and moved on through the estate. I was more relaxed now, both in respect of my own safety and the presence of troops on the streets in Britain.

A small child then illustrated the reality of the situation. Under the tutelage of his father, he picked up a half-brick and struggled to throw it at me. It dropped just two feet from him. I nearly laughed but then the toddler, who could barely talk, yelled in high-pitched voice:

"Fuck off ya Brit bastard!"

Republican terrorists in the Ulster Province had a taunt for the British soldiers:

"To be safe, you have to be lucky all the time, but to be successful, we only have to get lucky once." The army's presence antagonised the situation and we became the target just by being there, but without us the police would have been very vulnerable. Several weeks prior to my arrival, an RUC[49] officer had been shot in the back of the head on a busy Saturday afternoon in the middle of the high-street with ordinary people walking past doing their shopping.

My maternal Grandmother had been born in County Antrim but I had been brought up in Yorkshire and felt little compassion for my ancestors. My Granny tried to indoctrinate me with tales of the Good King Billy who had come from Holland to succeed the English crown and then gone to Ireland to protect one Irish group from another who were supported by the French.

Sectarian conflict is beyond the scope of most six year olds and it seemed obvious, even to my childish mind, that there is little glory in death no matter how fabulous are one's heroes nor how heroic are one's fables. Military experience did not change that perspective.

The significance of being called *Billy* had also been lost on me as a child but as I patrolled through the Creggan Estate attracting vicious looks every time one of the soldiers called me, I began to understand.[50]

Two years in Londonderry was not appealing: Derry from a Nationalist perspective. In the Seventeenth century, Derry had been a run down port on the northern coast of Ireland. A group of wealthy London Merchants had invested heavily in the town in order to improve trade links with the rapidly expanding New World and they it renamed Londonderry, setting the scene for sectarian strife 300 years later.

---

[49] Royal Ulster Constabulary: The very name of the police force in Northern Ireland was inflammatory.

[50] Military rank was not used whilst on patrol because it made commanders more of a target.

Londonderry was the scene of many of the flashpoints of Northern Irish history. It was in the city that the infamous Apprentice Boys march helped to repel the forces of the Catholic King James II in 1688 and, three centuries later, it was where the present troubles began as a result of the Republican Marches in 1968. The city was also host to the Bloody Sunday fiasco in 1972. It had once been a prosperous city but now stood in decline, neatly divided down the middle by the River Foyle, Catholics on the West Bank and Protestants on the East. I was physically and morally right in the middle.

When I first went to the Province I had no idea what to expect and I stepped down from the small airplane on to the tarmac at Belfast City Airport with trepidation.

Nothing happened: no explosions, shots or even verbal abuse so I marched bravely towards the terminal building. Once inside, I felt awkward and conspicuous as if everybody was watching me. I was no stranger to airports but this time there were no parents or adoring girls or even that exciting man who stamps your passport.

My transport was also something of a shock.

"This is my wife, sir, we've been shopping," said the driver cheerfully. I had expected to be picked up by an armoured car, or at least an armed military escort; a fresh-faced youth wearing jeans, accompanied by his equally young wife in a saloon car was a little underwhelming.

My first impressions of Northern Ireland as we drove out of Belfast were surprisingly pleasant, if not disappointing for the lack of burning cars and rioting youths. In fact, the countryside looked, unsurprisingly, like the west coast of Scotland with its green hills, craggy rocks and grazing sheep.

Returning to my regiment was novel. For the previous year, I had been supervising the remedial training of recruits, a job that many people said I was suited to, and now I was being posted as the Intelligence Officer in Northern Ireland. People joked that Billy Hanson being the intelligence officer was a contradiction in terms but I never laughed, partly because it was so obvious it was not funny, but also because I secretly feared that it was true.

"Welcome to your new home for the next two years, sir." The driver smiled as he dropped me at the officers' mess in the heavily fortified camp. My room was a small, pokey cabin at the back of the mess with a view from the window of corrugated steel topped with barred wire. Two fucking years: criminals get less for burglary.

I arrived on a Saturday and was surprised to find that most of the officers who were not on duty were watching a football match. I found one of the mess staff and asked for directions.

"Don't I need an escort or weapon or something?" I asked the bemused soldier.

"It's only a football match, sir."

"I just got here."

I walked to the sports pitches and saw the junior officers on the far touchline. I hurried over but as I approached them from behind, I realised that I did not recognise them. All I could see was a row of homogenous army officers dressed in Barbour jackets, corduroy trousers and flat caps. In the middle of the group was a man whom I vaguely recognised to be the Commanding Officer.

"Oh, well played, corporal!" he said. "Wasn't that a good run, Justin?" The Colonel turned to an officer whom I had last seen being ejected from one of Belize City's finest whorehouses.

195

"Indeed it was, sir," replied Justin on cue. "Corporal Ellis is a damn fine player." From where I was standing, Corporal Ellis looked to be at least thirty pounds overweight and had turned puce with the effort of running up the wing.

I hesitated before joining the fray, suddenly uncertain that I wanted to be part of it.

"Hey, Billy!" called one of the officers, "welcome back." Just for a moment I was the centre of attention amidst handshakes and bonhomie but it did not last long as my fellow officers returned to their sycophancy. I sensed the Army Bitch smile.

My working environment was more promising. I had a large team of experienced soldiers and NCOs, I worked with a great deal of autonomy and spent much of my time liaising with the RUC and specialist military intelligence units. I wore civilian clothes, drove an unmarked car and every morning I hung a 9mm pistol under my arm. The smoke grenades under my car seat added to my protection but I was mindful that I was thus protected in a land that flew my flag amongst a people who spoke my language.

The first time I went on leave to the gentle hills of Yorkshire I was saddened to realise that I actually felt vulnerable without the reassuring weight of the 9mm under my jacket. I could not relax and was nervous and twitchy and constantly looking at the door.

"Billy, won't you dance with me?" asked Carla, a favourite old girlfriend at a wedding in Belfast. I declined, partly to avoid the displeasure of her glowering husband, but also because I was concerned that she would feel the pistol under my arm. I did not want the groom to know that I had brought the tools of conflict into his marriage celebrations.

"How has life been treating you?" she asked.

"Okay."

"You seem nervous, Billy."

"I am a bit." As we spoke I was scanning the room.

"Billy Hanson nervous? Why have you got a gun under your jacket." Carla had always seen through me but her teasing in this case made me uncomfortable: I obviously was not cut out for plain-clothes work. She was sympathetic enough not to dwell.

"No lady in tow?" she asked to change the subject. It was a fair question I suppose, even though she was mocking me a little, for it had been Carla who had first prophesised the longevity of my bachelorhood.

My role as the intelligence officer required higher levels of security vetting. For weeks afterwards friends would me ring up and complain about strange men in dark suits turning up and asking them odd questions about my sobriety, morality and other things that I hoped they had not told the truth about.

"How are you financially?" asked my vetting officer, an old school retired military man complete with cords and tweeds.

"Okay, really," I replied in half truth. "I'm a bit overdrawn, but, nothing to cause concern."

"Well, what about your £5000 Visa bill?" It went down hill from there. "What about sexual preferences?" he asked.

"Yes, I prefer sex," I replied, not realising that the chap had no sense of humour.

"Have you ever engaged in unnatural practices?"

"What would you call unnatural?" I ventured cautiously, not wanting to incriminate myself.

"Buggery."

"Oh, no, I didn't go to boarding school." He gave me a stern look; obviously he did.

"What about with women?"

"No. I think it's a bit of a waste really. I mean if you were in to that sort of thing you might as well be gay, save yourself a lot of trouble with girls."

"Have you ever had any homosexual experiences?"

"No." I was starting to get a bit bored by then and so his next question caught me off guard.

"Have you ever had sex with a prostitute?"

"Er, no. I nearly shagged a whore though."

"What's the difference between a prostitute and a whore?"

"About fifty dollars, normally." It was too good to miss but there was not even the hint of a smile.

"Perhaps you had better explain."

Despite the physical difficulties and my moral objections, there were some advantages to the job. Intelligence work attracts service women since they can contribute on an equal basis without the need for physical strength. It was a very positive change from normal infantry work, although I did find it extremely distracting. It was impossible to concentrate on mundane issues like patrol programmes or summaries of terrorist activity when a warm, scented woman was at the end of the table.

I went to give a briefing in the headquarters near Belfast soon after I arrived in Province and met a young woman from the Intelligence Corps. As I had been leaving the office in Londonderry a colleague had joked about meeting Amanda at the Headquarters.

"Don't let her put you off your briefing," he said cryptically and I assumed that she was fiercely competitive or something.

But Amanda was tall and lovely, with a smile that rendered my carefully rehearsed presentation into Telly Tubby speak. How could I concentrate with all that womanly flesh calling out to be unfettered? She wore civvy clothes and under her straining blouse I could see that she had perfect tits; it was a shame to keep them cooped up all day. I imagined them spilling into my world at the merest flick of a bra clip.

I swallowed hard and droned on:

"We've seen concentrations of PIRA activity around this area here and we think they are planning.....to bend Amanda over the desk and take her roughly from behind." The dullard grown ups just stared at me, apparently listening to what I was saying.

Amanda, sitting high up at the back of the audience, crossed her legs slowly, raising her skirt and torturing me with a view of her stocking tops. I went blank for a moment, perspiring with the effort of concentration. The grown ups maintained a polite interest in my presentation but how could they concentrate? How could they ignore her siren charms, her emanating lust? Were they dead?

My own office had similar distractions. The intelligence and surveillance platoon included a team of female Military Police soldiers who dealt with female suspects. My favourite was Molly. She came into the office one day after a patrol. It was unusually warm outside and Molly had removed her combat smock and body armour and was just wearing a t-shirt that was damp with perspiration, clinging to her curves.

"Hello, sir."

"Hi, Molly. Had a good patrol?"

"Yes, sir, but I'm ever so hot now." I smiled lamely and turned my attention back to the computer. Molly crossed the large office to where I was working in the corner and reached across me to retrieve a notebook or some similarly unnecessary item and squashed her bosom into my ear. I nuzzled there for an unnecessary length of time before I found the resolve to extricate myself and remonstrate with her.

"Corporal, do you have to rub those..." I realised what I was about to say, the office was tense with amusement, "sweaty patrol clothes in my face?"

"Oh, sorry, sir, would you rather I took them off?"

Of course I want you to take them off. I want you to take all your clothes off, apart from your boots and red beret, and bend over the computer while I grab your pony tail with one hand, a heavy tit with the other and fuck you from behind.

21

"I'll have number three, please Cilla," declared one of the subbies[51] with his hands over his eyes.

"Loser!"

"What a growler!"

"She's your girlfriend!" It was rather sad, the highlight of the week for the cream of the nation's manhood (as we considered ourselves) was watching Blind Date on Saturday Night.

The social life in Northern Ireland was grim. Londonderry is largely a Republican area and so we were unable to go to the local cinemas, bars or restaurants and had to drive some distance simply to have a beer. Since we were normally on some sort of stand-by routine, this was not generally feasible. We watched a lot of television.

We hosted dinners and parties in the mess to which no one came and we would get pissed. Every Thursday night we held a Black Tie dinner and asked the chef to cook a themed meal - Thai or Mexican or something - and try to coerce some local totty to turn up. This usually failed and so we would get pissed.

Sometimes we just got pissed.

It was on such an occasion that I met Sally. I had arrived late, had not changed into dinner jacket and was on call so not drinking. I felt left out of the party. I assumed Sally came to talk to me out of pity. She was gorgeous; dark, almost Mediterranean, looks, shiny hair, voluptuous figure and enigmatic smile.

"Hello Number One, what's your name and where are you from?" She did a fair imitation of Cilla Black.

"Er, Billy."

---

[51] Subaltern – junior officer.

"Pleased to meet you, Billy," said Sally shaking my hand.

Sally was a legal officer working in Belfast. She had driven the two hours to 'Derry just to come to our dinner party and now she was talking to me, much to the chagrin of the chap who had invited her.

"Apparently, there is a party here next Saturday night," said Sally. "I think you should invite me."

"Right, okay then. Would you like to come to the party?" My reticence was only because I did not actually know there was a party.

Charles, who had originally asked Sally up to the Mess, joined us at the bar in an attempt to reclaim his woman. It was the unwritten rule of the Mess and I was obliged to accept his clumsy interruption.

"Hi, Sally, how you getting on?" Charles shouldered me out of the way.

"Fine, thanks." She smiled sweetly at him and the poor fool beamed at me in triumph.

"Great," he said, clearly misunderstanding Sally's body language. "We're having a party next weekend, why don't you come up as my guest?"

"Oh, that's so kind, but Billy has already asked me." That was going to cost me. Sally took his arm and led him away whilst smiling at me.

The "Back to School" party caused a lot of excitement in the Mess, an interruption of the mundane reality of our social life. Many of my colleagues took the opportunity to wear hockey skirts or something similar but the peculiar penchant amongst the military for being in drag never really appealed to me.

I had to go to work during the morning of the party and was late getting ready. I threw on a pair of shorts, white shirt, stripy tie and an old cricket cap that I found in the storeroom. I added a large plaster to my knee and

202

some freckles to my face and looked in the mirror: something missing.

I went to find a shop but the East Bank of Londonderry was not well served with toy stores. There was a newsagent that sold cheap toys and I found a fat, fluffy white teddy bear, sitting alone on a shelf. He wore a Christmas jumper and matching hat so he had obviously been sat there for most of the year. I thought the incongruity of a white bear might have some appeal.

Besides, the bear's mournful expression bothered me and I could not leave him in that dreadful shop to suffer the ignominy of another Christmas without being bought. My own dress and purchase hardly raised a flicker of interest from the storekeeper. People in Northern Ireland were adept at turning a blind eye.

Only about 50 people actually turned up for the party and many were already drunk when they arrived. There were some flamboyant outfits amongst the girls, totally impractical for school wear, and I wished that I had been to the same school as them.

Sally was resplendent. There is something irresistible about an educated woman dressed provocatively but behaving so demurely as to appear positively sluttish. It is a rare talent and one that Sally exploited beautifully. In fact, her beauty filled me with wonder; especially wondering whether or not I would get to see more of it.

At first, I felt very self-conscious, standing alone at the bar clutching the teddy bear but, apparently, there is something irresistible about a grown man, dressed as a schoolboy, displaying macho vulnerability by clutching a teddy bear. It had worked for Sebastian and Aloysius in *Brideshead Revisited* although that was not really much consolation. Sally liked it, which was all that mattered really.

"Hello, Billy," she smiled at me.

"Hello, Sally, glad you could come."

"Thanks. I've been looking forward to it." There was silence between us then as we both smiled, wondering how to begin the affair.

"Who's your friend?" she said eventually, looking at the bear. It had never occurred to me to give him a name.

"He's called Fang." Sally raised an eyebrow.

"He doesn't look much like a *Fang*."

"Well, he can be quite vicious."

"He doesn't look vicious."

"Looks can be deceiving." Sally raised another eyebrow. This was not going well.

"I suppose they can," said Sally smiling innocently. "Do you think I might have a dance with him later?" Ordinarily I would have replied with something very dumb but Aphrodite was smiling on me that night.

"Yes, of course, but he does get very nervous with girls so I'll have to come too." I smiled at Sally. She smiled back.

"Okay," she said stroking Fang's ear. "In that case I will see you both later." She winked at me slowly and walked away on her high heels.

I swallowed hard with the release of tension and, holding Fang by the leg, walked to the bar.

"Whisky and soda, please," I said to Private Walker behind the bar, "and a double for me."

I spent the early part of the evening circulating with Fang. Life as the Intelligence Officer meant that I spent a lot of time alone. The specialised nature of my work and my own natural reserve ensured that I had become a rather solitary figure. Still, I had Fang to talk to and, as we both got slowly drunk, the evening began to warm up.

It was during that evening that I first properly met

Bethany. She was an officer at a neighbouring unit, attractive and sophisticated, with porcelain skin and long, shiny hair. Such was the dearth of good-looking women in the Province, she always had a large following of attentive and hopeful junior officers and I had never had the opportunity to engage with her fully.

However, dressed as another pig-tailed and freckled schoolgirl, she seemed to be making a particular effort to talk to me that evening.

"Nice Bear."

"Thanks." Her radiance stunned me into monosyllabic responses.

"What's his name?"

"Fang." The bear was proving to be a great conversation starter, a bit like Deefor had been really.

"Does he bite?" asked Bethany.

"Well, only people he likes, really."

"Do you think I'll be at risk?"

"Probably." I smiled. So did Bethany.

"I'd better be careful then." She scratched the bear's ear, smiled at me and walked off. But not without throwing me another smile over her shoulder.

Fang and I went to the bar again.

Supper was mash, sausages and beans with jelly and ice cream for pudding. I sat down at a table with Sally and some of her legal friends. Sally's cheeks glowed under her painted freckles from too much wine. She talked with great animation and her pig-tails bounced with enthusiasm. So did her tits, straining the white blouse. She played the role of wanton schoolgirl slut very well. Damn, I wanted to fuck her.

The food fight began almost at once. Mash and beans flew across the room, even the occasional gateau was squelched into some-one's face. Sally and her friends drew a lot of fire. The aim was appalling for an infantry unit and I got covered as well. Even Fang got tomato sauce and chocolate on his fur but being machine washable, he did not seem to care.

Sally's blouse was not fully buttoned, revealing most of her ample cleavage and one of the bolder captains came up behind her and dumped a large handful of chocolate and vanilla ice cream down her front. She gasped with surprise, scolded the officer briefly and then leant forward towards me whilst making a pretence at removing the goo from her bosom.

All she did was smear her breasts with coffee-coloured ice cream, staining her lace bra and causing her nipples to become instantly erect.

"Ooh, Billy," she said in mock pain. "Look what a mess I'm in."

Me too.

The party was a tremendous success, especially for me. I was on an almost certain promise, if not two. Life rarely gets much better. There was still the matter of conducting the seductions, however, for no matter how willing a woman may be, she still needs to be seduced, if only for appearances' sake.

I danced with both Sally and Bethany (and Fang) and my liaisons were going equally well with both, although I was drunkenly conscious of trying not to alienate either. It seemed that I was going to have to choose between them: a rare dilemma, particularly in Northern Ireland.

When I was a teenager I went on a ski holiday with school and found myself on New Year's Eve dancing with a young lady on either arm. I was greedy and wanted to snog both of them although even I realised that this was not feasible. I really fancied the girl on my right who was a brunette but, not wanting to squander an opportunity, I leant to my left to snog the blonde girl first. A simple plan but as soon as I snogged the blonde, the brunette vanished in a huff.

By no means a disaster since I still had the blonde girl but it goes to show how women misinterpret the smallest of actions. Anyway, I was keen not to let this happen again but how to decide? Sally was vibrant and vivaciously seductive but she was also leaving the Province soon and so this was a decidedly short-term option. Bethany, by comparison was beautiful and coyly seductive and definitely had FMH potential.

Aphrodite was definitely smiling on me that night.

"Oh, Billy, I have bad news," said Bethany all woeful.

"What, what?"

"I have to go home already." She looked so upset as to be positively flattering. This was bad news although it did resolve my dilemma somewhat.

"Perhaps we could meet up for supper or something," ventured Bethany.

"Okay, sure, sounds good," I replied, stumbling for words because of disbelief at my own good fortune. Bethany scribbled her 'phone number on a beer mat which she thrust into my hand and then threw her arms around my neck and kissed me on the cheek.

I stuffed her 'phone number into my pocket with my conkers and bits of string and then wandered to the bar. Sally intercepted me.

"She seemed friendly." Sally nodded at Bethany's retreating figure. I had hoped that Sally had not noticed me snogging Bethany. "Well, she seems to have warmed you up for me. It's my turn now." Sally dragged me by my ketchup stained school tie into a dark corner. Soon I was going to wake up, I was sure of it. Well, so be it, just so long as I shagged Sally first.

"Hold me tightly, Billy," Sally urged. I nuzzled her neck and she moaned with pleasure. My nose was inches from her cleavage but I restrained myself for fear of being too forward.

"Oh, Billy, don't hold back." I raised a hand and tentatively brushed her blouse causing her to sag in my arms and groan deeply. Needing no further encouragement, I squeezed gently but firmly and I thought Sally was going to pass out.

I squeezed her bum. Sally responded by pressing against me even more firmly.

"Please, Billy, touch me." I slipped my hand under her skirt and stroked her soft skin. Under her prim schoolgirl outfit, Sally was wearing the full rig: stockings, suspenders and some sort of basque.

Holy fuck!

If this was a dream it was a corker. Suddenly, Sally pushed me away, breathless but adamant. She stared at me with big, dreamy, brown eyes.

"It's time for this lady to go to bed," she said and abruptly left me. I was devastated, confused and in turmoil.

What do you mean, "go to bed?" Is that an invitation or an excuse? Should I follow or have I been blown out? Did she, or didn't she?

The indications were that Sally wanted to get laid, but had left abruptly. Had she suddenly had a fit of conscience (it was rumoured that Sally had a fiancé somewhere), had she begun to sober up, was she playing hard to get, what?

Perhaps it had something to do with feminine sensitivities, wanting to get laid but not wanting to be seen to want to get laid. If I went to her room now I risked rejection, embarrassment and possibly retribution for my outrageous presumption. I could play it safe but then I would spend a sleepless night nursing an elephant of a hard-on. The trouble with girls is that they never say what they mean.

Eventually I decided to take the safe option.

Frustrated but dignity in tact, I wandered slowly back to my lonely cabin.

Bollocks to that! I went back downstairs to Sally's guest room and knocked on the door.

She was sitting in an armchair wrapped in a silk gown, sipping coffee.

"Oh, hi, Billy," she said as if she had not seen me for a while. I stood by the door for a moment, resolve suddenly deserting me.

"I came to tuck you in," I said eventually.

"Oh, I see." Sally looked at me quizzically for a heart lurching moment. "In that case I'd better get into bed." She stood up, dropped her robe to the floor and walked naked to the bed, magnificent breasts quivering with each step. I made it in one mighty leap.

22

Bethany wandered out of the bathroom into my room. One of the Company Commanders saw her and she giggled, wrapping her towel more tightly around herself. We were not supposed to have girlfriends in the mess and I was half expecting a rebuke.

"She's very suitable," was all that he said. I presumed that *suitable* was meant in the context of marriage and I could see his point: Bethany was stunning, fun to be with and charming in company. Moreover, being a serving officer herself, she would not make the Army Bitch jealous. We had become almost inseparable.

We had our first date in the only local bistro that was safe and we were together for over a month before we had sex for the first time. That was a novel experience for me and I actually appreciated the strength of feeling that the abstinence had developed in our nascent relationship. It was also a positive reflection of the possible longevity of the relationship.

"You're the bloke that goes out with Bethany Morris!" exclaimed an incredulous and jealous officer from another unit during a conference. Billy Hanson was defined not by the value I added to the intelligence war in Province but by virtue of the fact that Bethany was gorgeous. This was not a bad thing and I suppose I was actually a bit smug, like the *marrieds* in *Bridget Jones' Diary*.

Our relationship had a domestic balance to it. We spent regular nights in each other's messes.

"Hi Billy," Bethany's Regimental Second-in-Command greeted me with casual disdain at dinner one evening. He did not even shake my hand; so familiar was my presence in his mess.

Privately, our time was spent in more intimate

activities. Days out to the beach were a favourite even though the Ulster coast is not the most obvious place for beach resorts. The howling Atlantic wind, persistent rain and cold sea did not really pertain to skipping barefoot through the waves but, for two people developing a romance, it had a rugged appeal.

"Billy, I'm cold." Bethany huddled naked into my arms and I turned the shower up so that the steam billowed out of the bathroom. The warm water was a delicious contrast to the cold, buffeting wind we had just run in from. I washed her hair with slow, firm movements whilst she purred like a kitten. Then we wrapped each other up in big, fluffy towels and sat on her bed drinking tea.

"This is nice, Beth," I mumbled.

"Tea and chocolate cake?" She had a smudge of chocolate at the edge of her mouth and I leant forward to kiss it away.

"Well, yes, but I meant being here with you." I brushed her hair away from her lovely face and she relaxed against me.

"I think so too," she whispered, closing her eyes and we lay curled up watching TV together.

"I'll have number two, please, Cilla," declared the hopeful contestant and I was so personally contented that I did not even bother to check if he had made the right choice.

Bethany Hanson did have a nice ring to it but I had a lingering concern about our relationship. I wanted more than *suitable* but I felt that we did not quite connect somehow.

"Surely you did not come here just to make love with me?" said Bethany one Saturday afternoon. I had gone to join her for horse riding lessons. I was early and Bethany was still getting ready, wearing only boots, jodhpurs and bra. She provoked an inevitable reaction.

"No, of course not," I replied but wondered why I had gone round. I certainly had no interest in formal riding lessons. I grew up riding across the heaths and moors of Yorkshire and had subsequently ridden wild in Central and North America. I once went riding with Emily Fisher over the North York Moors, cantering through the gorse and bracken on sturdy horses that enjoyed the freedom to roam as much as we did.

Afterwards, flushed with excitement, I pulled down Emily's jodhpurs, bent her over a rock and did her from behind as we both enjoyed the utterly splendid view of rolling hills and distant horizons.

Plodding around a sandy paddock on a robot horse in a military camp in Northern Ireland held little excitement for me, especially if I was not going to get to ride Bethany either before or afterwards. Sex was a fundamental part of a relationship for me and Bethany was generally fairly keen but sometimes she had other things on her mind, I suppose.

We were both in our late twenties and no doubt Bethany felt she was wasting time in not getting married. I felt like I was wasting time in not getting laid: a grown up relationship was a bit dull. This feeling was not helped by an inadvertent meeting with Emily Fisher.

"Billy!" exclaimed an old comrade from Strensall and Sandhurst. "What brings you back?" I was sat outside a pub by the river in York.

"A memorial service. Mull of Kintyre," I said. He nodded.

"The Chinny crash?[52] That was a real fucker. You need something stiff." He returned from the bar with

[52] In June 1994 a Chinook helicopter carrying intelligence experts from Northern Ireland crashed in the Mull of Kintyr killing all 29 crew and passengers..

212

beer and whisky chasers. He raised his glass. "Fallen comrades." I was dressed in parade order and should not have been walking around in uniform for security reasons and should not have gone to a pub for reasons of protocol but I only intended to have a quick pint.

"Why are you here in the middle of the day, Chris?" I asked him.

"Charlotte's just left me." He stared into the slow muddy water of the River Ouse. I was afraid he might jump in.

"Double fucker." I went for more whisky.

Whisky and sad men do not mix well. By late afternoon we were slumped against each other on chairs outside the pub. There was an array of empty glasses scattered over several tables. Bits of my uniform were equally discarded with my hat, Sam Browne belt, gloves and jacket providing evidence of our migration across the pub terrace from sober and sombre officers to miserable, drunken wankers.

"I thought it might be you." I looked up through the haze to see Emily Fisher standing there, slender, sweet and sympathetic.

"I've been to a funeral," I said. Emily collected all my kit and put it on the table. She sat down next to me and gently rubbed my cheek.

"Shall I get you a drink?" I asked slowly as if I had seen her that morning. Emily looked at me and tried to hide a smile.

"I'll go," she grinned, "you'll spill it." Chris watched her disappear into the pub.

"She's gorgeous," he said, "I thought you broke up?"

"We did," I replied with more sadness than I would have expected. Chris nodded slowly.

"Do you mind if I shag her then?"

"Yes, I mind, you wanker," I replied vehemently

213

although with no actual hostility; you could not blame him for that.

"How've you been?" Emily asked as she sat down again.

"Okay, I suppose, Northern Ireland is hard work." I paused in my explanation, wanting to say so much but not knowing how to say it. "It's lonely." That was disingenuous. I had not been lonely at all but I did miss Emily but was not able to say so.

"Well, you're here now," she whispered, "there's no need to feel lonely." Emily smiled at me and it felt like the kiss of a thousand angels.

I went back to Derry, to Bethany, in a state of confusion. Being back with Emily had been wonderful; great fun, great sex and happy reminisces but those sentiments were largely nostalgic. Emily and I had tried twice over several years to maintain a relationship and failed. It seemed that fate did not plan for us to be together. I was slowly beginning to realize that the common denominator in these failed relationships was me.

So Bethany and I carried on, if only because shared experiences were better than solo ones, particularly in Northern Ireland where the opportunities and time for socializing where limited. Indeed, my relationship with Bethany was developing against the context of accelerated sectarian strife in Londonderry, and that was my focus; or possibly it was my excuse.

23

My pager woke me up in the middle of the night.

"Mark 16 IED on Strand Road, one fatality, an RUC officer," the message from the Operations Room when I called in was curt and concise.

"Any warnings of further devices?" I asked, trying to clear the fog of sleep.

"Nothing declared, sir," the duty signaller's voice was strained with the responsibility of waking people up to tell them a colleague was dead.

"Ok," I replied, "warn the responding callsign to search the cordon[53] for hidden devices. I'll be in within five minutes." I dressed and stumbled through the rain across to the Ops Room. It was starting to get busy. The Ops Company Commander was already there, briefing the Ops Officer.

"Defilade shoot[54], side impact to a Police Landrover, the officer was killed instantly," the major briefed in terse, efficient tones but then lowered his voice. "He was actually blown in half." We carried on, following the drills that were developed through experience and practiced repetitiously in the hope that we would never have to follow them for real.

The level of incidents like this was relatively low; the IRA restricted their attacks in Londonderry to the security forces so that they were less likely to alienate themselves from the community that they purported to represent. Despite this, the reality was that they simply coerced the people in to silent compliance.

During my tenure there were occasional bombs

---

[53] A cordon is a ring of troops placed on the ground to secure the immediate area. There was always a risk of a secondary device being left to target static troops.

[54] A side on attack intended to avoid the more heavily armoured front of the vehicle.

targeted against soldiers, attacks against vehicles and mortar attacks against patrol bases.

We played the game: We patrolled, we observed, and we reported activity. We limited the violence but no more than that and it was an uneasy stalemate, neither side being able to dominate the other. The sadness of the situation was that there was no reason for it. No worthy cause is enhanced by violence.

The violence did provoke a Loyalist backlash.

"Sir, I had a meeting with the local Support Detachment[55] yesterday. They warned me about Loyalist paramilitary activity in our area." I paused in my morning briefing to the CO, waiting for the gravity of my statement to register.

"We've not had Loyalist activity here for a long time." He dismissed my briefing almost without consideration.

"I know, sir, that's why this is so significant. The Det have not been so specific with me before and the fact that they volunteered the information implies great concern. They suggested we increase our patrol profile on the East bank." Perhaps I delivered my briefing in an inappropriate way, or perhaps the CO's ridiculous ego clouded his judgment.

"Tell them," he almost spat at me, "to focus on their role and leave patrol programming to me." He glared at me, precluding any further discussion.

Two days later, Loyalist gunmen stormed into the Rising Sun bar in a local village called Greysteel shouting:

"Trick or treat!" They fired indiscriminately into the group of drinkers, killing six men and two women. Protestants and Catholics died together but none of them had been overtly Republican or Loyalist. Indeed,

---

[55] A specialist intelligence agency.

there were no sectarian causes in that place, just people socializing together and that had been their crime because hooded men of both sides seemed to need death to justify their existence. There was no contrition on behalf of the CO either; he just dealt with it as any other "incident".

The following year, the IRA announced a complete cessation of violence. This was followed by a cessation of loyalist hostilities but a cease-fire did not bring peace. In fact, we had widespread riots as people celebrated victory, simply in order to deny that they had lost.

"Sir, the protests actually had little real support. I think Sinn Fein used the tactics of Gideon[56]." I was briefing the CO who was a practicing Catholic.

"That's an outrageous metaphor, Billy." At least he smiled.

"It seemed the most effective way of explaining it, sir. The press seemed to have been convinced. Still, they were looking for a sensational story."

A personal sideshow to sectarian strife was my relationship with Bethany. We had not moved forward much during that summer since I was preoccupied and so the advent of a peaceful Christmas together offered hope that we might mature as a couple.

Christmas in Londonderry, however, was a sad event. Bethany and I awoke together in my cabin, unwrapped presents, made love and did normal Christmassy things. I felt at peace for a moment but then Bethany went back to her mess for lunch and I had to go visit my soldiers who were still on duty in the watchtowers looking over the City.

I collected my pistol, felt its reassuring weight under

---

[56] Old Testament – Judges 6-8 – The Hebrew leader Gideon was able to emphasise the small number of his followers in an attack against their Midianite captors using deception and noise.

my arm, and stepped out into the Christmas morning. Strangely, I felt more vulnerable than usual. There was much less traffic to hold me up and I had the comforting knowledge that PIRA's Christmas cease-fires were sacrosanct. But I still had a feeling of paranoia. Perhaps it was because I was all tooled up going to iron clad watch towers to wish greetings to my armed and vigilant soldiers on Christmas Day: This was not the Soviet Union or a mythical Sci-fi city, this was the United Kingdom.

I joined one young, cheerful soldier at the top of his eyrie, watching over the City. Watching the local people, looking into their windows, sharing Christmas with them from afar. Some people were sympathetic, possibly quite grateful for our vigilance. Boxes of chocolates were common and it gave me hope that gestures of goodwill were still made in this torn city.

Sadly, those who offered goodwill were so terrified of being identified by the Republicans that they would not stay to talk or exchange festive pleasantries. They hurried on, shoulders hunched, faces obscured. Sadly too, we checked all the gifts for booby traps. How badly have we tainted things that even Christmas is not immune from prejudice?

There was one woman who was able to offer comfort and cheer without concern for either side. Her bedroom lay in the shadow of the watchtower. Many residents in similar positions kept their curtains permanently closed but this young lady had no such inhibitions and she threw open her curtains with an expansive *Happy Christmas* gesture and then proceeded to remove her pyjamas; slowly, tantalizingly and generously. She did a whole lot more really, putting on a display to lighten the saddest of hearts. I left the soldier to his fantasies and powerful telescopic lens and hoped she was not a decoy for a major arms move in the City's hinterland, where the soldier was supposed to be watching.

For the remainder of my posting to Londonderry, the Peace Process gathered momentum and there was great excitement that, barring some isolated violence, the Troubles would come to an eventual end. Indeed, it was clear that they would in the short term but, even as the self-congratulatory backslapping was going on in Stormont and Westminster, it was equally apparent to the well informed that this was a transient situation.

In the years to come, once New Labour's well intentioned but naïve interference had culminated and the PIRA leadership had secured themselves well paid sinecures in the new government, Dissident Republicanism would emerge anew; the IRA use the Phoenix emblem for a reason.

But that was not my problem and Bethany and me went on a Caribbean holiday and discovered, I thought, that we were good together. We walked on the beach, we dined by candlelight on open verandas, we wandered through a street carnival enjoying the unbridled, infectious fun of the local people and we went SCUBA diving together, swimming along underwater holding hands.

The only friction was that I insisted on going running in the evening.

"Must you go?" Bethany's voice had a hint of exasperation. I was unsure what she meant; of course I had to go.

"When we get back the Battalion moves to Catterick and converts to a conventional infantry role. I need to be fit." We both knew that my fitness was good. Throughout my two years in Londonderry, I had run endless circuits around the small perimeter of the barracks and spent hours in the gym, but I went running on holiday for an hour's solitude.

I left 'Derry with mixed emotions. I was glad to be leaving Northern Ireland, glad that I would not have to look over my shoulder, and I stood on the ferry deck watching the coastline of Larne recede into the distance.

But I was sad to be leaving Bethany. Our relationship had not developed as completely as we both may have wished because, although we were good together, Bethany creased my shirt. I realized that I had to confront my own euphemism and accept that a permanent girlfriend required concession. Now I understood the company commander's advice that Bethany was suitable; love in itself was not sufficient.

I waited on the top deck of the ferry until Ulster disappeared from view. I felt safe then, but from what I wasn't sure.

Part 6 – God's Country

"...until I can find me, a girl who'll stay and won't play games behind me, I'll be what I am..." Solitary Man – Neil Diamond 1966.

24

I was working late in my office when the 'phone rang. The rest of the HQ building was in darkness, all the staff having left three hours previously.

"Hello, adjutant."

"Billy, it's Bethany." There was no *Hello Darling* or sentiment of any kind.

"Hi, Sweetheart, how're you?" I tried to sound cheerful, as if I could halt the inevitable. There was silence for a moment too long.

"Okay," she said eventually.

"So, what's up?"

She hesitated again before replying.

"I'm not coming over to see you this weekend."

"Why, what's happened? We're supposed to be going on holiday." I expected her to come up with some thin excuse of working or something; girls are generally crap at such things. Bethany, however, was more practised.

"I've met some-one else."

"Oh, right. Who's that?"

"A chap I had known before." The silence between us was heavy then as I tried to rationalise her words.

"How did that happen, I've only been gone for eight weeks?"

"Well, we just bumped into each other recently and then he kept in touch with me." Bethany explained that, having met this bloke, she realised that she just did not love me as much as she had thought. It seemed hollow.

"Beth, you're in Northern Ireland, how did you *bump* into each other?" More silence.

"He had been writing to me for a while," she eventually confessed.

"What's a while, exactly?"

"A few months."

"We've only been together for ten months, Bethany. How did you meet up?" I probably should not have asked.

"He came to visit me."

I lost control then and let go of the rant that had been building deep within my soul.

"So, you'd actually been involved with this bloke for about half the time we were together and as soon as I left Province you got him out to visit." She did not try to challenge my assumptions, preferring to weather my storm than to face the truth. That incensed me even more.

"Why did you do that, Bethany? You knew I had doubts about our relationship and you could have ended it weeks ago, not dragged me to St Lucia, making promises about our future together. Presumably, if it hadn't worked out with this guy you would have continued our relationship until the next decent offer came along."

"No," she said almost beseeching me, "no, that's not how it was"

"So, how *was* it, then?"

But she could not respond quickly enough to assuage my assumptions. I put the 'phone down, shut my office and went to the Mess bar. Suddenly, I was a single man again.

Sleep was a stranger. I lay alone in the bed that should have seen Bethany there, naked and resplendent next to me but she was with another man and that thought tortured me all night long. I could not reconcile the warm, caring woman that I had known with the cold, distant person who had so easily transferred her affections to another man.

Next morning I had to rise at dawn for a training exercise. I could really have done without it and, for a short while, I considered throwing a sickie but that is not what real men do and, alarmingly, I also realised that I had nowhere else to go. Suddenly, the Army Bitch was more appealing.

I shaved closely, drawing comfort from the peculiar masculinity of the act and then I put my boots on, set a firm grimace on my face and went back to the arms of the Bitch, once again finding sanctuary in the dubious company of the army. She smiled cynically to herself.

Eventually my misery became so obvious that even my usually insensitive colleagues noticed.

"Why so glum, Billy?" the Regimental Second in Command asked me late in the day.

"Nothing really, I'm just a bit tired," I replied, not wanting to be bothered with explanations.

"Well," he said good-naturedly. "You'd best get some rest before Beth gets here at the weekend." I felt that I might as well get it over with now that the subject was in the open; besides, I could have really done with some male bonding just then.

"Actually, Bethany is not coming at the weekend." There was a brief silence before they smelt scandal.

"Oh, that's a shame."

"What's happened, Billy?" asked one of the more perceptive officers.

"Well, actually," I hesitated then, probably because I found it hard to admit, even to myself, "she dumped me." Then it started.

"Oh no, why? Is your cock not big enough?"

"I'd heard she was getting it from some fellah called Winston."

"Do you think she'll go out with me then?"

That set the tone of life for the rest of the summer. I lost what little interest I ever had in my work and it even became something of a chore to socialise. The only escape I could find was in the gym or out on the moors, running long distances, my body always at the point of stress. It became my cave.

Bethany had drawn me in to the relationship and, at the precise moment of my acceptance of our long-term future, she abruptly ended it. The intrusion of an old boyfriend was strange. Being usurped by another bloke is easy enough to understand but what was difficult to accept was why Bethany had been so ostensibly confident about a relationship that, in her mind at least, must have actually been so fragile.

Men and women have fundamentally different views on finding a partner. Men plod along until they meet a woman who is a prospective partner. Women, however, appear to have a pre-determined view of the environment in which they want to live and seek to find a man to fill the hole. Presumably, if they do not find an ideal candidate, they accept an inferior model and try to round off the corners until he fits.

I tried to focus on my work as the Adjutant, the senior Regimental Captain, but it was a strange experience to which I was entirely unsuited. It was a high profile position that could have developed my career but I had not sought the appointment, it was thrust upon me, and I found it difficult to reconcile my personal views with the responsibilities of the job.

I worked late into the night nearly every day. The telephone rang with the incessant annoyance of a dose of crabs, people queued outside my office in order to blame me, berate me or give me more work. I spoke to people on matters as important as the manning of the Regiment on overseas operations and issues as inconsequential as why we could not spare any troops to help at the local village fair.

Some days were so bad that I felt like a laboratory experiment. Clearly there was a hidden camera in my office and each time the 'phone rang a monitor in the earpiece would register my stress levels. The scientists running the experiment obviously had a very perverse sense of humour and when they could see that my office was crowded with the senior majors all giving me a hard time about things over which I had no control, they would ring up and pretend to be the headmistress of the local primary school demanding soldiers to erect tents at their school fete and saying things like:

"I'm a tax payer, I've got rights you know."

This general situation could only be made worse by having to work for a totally unreasonable commanding officer. I once had an argument with a civilian girlfriend who said vehemently that stress at work was primarily caused by trying to satisfy the unreasonable demands of an irascible boss. I countered that nothing could really compare to the pressures of managing military operations in life threatening situations. However, in Catterick, I began to realise that she was right; nothing causes stress like working for a complete bastard.

A commanding officer in the army has much power. Autonomy in management can be effective if it is handled sensibly and it is generally expected that fifteen to twenty years service should make an officer a reasonable and balanced individual. Unfortunately, men who have the ambition to succeed in the military rat race often have egos like Cassius Clay. My CO was especially arrogant, overbearing and, unusually for a senior officer, lazy.

Lieutenant Colonel Taylor also seemed a bit mad. He would instruct me to do something against my advice and then, when it went wrong, he would blame me for it.

"Why did you not discharge those soldiers who were medically certified to be temperamentally unfit for duty?" he once asked me.

"Because you told me not to, sir," I replied, rather bemused that he did not recall our long conversation about it less than a week previously.

"I would not do that," he said in mock horror.

"Well, actually, sir, you made me refer the cases to the Brigade Headquarters."

"What did they say?"

"That we had to discharge them."

"So, why didn't you?"

"Because you said that they were your soldiers and the medical report was only a recommendation and you did not have to discharge them if you did not want to."

"Well that's against Queen's Regulations, apparently."

"I know, sir, I told you that." Taylor glowered at me for my insolence.

"Well, I've told the Brigade Chief of Staff that it's your fault, so you better have an explanation ready."

I naively imagined that the Brigade Chief of Staff would consider the matter sensibly but he too was a busy man and obviously felt that it was easier to blame a lowly captain than try to wrangle with a Lieutenant Colonel who was technically senior to him.

"I understand your problem, Billy," he told me whilst I was stood nearly to attention in his office, "but, even so, you are ultimately responsible for personnel matters in the regiment and you should have prepared the discharge paperwork."

"I did. He would not sign it."

"Why didn't you raise the matter with the Brigade HQ?"

"I did, your staff referred me to Queen's Regulations which I quoted to the Colonel who told me not to quote regulations at him."

At this stage the Chief of Staff had two options. He

could launch an investigation which would be time consuming, costly and embarrassing, or he could blame me, administer some sort of caution to me, annotate the file accordingly and close the case. So many of life's problems seem to be caused by the petty politics of little men trying to make themselves bigger.

Before I had joined the Army I had assumed that senior officers would be splendid men of high morals and many talents; which was usually the case. However, competition to be a senior officer was so intense that middle ranking officers were often shameless in their attempts to climb the rank structure and I soon came to realise that many of them had few morals and scarce few talents other than sycophancy, hypocrisy and expediency.

I discussed it with a friend who was a merchant banker and used to such petty politics.

"It's like a game, Billy," he mused, "and if you don't like the rules, then you shouldn't play." We were drunk, of course, philosophy does not suit the sober man, but his logic was clear, nevertheless. Consequentially, I determined to be my own man, to be independent of the quest for promotion, clear in my mind that a man should be measured by his manners, his humility and humour and, perhaps most importantly, the strength of his own values.

"Be true to yourself," my grandfather had exhorted but I did not have the strength of character to follow his advice. Being dumped by Bethany and then working for Taylor had made me irascible and paranoiac. I was bitter and pre-occupied and my relationships with other people were, at best, acrimonious.

I began dating a girl that I met in a shop but the relationship died before it had ever really been born. I found it increasingly difficult to drag myself away from my office in the evening because I was obsessed with my in-tray and my dates with the girl quickly became perfunctory. She could not tolerate my distracted and inattentive company.

How low can a man sink that he would rather work late, alone in his office, than dine with a beautiful woman? I was at the very edge of despair.

"Come on you fucker," I demanded of the computer one evening. The army was slow to capitalise on desktop computers and when we did get them they were obviously provided by the firm that had tendered the lowest priced contract. There was no formal training either, which just added to the comedy value of me trying to manipulate the machine.

"Talking to your computer is the first sign of madness, sir," quipped the Chief Clerk as she was passing my office. She was one of the most supportive Warrant Officers with whom I had worked, although I was not sure whether this was because she was a woman or a clerk.

"What's the second sign of madness then, Chief?" I asked with the first smile of my day.

"When it starts talking back to you," she smiled in return. I nodded grimly.

"It's been doing that for a while."

25

I sat in an open bar in the teeming streets of Phuket with only my beer and melancholia for company. The rain poured from the roof and bounced off the road and all around me was social mayhem; noise, light and drunken, laughing people. It was reminiscent of an old Vietnam movie: The brown slope-eyed native girls, the sunburnt lurching white men nursing bourbon and misery and the incongruity of their relationships most stark.

I sipped from a tall glass that I emptied frequently and which was filled just as quickly by the grumpy and taciturn woman behind the bar. We had a perfect relationship. She fulfilled all my immediate needs, physical and emotional, and we did not have to speak or even look at each other.

A smooth-skinned girl came and sat on the stool next to me and gently laid her hand on my leg. It was a while before I was able to register her presence.

"Buy me a drink?" she asked in well rehearsed but still halting English. I nodded to the bar tender lady and she poured the girl a beer. She sipped at it dutifully, clearly disliking the taste.

"You want girl?" she asked hopefully.

"I had a girl, once," I replied, "then she betrayed me." The smooth skinned girl did not reply, but just nodded her head.

"I loved her," I said in response to the whore's silence, "but I never told her that." I hung my head back over the friendly beer glass. Ice cool, perspiring beer glass; always full, always reliable.

"I love you lots," said the whore enthusiastically and I was touched by her simplicity. She did not need love or commitment or even any affection; she would love me for money.

Joe Wilson, a regimental friend, was watching me.

"Christ, Billy, she's not an analyst. Go and shag her, she needs the money." I shook my head, left some money on the bar, gave some more to the disappointed whore and wandered clumsily back to my hotel. The regiment had been on exercise to Malaysia and we had a week off at the end so a few of us had gone to Thailand to get drunk.

The exercise had been torture and the forced frivolity of drinking in Phuket did not raise my spirits so the next morning I went diving in the hope that some adventure might lift my mood. The boat ride out into the gulf was tedious, packed with backpackers and egocentric Americans all trying to be cooler than each other but when I jumped over the side into the warm water, I felt silence and isolation wrap around me like a comfortable blanket.

The first event was a wall dive and I hovered slowly in the water looking at the life that clung horizontally to the limestone cliffs in vivid colour and animation. Small clown fish weaved their way through forests of anemones and twisted antler coral. Larger fish swam in the deeper water away from the cliff and they dispersed rapidly to avoid the plunging humans as they leapt like lemmings into the water. The sea was soon as congested as the boat had been so I allowed myself to drift downwards away from the group.

When I rolled over and looked up through the surface I could see light dancing on the waves and when I looked down I saw the wall descending into dark nothingness, several hundred metres below. It seemed like a living metaphor for me although for what exactly, I was not sure.

Perhaps it was the sense of crowding, perhaps it was the exhilaration of feeling inconsequential in the deep water, perhaps it was the mesmerising lure of the darkness below, but something made me raise my legs and begin to descend slowly down.

I did not feel the slowly increasing pressure on my chest, it was the lack of coral on the cliff wall that alerted me to the depth to which I had sunk. I checked my gauge and had a momentary panic; I was well below compression depth. I looked around for the group and saw that they were high above and ahead of me so I swam a slowly upward line to try and obviate the need for a decompression stop. The dive leader had not noticed my absence and it was not until she checked our gauges before ascending that she raised an eyebrow in query.

In the afternoon we ran a rift dive, hanging nearly motionless in the water and being swept along in the current without any effort. Below us were seemingly huge leopard sharks cruising the seabed and actually the sense of adventure did provide a momentary release from my misery: I emerged from the water feeling much easier with myself.

I carried my new resolve back to the UK. I went on holiday with an old friend.

"Beer, please," said Adam as we sat down at a bar. The barman cast us an amused glance. Almost immediately there were two women at our sides. One ran a hand over Adam's arm.

"You buy me a drink?" the lady asked in halting English.

"Yes, of course," he replied, quite delighted to have some female company at last. "What would you like?"

"Champagne." Adam did not even flinch.

"Barman, champagne," he ordered with a flourish. The Frenchy had a bottle open immediately and poured us all a glass.

"Thank you," said Adam's new girlfriend in her clumsy English.

"My pleasure," he replied emphatically, although by then his English was as clumsy as hers.

The barman produced a bill for Adam to sign. He peered at it drunkenly.

"Billy, how much is two thousand, five hundred Francs?"

"About two hundred and fifty quid, I think"

"Fuck me!" said Adam.

"If you want," said his lady. He looked at her with further surprise, realisation coming slowly. Then he looked at me. He tried to whisper, but drunks cannot whisper.

"Billy, do you think they're prostitutes?"

"I think so."

Adam thought about this for a while.

"Have you ever shagged a prostitute?" he asked, still trying to whisper even though the ladies neither understood nor cared what he was saying.

"Yes," I said because it was too difficult to explain.

"Do you think it's wrong?"

"No," I replied earnestly, for I was too drunk to pronounce "moral" let alone discuss it.

"You sure?"

"Well," I began a mumbled explanation, "they have to earn a living somehow and so long as no-one gets hurt..." my voice trailed off as my treatise on whoring began to confuse even me. Besides, these women were mature (to say the least) and certainly did not appear to be victims of exploitation in the way that the youngsters in Malaysia had been.

"It's fine," I summarised, "and it'll give you something to talk about when you're an old fart in a home."

"Okay, Billy," said Adam cheerfully brandishing his company credit card, "it will be my treat. It will take your mind off Bethany." I doubted that but it was worth

235

a try and before long we were sat naked in a Jacuzzi slurping champagne with two French hookers.

"I am skiing," giggled one of the women as she sat between us and took us both in hand. I did not even try to get laid. The prospect held no attraction for me so I just sat in the froth slurping overpriced champagne whilst the woman pumped me enthusiastically. In truth, although I had no actual interest in sex with her, I did quite enjoy her attempts to raise my level of interest.

What the experience really illustrated to me was the importance of true friends. Friends do not judge or criticise or say *I told you so*. Friends know when to get you drunk, when to keep you sober, when to cheer you up and, most importantly, when to leave you to the misery of your own making. Nothing weighs so heavily in the heart of a sad man as the attempts of a fool to cheer him up.

Adam and I had gone to a Mediterranean resort where the sea was blue and the sand was warm and the wine was generally cheap and there was just the two of us; friends from long ago when our pants were short and we knew nothing of the trouble that girls could cause.

Inevitably, however, most of our time was spent trying to seduce girls. We were very unsuccessful. Realistically, any successful seduction would have to have been completed before supper. Afterwards, I was just too damn drunk. It could be argued that I should not have drunk so much but to a jilted man that is just foolish logic: drunkenness is a good place to hide.

The French have many faults but you cannot fault the quality of their whorehouses. We had not actually intended to go to one and perhaps when I asked the taxi driver to take us to a bar with lots of girls, I should have been more specific. It took us a while to realise our mistake although the velour wallpaper and crimson velvet furnishings might have been a clue but this adventure occurred long after supper.

Although I did not exploit the situation, I enjoyed playing the whoremonger and, oiled (literally) by that minor victory, I emerged yet further from the gloom to discover that there were actually other women around who were kind and witty and foolish enough to like me without being paid to do so.

Ironically, it was trouble with girls that helped me keep things in perspective. It seemed that, even if my ego was being routinely abused by the Army Bitch and Bethany, I could endure it so long as my libido was being regularly stroked; so to speak.

The end of my dry spell inevitably happened when I was not expecting it. I met a girl called Lucy who had a bright, pretty face and a wonderfully vivacious smile. We found ourselves sitting next to each other in a friend's garden with barbecue meals on paper plates balanced on our knees at his party. She caught my eye and smiled at me over a chicken leg.

"Hello."

"Hi," I said, caught in need of something more significant to say. Lucy, however, had no such worries; she was young enough simply to be spontaneous.

"I'm Lucy," she smiled.

"Billy," I mumbled through chicken and rice. Lucy smiled. She had ketchup on her chin and on such a young, pretty face it made her look very sweet.

"Hello, *Billy*." It was my turn to smile, I couldn't think of anything else to say. "How do you come to be here?" enquired Lucy.

"I'm an old friend of Martin."

"Who's Martin?" she asked.

"Birthday Boy." Lucy nodded. Eventually I took my cue. "What about you, what's your claim to fame?"

"I'm a friend of Jenna, who's a friend of Martin,

apparently."

This was not good news since I had previously been involved with Jenna whilst on leave from Northern Ireland. She was an impressive young woman who, despite her voluptuous figure and early career success as an accountant, was in the habit of sucking her thumb whilst she was getting laid. That was not her only interesting diversion.

"What's your favourite animal, Billy?" she asked me once as I was slowly humping her and watching her breasts wobble and independently vie for my attention. I was not really sure what she meant. I shrugged.

"I quite like horse riding."

Jenna wriggled away from me and turned over onto her hands and knees. She whinnied.

"Ride me then, Billy, ride me like a horse!" So I gripped her hips, slapped her arse and rode her like John Wayne whilst she whinnied and harumphed her way back to the paddock.

As it was, I began to colour with embarrassment. Lucy was less trifled.

"She's told me all about you," she smiled with malicious humour.

"Oh, right."

Her humour was infectious and it was a delight to be able to talk to a girl without concern for the future. Soon, we were leant close together, laughing confidentially at other people. I enjoyed her company, her smile, and her sweet smelling hair.

Finally, we had chatted too long and Lucy had to go. I was gutted. I wanted to kiss her deeply, to feel the softness of a woman again, but I was afraid that this would be an intrusion, a betrayal of her trust. For men, this recurring question is truly the meaning of life.

As we lingered too long I found a compromise at last.

"What are you doing tomorrow?" I asked.

"Helping my mum with chores," she replied with a teasing smile.

"If I write you a note do you think you could be excused?"

"Why should I want to be excused?"

"So that we can go on a picnic together."

"Okay." After that the embrace was inevitable. We dated for a short time and our relationship was a pleasant interlude but it had a very limited shelf life: *Lucy Hanson* just did not seem to chime very well.

My next amorous adventure was equally spontaneous. I was drinking with an old army friend in a convivial bar near London and idly looking around the pub. I kept catching the eye of a blonde woman in the corner. She was chatting to a large group so I assumed it was my imagination or ego that made me think she was watching me.

My friend, Mack, saw her looking over as well.

"She's nice," he said with enthusiasm, "I think she's watching us."

"Aye, she has been glancing at me for a while."

"You've such an ego, Billy, why do you assume she's interested in you?" He was obviously a little vexed by my assumption, which was fair enough so I just shrugged.

"She seemed to be. I am not interested."

Eventually she wandered over.

"I'm Mack," said my friend, extending his hand and muscling me out of the way. I was happy enough to step aside and let him try to chat her up although I could not resist a wink. She smiled coyly.

"Ffyon," she smiled, shaking hands gently. They chatted amicably enough although I was not sure how to tell Mack that he was headed for disappointment. Somehow, she was persuaded to come home with us so perhaps I had been wrong and my ego was clouding my judgement. My sprits were lifted briefly by possibilities this presented but Ffyon was way ahead of me.

"There'll be no threesomes fellahs," she declared on the way home. She smiled at us brightly, never faltering in her stride, and I was amazed by the confidence of a woman who could wander home with two strange blokes and was candid enough to talk about group sex without feeling threatened.

When we got back to Mack's flat I went to bed alone.

"Bollocks!" Mack stormed into my room moments later.

"What's up, won't she shag you?"

"No, the bitch wants you," he grumped and left to be followed by Ffyon who was dressed in her underwear.

"You're gorgeous," I breathed as I ran my hands over her firm curves. She dropped her underwear to the floor.

"I'm a dancer," she said and did a heart-stopping naked pirouette. She turned back to face me and held the palm of her hand against my cheek.

"There'll be no sex tonight, Billy," she said quietly, "we've only just met." That was fine by me, I was not up for one-night stands, and we spooned up in Mack's spare bed.

"I want to go on an adventure!" she declared when she woke up.

"Doing what?" I asked.

"That's your job." So we went and had a cooked breakfast and a walk along the Thames arriving neatly at the pub for lunch. We had fish and several glasses of wine and the afternoon carried on until the evening by which time Ffyon was well marinated.

Next morning we bathed together.

"Wash my hair?" came the inevitable request. So I rinsed her thick long hair and then began to gently rub shampoo into it.

"Mmm, that's nice, Billy," she purred quietly, "but can you rub a little harder?" Girls are always so impatient for that.

"Yes, Fifi, I will but the shampoo needs spreading around first." I continued to rub her hair softly until I was ready to massage it more firmly, drawing my fingers slowly but firmly through her hair.

"That's sweet, Billy," she sighed going limp in the bath so I had to hold her head whilst washing her hair. I rinsed the soapsuds out.

"Conditioner?"

"Please," she whispered. So I massaged it in and combed it through gently for a while.

"I'll just leave it to soak in for a while," I whispered in her ear. Ffyon nodded almost imperceptibly. I rubbed some creamy soap into her neck and shoulders and massaged them firmly. It was a strain to stop my hands straying around to her breasts but this moment was about building intimacy and trust, not clumsy groping.

Once I had rinsed her hair Ffyon looked at me lazily as if I had woken her from a deep sleep.

"Where did you learn to do that?" she asked eventually.

"I used to work in my Mom's hairdressing shop as a kid."

Ffyon wanted shagging in the kitchen, from behind whilst leaning over the table. She was very specific about how I should proceed and inevitably we were compromised when one of her flatmates came stumbling in looking for morning coffee.

"Oh, I'm sorry," she gushed but Ffyon never missed a beat and just continued pushing back against me. It seemed as if that had been her intention all along, to illustrate her Bohemian style. For an excited moment I again thought I might get a three-way shag but the flatmate promptly withdrew. Still, the episode also raised a hope that Ffyon's sexuality, confidence, intelligence and curvy aesthetics might translate into FMH potential.

We went out for Sunday Lunch and then back to her room to watch movies. Ffyon opened some wine although I initially declined, still feeling the previous day's indulgence.

An hour later I reached for the bottle.

"I'll have a glass now."

"You'll need to open another bottle then," she slurred and let the empty wine bottle drop to the floor. Ffyon was slumped on the bed at three o'clock in the afternoon and looked altogether less appealing, even for a drunken letch such as me. That night I left London for Yorkshire, feeling as much like an island as a man can get.

The following week I met Caterina in the Jacuzzi. I was sat on my own. She wandered in and lowered herself into the bubbles so that her breasts were just visible above the water. They jostled up and down like excited children. She was wearing a pink PVC swimsuit that was pulled together at the front by a straining zip. Damn, I wanted it to break.

"Hot, isn't it," she said, beginning to perspire in the angry froth.

"Yes."

"I like to come and sit in here after a good work out." She smiled at me. I just nodded. She held out her hand, "I'm Caterina."

"Billy."

"Do you work around here?" I nodded, aware that I was beginning to appear a bit stupid but afraid to speak lest I uttered strangled expletives of awe. Caterina smiled and her beauty and quiet confidence served only to remind me how lonely I was.

I went to a local gym even though we had basic fitness facilities in camp. I preferred the material comforts of a private club since the rhythm of the running machine and steady exertion of weight training were like therapy. There were girls in the gym as well, lots of them, and they were civilians, not tainted by the Army Bitch. Caterina was the most splendid: Danish, tall, dark and voluptuous with velvety brown eyes and an enigmatic smile. I never imagined she would be interested in an intense and overworked soldier like me.

"You're very quiet," she said.

"Well, I'm the strong silent type." It was the best I could manage under the pressure. She smiled again.

"I have seen you training," she said. "You work very hard."

"I am stuck behind a desk all day. It gets a bit frustrating."

"You should go out more, then." Caterina smiled at me again.

"Yes."

"I have just arrived here," she said nodding. "I don't get out much either."

Eventually I got the hint.

"Would you like to go for a drink then?"

"Yes," she said and stood up out of the Jacuzzi. "I'll go get changed." When she stood, Caterina towered over me with the water shimmering from her pink latex clad curves and I had to wait until she had left before I could decently emerge. Soon after I was sat in a dingy North Yorkshire pub with the most beautiful woman I had ever met.

We were both wearing tracksuits

"I was not expecting to go out tonight," Caterina

confided, leaning close so she could whisper, "and I forgot my underwear." She smiled coyly. I nearly choked on my Guinness. I failed to prevent my eyes glancing at her gently heaving breasts. I feared a reprimand but Caterina seemed sympathetic to the weakness of man and she offered me an almost imperceptible shake.

Our subsequent dinner date ran exactly as I would have wished. It ended with us sitting in front of a roaring log fire slowly exploring each other. Caterina was staying with her Aunt who was married to a wealthy Englishmen, complete with country mansion in Yorkshire, and as I sat and smooched and caressed this stunning Viking maiden I thought I had finally made it to Valhalla.

I had declined several glasses of wine because I had to drive home and Caterina had not insisted so I realised that the intense petting was simply an initial foray; full engagement to be had later. Physically, that was obviously disappointing but initial abstinence augured well for the long-term development of our relationship; Caterina Hanson did have a pleasantly exotic ring to it.

She walked with me out to my car. I kissed her slowly as I made my final farewell and she faltered, breathing in heavily.

"Oh Billy, come back inside," she urged pulling gently at my sleeve. I made to follow but Caterina hesitated again. "No," she muttered. "We must do what's right." She bustled me back into the car.

And, bizarrely, that was the end of my affair with the Great Dane. She called me later to say she did not think it would work. I was confused and despairing that I had come as close to loving her as a man can come to loving a woman without actually doing so and the lack of carnal adventure nearly broke my heart. It may be better to have loved and lost than never to have loved at all but it is certainly not better to have held a magnificent pair of breasts and not shagged their owner.

But what really concerned me was that this was becoming a pattern. There seemed to be plenty of girls, but none of them appeared to have FMH potential, either because they did not want to be with me or vice versa. I began to assume that I would be forever lonely.

26

"Stay there and don't move," the girl ordered, stroking my cheek and kissing me softly on the lips. Her touch was pleasant but not particularly engaging and as she went to dance with her friend, I was already planning my escape. Her lingering look as she left me promised a night of sex but, even though she was pretty in a modest way, I had no desire for a casual fling.

I slipped away from the nightclub and returned to our holiday apartment. My two friends were already back.

"Wow, Billy, she was a howler," yelled one cheerfully.

"Why did you go off with her?" laughed the other. Their jocular teasing annoyed me.

"I didn't go off with anyone, that's why I'm back here."

"Yeah, well I'm not surprised if she's the best you can do," continued one of my friends. His criticism of the girl was unfair, she was just trying to have some holiday fun, but they were too drunk to reason with so I just shrugged them off.

"You two were back here first," I pointed out but the irony of that fact was lost on them.

We were on holiday in Kardamena, Greece, and there had been several similar incidents when I had *failed* to get laid, leading to increasing derision from my friends. We met the jilted girl again the following evening. She was quite offhand, to the extent that she went off with one of my friends.

"I thought you said she was a howler," I hissed in his ear as he made to leave. He shrugged.

"Shag's a shag," he parried.

"You're a hypocrite," I declared but his libido was obviously stronger than his ego and he let the girl lead him away by the hand.

Notwithstanding my inevitable trouble with girls, I enjoyed the holiday. I was a Grecophile, having first visited the country when Emily Fisher worked in Crete. I loved the gentle folk, beautiful beaches, rugged interior and baking summer climate. I also loved the fact that Northern European women walked around the beach in a state of near nakedness, just as Eve would have done.

One morning I sat watching a girl unselfconsciously rub sun cream into her breasts. She cupped her left breast gently and raised it up whilst carefully rubbing the skin with cream. She extended a delicate index finger to focus more closely on an increasingly erect nipple.

"Do you want a hand doing that?" I could not resist a comment. She looked up, a little startled, and regarded me silently for a moment. I thought she might think me impertinent but she just laughed.

"No, but thank you for asking. Maybe next time." She smiled a little and her two friends also turned to look and all of a sudden we were a group: three blokes and three girls on the beach together had a natural synergy to it. I bought some ice lollies and dished them out as we sat chatting, sub consciously pairing up.

One of the girls, Andrea, was truly beautiful: dark, shapely, intelligent and confident. As we all chatted together I tried to subtly aim my conversation in her direction, trying to engage her more than the others. She was impervious to my attentions, expertly but gently brushing aside my clumsy flirting like a woman used to receiving the impotent doting of a thousand foolish admirers.

There was another girl in the group who seemed to hang on my every word. She was pretty and quite pleasant, but in my overly critical way she seemed to lack spark and she was clearly never going to be the FMH. I realised then that even if Andrea might have held some attraction for me, she would not move in the way of her friend and another potential relationship faltered before it began.

Drink and dark nightclubs brought no distraction either, just more trouble. That was where I met Ella. We were sat near each other and started chatting with a natural ease that suggested to me that we were meant to be together. She had a beautifully sweet face, soft brown hair and an easy manner that quickly burst into infectious laughter.

"You're all quite brown already," she commented looking at my friends. "Have you been here for a while?"

"No, just a couple of days but we're all outdoorsy types," I replied.

"What's an *outdoorsy* type."

"Army," I confessed. Usually I waited until I knew someone before I mentioned the Army Bitch as it turned some women off but Ella was so engaging that I would have immediately told her everything about myself.

We talked easily, laughed a lot and as we grew closer Ella demonstrated little intimacies by leaning against me, resting a hand on my thigh and frequently touching my face.

"Oh I could fall in love with you," she smiled, stroking my cheek with an electric touch and then kissing me with breathless passion.

"I've already fallen in love with you," I said and she smiled at me with a warmth that enveloped me like a post-coital hug.

As we were walking back to her apartment, I was making all manner of inappropriate assumptions about our future and something in my over excited rambling suddenly seemed to concern her.

"Billy," she whispered seriously, "I have to tell you that I have a boyfriend at home." Reality crashed violently through my consciousness with a depressing familiarity.

"But I thought you said you were falling in love with me." I felt very broken. Ella studied my face.

"No," she corrected gently, "I said I *could* fall in love with you. You're a very special man but just a bit too different." I flopped miserably onto a low wall.

"You said you liked that." Ella sat beside me and held my hand.

"I do, Billy," she consoled, "but only for now, not forever!" There was an incredulous ring to her voice that made me suddenly realise how ridiculous I had been in my drunken, lonely optimism.

"We could still have a holiday fling, though," she offered. She was smiling at me and her bright eyes shone in the dark with very tempting promise.

"I'll not be a holiday distraction to be cast aside once you've had your amusement." My words were perhaps unfair, Ella just wanted to get laid and I should have been flattered but *Ella Hanson* had immediately resonated strongly with me and the sudden reality was hard to bear.

I walked her silently back to her apartment where she stopped and kissed me very tenderly.

"Come inside and hold me, Billy," she urged with a quiet passion that tore at my whole being. I shook my head and stood away from her with more emotional muscle than I thought I possessed. Ella went inside and I went to the beach and sat on some rocks to listen to the gentle waves lapping at the shore. I sat there too long in the dark and the quiet lullaby of the waves turned inexorably into the haunting words of Carla, a university girlfriend:

"You're an easy man to fall in love with, but you're impossible to love."

As had become my habit when feeling isolated, I took to the sanctuary of running. I ran in the relative cool of the evening and the exhilaration of sustained exercise helped me to rationalise the situation and put things into perspective.

Greece is a good place to run. The land is open and not fenced off as it is in England. There is little traffic and you can run unhindered across hills and through fields and people wave at you as you run past. There are olive groves and sweet smelling fruit plantations to run through and the farmers use donkeys and thresh wheat by hand so that the countryside has the sort of charm that an Englishmen imagines his own land would have had two hundred years ago.

Kos is also rich in history with castles and ruins in abundance. On the escarpment, overlooking the beach at Kardamena is a grand castle. From my scant knowledge of Eastern European history, I assumed it to be a Crusader fort, perhaps built in the Twelfth Century by French or English knights heading East to fight the Moors. It had stood for nearly a thousand years, protecting against invasion and now the castle seemed to be presiding over the latest invasion and example of Northern European foolishness as it frowned over the frivolity of the tourists who frolicked pink and naked on the sands below it.

It was compelling. It took me three days to find a route through the countryside to the fort. During the day I studied the land from the beach, trying to follow the form of the hills to see which crest lead to the next. In the evening I would try to follow the line that I had identified earlier and I eventually found a path that lead through the low lying farmland up into the hills and then I was away, running freely, ever upwards.

It was a twenty-minute run, about three miles, and I crested the last peak unexpectedly, arriving at the Fort and startling the tourists who were newly arrived in their air conditioned coach.

I stood looking up at the walls, imagining the chain-mailed knights guarding the ramparts whilst steadily gazing East, fearing the violent attention of the Moors. I ran around the walls sweating heavily but running easily, picking my feet high over the rough ground and stepping lightly amongst the labouring tourists.

Finally, I came to the gate and entered the fort. Humbled by its presence, I climbed up to the ramparts where the tourists did not go and there, high on the hill, I saw Greece at its best.

Below me, endlessly shimmering, was the Mediterranean and behind me the hills rose inexorably up to the peerless blue sky. The breeze cooled my skin and my breathing steadied and I was lost in the world of the Lionheart, St George and the vivid possibilities of my imagination and history's endless fables.

My friends thought it was strange to spend a holiday exploring castles when there were women to pursue but for me it was infinitely more rewarding, and I enjoyed the respite from trouble with girls.

That ended as soon as I got home. I wore my smart uniform to a friend's wedding. It was rather cumbersome trying to squeeze my leather boots under the tight trousers and fasten the heavy sword to my belt but the end result was rather pleasing: I felt like a character in a Flashman novel.

Especially when Alison, the bridesmaid, came to explore.

"Ooh sir," she said stroking my arm, "why are you wearing such sparkly spurs?"

"They make my mounts go faster," I replied.

"Really, do you find they need such encouragement?"

"Not usually, it depends how I ride them, but a good prick helps to keep them keen."

"Is that why you've got such a big sword?"

"Not exactly," I replied tentatively, wondering how far I might push this innuendo without causing offence. "This is an Infantry pattern sword, it's used mainly to thrust rather than slash."

"Do you have to thrust hard then to get the best effect?" It seemed the innuendo had no limits.

"Yes and deep."

"I bet that would make a girl's eyes water," she mused with a slight flick of the tongue across her lips.

Alison, cast her eyes for a moment and then squeezed my arm as she offered me a long, slow, shy smile that held all the promise of Pandora. She walked away. I did not move for a while, unsure as to whether I was about to have sex or, indeed, had just had it. A waiter came past proffering a silver platter of champagne. I took two and drank them in quick succession. Then I took another.

I rejoined the party to host the guests but they were all relaxed and it seemed that my role as best man had run out of steam. I went outside to enjoy the quiet Yorkshire air. The summer breeze rose over the lake and caressed my warm face so I undid my tunic to let the air cool me as I sipped the champagne and contemplated the view, enjoying some solitude.

I heard the click of stiletto heels on the stone flags behind me and then felt gentle fingers on the back of my neck. Alison moved in front of me and took the champagne flute from my hand. She took a long sip and then lent up to kiss me with the champagne still in her mouth. The cool tingle of champagne mixed with the soft warmth of her mouth was intense and I had to still my breathing as the fire began to rage.

She ran her lips across my jaw up to my ear.

"Take me," she whispered and her intensity overcame all my reservations about getting into trouble again.

We walked in silence to the cottage I had rented for the weekend. Once inside she stood demurely but provocatively as I removed my belt and tunic and then drew my sword from its scabbard. I raised the blade and it pointed towards her, trying to gauge her reaction. She consented with an almost imperceptible nod of her head.

I flicked the buttons of her blouse with the tip of the sword and she slowly undid them. Once the swell of flesh was partly exposed I explored it further with the sword. Alison demurely followed my unspoken commands until she stood naked before me. Her breathing was shallow and her breasts rose and fell with quick rhythm as the colour rose to her checks. I traced the sword tip down her skin and then ran it between her legs with the flat of the blade pressing gently upwards.

Alison shivered and pressed harder against the sword so that I needed both hands to hold it firm. Eventually she pushed the sword away and pressed herself against me.

"Now!".

Our impromptu tryst quickly developed into a thriving relationship. Alison lived in a rented cottage on the edge of the Dales and her vivacious company in such cosy seclusion was enough to drag me from my career and romantic doldrums. Elegant dinner dates were matched with athletic sex and for a while we flourished together as an ersatz couple.

Alison also had a dog and we went walking in the woods. It was early summer and Yorkshire was at its best with a carpet of bluebells growing thickly under a roof of deciduous leaves and I held hands with a pretty woman as we walked alongside a tinkling stream in dappled sunshine with a friendly dog running along.

But there were too many contradictions for the relationship to endure. Alison had been engaged to a man I had worked with in Northern Ireland. He had been killed there and when I first went to visit her cottage there was a picture of him on the mantelpiece. I forever felt in his shadow and one evening as Alison and I were smooching in the woods, I had a sudden and terrible realisation that I was living another man's life: kissing his woman and walking his dog. I was even wearing his coat.

We tried to make it work but Alison seemed to sense my reservations and my lack of commitment inevitably made the relationship unfulfilling for her.

27

I trundled along in the dark in an old tracked vehicle that was made in 1963. I had not slept for three days. We were in severe danger of missing the next morning's battle because we were lost. Meandering slowly over the Canadian Prairies meant that we were unlikely to make the line of departure[57] in time, even if we found it.

In the cold, lonely night, I could not use my compass to navigate because the vehicle's steel case made it go mad and Vickers Industries who made the shitty machine had neglected to put a vehicle compass in it.[58] I was leading Battle Group HQ in a Dad's Army circus of ancient vehicles on a large-scale training exercise in Canada. The Rifle Companies had gone charging ahead at 30 KHM in new Warrior Fighting vehicles and were nowhere to be seen.

I could not even read the map because we were on *Hard Routine*, which meant no lights. I was reduced to describing the landscape over the vehicle's screaming intercom to my sergeant who was sat in the back reading the map.

"Okay, we're crossing a river now," I had to shout into the mike in order to compensate for the engine noise interfering with the intercom.

"How wide is it, boss?" Sergeant Ellis yelled back.

"I don't know it's fucking dark."

"Well, what else can you see?" he asked, irritation clear in his voice.

"I think there's a track junction ahead."

---

[57] Starting point of an advance into battle.
[58] One of the few certainties of army life used to be that the equipment was made by the lowest priced contractor.

"Right, got it. Take the middle track at the fork."

"There are about five tracks."

"Well, take the one that goes in the most northerly direction."

"Smashing. Which way is north?" He paused then.

"Can you see the stars?" I looked up into the sky. There was a myriad of twinkling lights in the clear, Northern sky.

"Yes."

"Well, follow the Pole Star."

"Are you fucking pissed? I'm not Gallileo." I began to wonder if the diesel fumes filling the back of the vehicle were making the Sergeant light headed but after a short while I felt a hand reach up between my legs. I expected to be given a brew but instead a piece of paper was thrust at me. I crouched down into the cockpit to read it. There was a rough diagram of a constellation which looked liked the Great Bear.

"Boss, are you familiar with Ursa Major?"

"Yeah, I think so." Sergeant Ellis explained the position of the Pole Star and I used it as my reference point.

So, the headquarters of a British Army Armoured Infantry unit stumbled along in the dark, following the North Star: it seemed like a rather tenuous way to train for war.

Going to Canada was always going to be bad. During the day it was 30 degrees centigrade and at night it fell below freezing. We were living on hard rations and working around the clock. It had even started badly. I was supposed to have been the last man out of the UK to ensure the final running of the Regiment until everyone had gone to Canada.

I had managed, I thought, to work this to my advantage. My 30th birthday fell the day before I was due to leave for Canada and I had made contact with

Sally (of *Back to School Party* fame in Northern Ireland). She was working in the Middle East but by good fortune was due to take leave in the autumn. She agreed to bring it forward a few days to meet me in London.

I yearned for Sally's embrace; it had been months since I had felt the tenderness of an affectionate woman. Moreover, Sally had starting writing to me. In one letter she told me that some girlfriends had dropped out of a ski trip so she had gone alone with six blokes.

"It was an interesting experience," was all that her letter said and possibly it was simply my tortured imagination, but the connotations were enormous and promised much excitement. The anticipation was almost unbearable.

"Billy, I need you out here immediately," demanded my CO when he rang from Canada.

"Why, sir, what's so important that no-one else can do it?" I was so incensed that my normal diffidence vanished and I demanded to know why, exactly, I had to go early bearing in mind the imminence of my 30th birthday and colossal shagfest with the lovely Sally. Genghis Khan might have had some sympathy with my point of view but David Taylor cared not. He told me so.

I telephoned Sally in Jordan.

"That's why I left," she said. "I was fed up with being messed about by idiots like that. It's a shame though," she continued seductively, "I was looking forward to seeing you again." I thought that I might start crying loudly then because I realised that I would never see Sally again.

Life on the prairie was as grim as ever I had experienced. After a month on exercise, our misery was compounded by the early and vengeful arrival of winter. It rained or snowed in alternate mockery of our

257

pitiful souls and the ground was quickly churned into a foul mud.

We slept under a single tarpaulin sheet stretched from the side of the vehicle and every night we had the *boots in sleeping bag dilemma*. If we did not sleep with our boots on, we could be badly caught out if we needed to get up in a hurry, but crawling into your maggot with mud caked boots on was depressing.

But such deprivation imbues in you a bizarre appreciation for minor comforts. Comfy bum[59] very quickly went into short supply, the Lea and Perrins Sauce that added some taste to the rations did not last long and a clean, dry uniform was a nearly forgotten luxury alive only in the most masochistic of minds.

One night, at about three o'clock in the morning, Sergeant Ellis and I were finally getting into our sleeping bags.

"You know, Boss," he mused, "when I leave this man's army, I'll miss the warm cosy feeling of getting into my sleeping bag on nights like this." I looked at him curiously and then I looked out into the dark, cheerless night. The stench of mud was thick in my nostrils, it was well below freezing and it was snowing hard with an icy wind sniffing around our ears.

"I doubt that I will, Danny." I slept fitfully, the cold seeping through my maggot.

My rebirth into the world, scarcely three hours later, was rude and brutal. Private Miller, one of the signalmen, shook me with the charm of a rhinoceros.

"What time is it, Windy?" I asked him. It was still dark.

"Sixish, boss."

"Fuck. Fuck! Windy, I asked you to wake me at five. There's an orders session at seven, I have to

---

[59] Soft toilet paper.

inform all the sub-unit commanders, set up the briefing tent..." my voice tailed off, dulled through lack of sleep.

"S'okay, Boss," said the implacable Windy Miller, "I've had radio responses from all call-signs, they've all acknowledged orders and I logged it down."

"That's a start," I said grudgingly. "What about the tent?"

"Me and Bogsy put it up during the night"

"In the dark?"

"Aye. Well, there was a half moon."

"Briefing map?"

"In the corner of the tent, we rigged a light too."

"Map traces?"

"Done." I thought about all of this and realised that there was little for me to worry about, I could stay in my warm maggot for another ten minutes at least.

"Thanks, Windy."

"No problem. One other thing, boss." He thrust a steaming mug of tea into my hand.

"Will you marry me, Windy?"

"Kind of you, boss," he laughed, "but I'm already married."

"Well, how's about just a shag then?" Despite the dark, I could see him grin.

"You'll have to ask Mrs Windy."

My dreams whilst on exercise in Canada were warmed by the prospect of returning to Yorkshire and the comfortable, alluring embrace of Alison. As my loneliness overwhelmed my consciousness, I resolved to make the relationship work.

"Billy, I'm getting married," she declared emphatically when I rang her as soon as I got home. Her declaration had an unspoken but quite obvious *so you can fuck off* ring to it and my libido and ego both took a familiar downturn.

So when the possibility of promotion and a move to Edinburgh arose, I jumped at the chance. It was such an attractive option that I decided not to leave the Army Bitch despite the warnings from more career minded friends that such a move could jeopardise my prospects. Who cared? Certainly not me, I was leaving the military rat race; the Bitch could go fuck herself.

Part 7 - Land of Plenty

"Well I need someone to hold me, but I'll wait for something more." Faith - George Michael 1987.

28

"Trouble with girls over thirty is inevitable," said Johno, the Company Sergeant Major, in response to my glum face one morning. "If they're married they become domineering and if they're single they become obsessive." He smiled at me, anticipating some amusing tale of girl trouble.

We had an unusual relationship, more informal than the Army Bitch liked. He ran the show and I signed the paperwork.

"What shit have you got yourself into this time?" he asked.

"I shagged Angie last night. Then we had a row."

"Your riding partner! I thought that was platonic."

"Well it was but she said we could have platonic sex."

"I don't believe you fell for that," he scoffed. "Good job you don't have a bunny rabbit."

I sat down in his office and took the consolation brew he offered: fresh, black coffee straight from the percolator.

"So, what's next?" he asked with a grin.

"This morning she asked if I was going to give up all my other girlfriends," I replied slowly. "She was quite intense."

"Well, was it worth it?" he smiled, getting straight to the point. It was my turn to smile.

"It was actually, very strong thighs. Bit of a shame though, I enjoyed riding with her." The CSM smiled again.

"Well, now you can enjoy riding her," he said happily. I shook my head.

"No, she turns out to be an all or nothing girl and I don't want to get married just yet; not to her at least. She's too manipulative."

"All women are manipulative," Johno said slowly.

"That's a bit cynical."

"I've been married twice," he shrugged, suddenly very serious.

I took my coffee into my own office to cogitate on trouble with girls. When I first moved up to Edinburgh I had picked up an old interest in horses and enjoyed riding around the majestic Pentland Hills.

I rode with a girl from the local stables and we quickly became friends. She was warm and bright with a freckled smile and soft skin. The film scene where Sarah Miles gets well rogered amidst the heather was always in my mind[60] but Angie seemed to be the sort of friend you cannot shag, so our relationship was simple and relaxed.

They were pleasant days. The only problem was that I had to ride the ugliest horse in history. He was a fatboy of a horse, lazy and belligerent and called Panda because, with canny Scots humour, he was a black and white palomino crossbreed; crossbred with an elephant, I think.

"Morning, Panda, you ugly bastard" I called cheerfully each time I saw him. He would just look at me sullenly. He was a solid beast of a horse but, with enough encouragement, he could turn out a fair canter and the best thing about riding him was that you did not have to look at his fuck-ugly face.

In retrospect, it seemed inevitable that my relationship with Angie would cause trouble. Lunch after riding became dinner after the theatre and we actually became quite close. Angie scrubbed up quite well and I suppose I had noticed that her outfits had become ever more revealing but she knew I was up to

---

[60] In he 1970 David Lean film *Ryan's Daughter.*

265

my eyes in trouble elsewhere so it never occurred to me that trouble was brewing with her as well.

"Come in for a dram," she insisted in her songlike voice after I had walked her home from dinner one night. We had gone to a pub near her house and I had planned to cab it home. We were both quite drunk. The whisky she poured me would have floored Panda.

There was something different about her, about us, as she sashayed around her cosy living room.

"Why don't you stay here tonight, Billy, then you won't have to come for your car tomorrow?" she asked.

"I suppose I could crash on your sofa," I replied hesitantly. Angie looked at me like I was stupid.

"No, Billy," she said with meaning. "I want you to stay with me."

"I'd love to, Angie, but I am not looking for a relationship." I spoke as carefully as I could, full as I was of Glenmorangie.

"Och, neither am I you soft bastard, I just want to get laid," she smiled, closing down the safe distance between us.

I realised immediately that this was going to end in trouble. I should have gently extricated myself and gone home, but then she would feel spurned. If I stayed and physically consummated the relationship I would be starting an affair that would never work and if I had sex with her and tried to maintain a friendship without commitment I would be accused of using her.

Whatever I did or said was likely to irretrievably break our friendship and, apart from all moral considerations, my libido had been stirred from under its blanket of whisky and would not now lie down. So, since we were no longer friends whatever I did, I figured I might as well get a shag out of the situation.

Angie was a good shag. In the morning we sat in bed drinking coffee and, just for a moment, it seemed like friends can shag and still be friends. We shagged again.

"Are you going to give up your other girlfriends or will I just become one of your harem?" she asked with apparent nonchalance. It was as inevitable as the rising sun. I felt trapped, even manipulated.

"Neither actually," I replied hesitantly, amazed at my own naivety.

"You bastard," she spat rising from the bed, "how could you make love with me like that if you had no intention of committing to a relationship?" I was amazed at the woman's duplicity and the vehemence with which she turned from a friend you cannot shag, to one that you can shag, to a poisonous ex-girlfriend.

"But you insisted. I said I didn't want commitment, you said that was fine." I protested like a soccer player to an impervious referee. Angie snarled like an angry dog.

"Oh, fuck off," she yelled, "you men are all the same." So I left quickly, ensuring I had all my stuff so that she could not cast a spell on me.

I sat in my office lamenting yet another failed relationship. It was a large office in a nineteenth century castle-keep. My windows overlooked the tree lined parade square. I had enough staff to do the job properly. Life in Edinburgh as a training company commander had changed remarkably from the desk bound lab rat that I had been as the Battalion Adjutant.

I had been promoted so received increased pay but I got fewer phone calls, what a result. The Army Bitch was warm and welcoming again and opened her legs in a flagrant attempt to seduce me back to her whim. It worked for a while so I decided to put problems with girls aside and focus on trying to rescue my career.

This job was much more satisfying than battalion life. Recruit basic training was well structured and therefore life was more balanced. I went out to the rifle ranges, on to the training area, and did all the other soldiery stuff that being in the Army was meant to be about.

I enjoyed the focussed effort of training soldiers as I had done in the jungle and in York but I was also responsible for the moral aspects of the young army initiates and that brought extra responsibility.

"Hello, this is Craig's Mum," said an irate sounding woman on the phone. "He's just told me that he's going to Northern Ireland when he's finished training." I was looking frantically down the nominal role.

"Could you give me a surname, please," I asked carefully, "there are five hundred recruits here presently."

"Riley," she snapped. I found her son's name on the roll.

"Yes, Mrs Riley, his regiment is due to deploy to Northern Ireland next year," I said trying to be sympathetic.

"Well, I don't want him to go," she said in near hysterics, "can't you send him to a different unit?"

"No, I am afraid that people are assigned to a regiment when they sign up. Besides, all regiments deploy to Northern Ireland at some point.

"Well, I want him out," she demanded, "send him home."

I was struck that, in a democracy, people often seem to support the need for a military option, just so long as it does not affect them. Still, I remembered my own mother's misgivings when I first went to Northern Ireland and tried to couch my words sympathetically.

"He's over eighteen, he'll have to decide for himself." She seemed to be crying. "I'll ask him to call you," I said gently trying to paint a picture in her mind of a caring organisation that supports its people. It was likely, however, that by the time the message got down to Private Riley through the NCOs it would be translated as:

"Riley, you soft fucker, call your mother and tell her to stop bitchin' to the company commander!"

At the other end of the spectrum were those who desperately wanted to stay in the Army but just could not make the grade.

"Miss Yates, my name is Major Billy Hanson, I am Danny's Company Commander up in Edinburgh."

"Hello," she said with surprise, "how is he doing?"

"Not very well, I'm afraid. He is struggling quite a lot with the physical training as well as the technical elements." I spoke cautiously, conscious that receiving an unexpected call telling you that your son is a failure would not be easy. Miss Yates seemed accustomed to it, however.

"Oh, well," she said matter-of-factly, "he's failed at everything else, this was really his last chance to do something useful." I arranged to send Danny home since he was under eighteen. I was again struck by how ironic it was that in a democracy where government funding is tight and pay is low, society's low achievers had inadvertently assumed responsibility for protecting the nation's interests.

They were youngsters away from home and exposed to the horrors of the world, mostly for the first time. I had little experience of administering formal discipline, other than watching my erstwhile CO blunder his way through it when I was the adjutant. I'd had no training.

"Why did you urinate against a garden wall?" I asked a forlorn and timid looking recruit in my first discipline session. He was almost shaking with nervousness.

"We'd been in to town and had a few drinks," he stuttered. "Then we had to queue at the guardroom to sign in…" His voice trailed off miserably. I had some sympathy; at his age I was still trying to get laid for the first time but he was now stood in front of me having to answer for the perfectly obvious. Johno, in the role of mentoring CSM, looked sternly at me behind the recruit's back, willing me not to be weak.

I looked at the recruit's file.

"You are only seventeen, you should not even have been drinking alcohol." I felt like a complete hypocrite. Johno was nodding at the back of the room. The recruit did not respond so I pressed on.

"What would your mother say if she saw some little oik pissing against her garden wall?" The recruit almost crumpled in front of me.

"My mother died last year," he sobbed, lip trembling. Behind him, Johno was bent double against the wall holding his stomach so as not to guffaw loudly.

As well as discipline, we also had to mentor the young recruits. The experience of being away from home and joining the army was quite a culture shock and many recruits needed convincing that they should stay. This was a responsibility that the Company Sergeant-major assumed enthusiastically.

"Why do you want to leave the army?" I heard Johno asking a recruit in his office.

"I've had enough, sir."

"Well, you've only just joined. What does your father say?"

"He doesn't really agree but he supports me."

"Do you think he means that?"

"Yes, sir," replied the recruit hesitantly.

I was listening to the interview from my own office. I was not sure where it was leading but I was becoming increasingly uncomfortable.

"How old are you, son?" asked Johno.

"Seventeen, sir."

"So for seventeen years you've been cramping your dad's style," Johno launched into his tirade, "and now, for the last five weeks, he's had the house to himself with your mom." I realised where this was leading and leapt out of my chair in cartoon style slow motion. I was too late.

"So your dad will have been wheel barrowing your mom around the house for weeks and now you're going to go home and spoil his fun just 'cos you don't like the fucking army. Bit jack[61] isn't it?"

---

[61] Selfish

29

A man's perception of the ideal woman changes as he gets older. When he is young the ideal woman is gorgeous, urbane, sexually active. When he matures, she is still gorgeous, but also sensitive, chaste in public but adventurous in bed. More importantly, she is a person with whom love develops naturally so that both parties accommodate each other's idiosyncrasies without question.

Edinburgh was where I finally got it. I took the opportunity to live in the city rather than cosset myself with the Army Bitch out in the countryside. I rented a shared flat and so I walked into a ready-made existence, complete with social life.

I felt like a real person. I did not have to wear a suit for dinner, had Sunday lunch in a pub and spent long evenings drinking in Edinburgh's many hostelries. On Sunday mornings Sandy, my flat mate, would sit on my bed in her pyjamas gossiping and drinking tea. I drank with her boyfriend so felt comfortable that there would be no trouble.

Civilian life had pleasures that were unknown to a single military man. Going shopping was, oddly, one of those pleasures. The supermarket was like a small village; you could do everything, get photos developed, dry cleaning done, and book a holiday. You could even buy groceries.

On my first trip I filled a trolley with all the stuff that my mom would not buy when I was a kid, like caramel ice cream and deluxe biscuits. Then I paid the bill and realised why she had not bought it. When I got home I also realized I had not actually bought any food.

I quickly got the hang of it and developed a slightly incongruous interest in cooking. I started with simple snack food like sausage sandwiches but these became more elaborate as I experimented and eventually breakfast was bacon and brie baguettes with cracked black pepper and fresh watercress. I progressed on to supper and baked chicken in a yoghurt and honey sauce or shallow fried rib-eye steak with a raspberry relish and garlic mash.

Cooking at home was an effective seduction technique, demonstrating more effort than a restaurant and immediately overcame the *your place or mine* complications. It had worked at university although then the imperative behind the plan had been dwindling funds.

There were some initial complications with the practice, however.

"This is unusual," suggested one of my first unfortunate dinner guests holding up a potato crisp.

"The recipe suggested a *crisp salad* as an accompaniment."

"I think it meant *fresh*."

My expertise developed quickly although my dinner menu remained limited to a few specialities. This did not really matter since few girls held their place on the guest list long enough to have to endure a repeat order.

Another special pleasure of civilian life that I embraced enthusiastically was having my hair cut in a unisex salon. My hair was washed by a girl of almost impossible beauty[62]. She was tall, slim and had wonderful ripe breasts; firm and full like bags of gold. She was the sort of girl that makes you want to just stop and applaud, especially since she seemed so willing to let everyone indulge in the wonder of nature. She wore a cropped vest that exposed her silky midriff and

---

[62] So it seemed to me at least, I was used to having my hair cut by fat sweaty blokes.

strained to contain her ample charms.

She washed my hair with warm water and firm, gentle strokes. I slid into a dream.

"Would you like conditioner on your hair?" she asked innocently.

"Yes please," I replied, not wanting the experience to end.

How about a soapy tit wank while we're at it?

Eventually it came to an end and when she removed the towel, they were there, hanging fulsome and magnificent in front of me. They wobbled gently as she dried my hair. Such torment. They were huge, the entire focus of my world; like your mom and dad leaning over your pram when you're a kid.

There were girls aplenty in Edinburgh but the tenacity with which I was approached quickly made me feel like fresh meat to hungry dogs.

"So *you're* Sandy's flat mate!" exclaimed a girl that I had just met at a party. I fooled myself that my popularity was due to my charm and wit but, in reality, I knew it was because I had a decent job and a lack of marital commitments; sought-after commodities in Scotland, it seemed. I had a girlfriend in Yorkshire so did not immediately indulge in the opportunities that were presented.

"Isn't it awful being *thirty*," said a girl I had just met in a Grassmarket[63] pub. I shrugged.

"Not really. I'm young enough to enjoy myself and can at least afford it." It seemed plausible enough.

"That's a really cool philosophy," she said. "What's your name?" We did the introductions. Vicki was quite appealing but she was also quite intense.

---

[63] An area of pubs and restaurants near Edinburgh Castle.

"Where's your ring?"

"I don't have one?"

"Did you take it off before you came out drinking?"

"No, I'm not married."

"Divorced?"

"No, I've never been married," I said nervously.

Vicki then asked me about my job, my past relationship history and my future intentions in respect of matrimony with particular emphasis on whether she might play a role in any such plans. She did not quite say it like that but her implications were obvious enough.

I excused myself to the toilet and tried to escape. Vicki saw me leave the pub and chased me down the street. I jumped into a taxi.

"Drive!" I beseeched the cabby.

"Where to, mate?" Vicki was running wild-eyed and shouting down the street.

"Away from her." The cabby picked out her reflection in the headlights.

"Oh, I see." He drove towards Vicki. "It's a one-way street," he called over his shoulder and drove slowly past her. She banged on the cab window.

"Don't leave me, Billy!"

The cabby pulled away as soon as was safe.

"Jilted girlfriend?" he asked cheerfully into the mirror.

"No, mate. I just met her."

On another night I was sleeping peacefully through the effects of beer and single malt in my flat when I was gently disturbed by a presence nudging its way under the duvet: A bit like Deefor had done before he went to doggy heaven.

"Billy," whispered the Siren as a hand curled around my shoulder and over my chest. Pressed firmly against my back were two very exciting girly lumps. It was a re-enactment of the Emma Briggs scenario and I swore after that incident that I would never again spurn such an opportunity.

I rolled over to meet Mary, a friend of Sandy. She had been drinking but she was still tempting. So very tempting.

"Mary, I am seeing some-one," I sighed, hardly believing myself.

"Oh, I'm sorry." She kissed me gently and slid away, which I thought was very sweet.

It was a hollow victory. I had forsaken what would probably have been an excellent shag in order to protect a current relationship. The succession of failed romances seemed like weakness on my part and I was determined to break the cycle but, in this case, my attempts at fidelity proved to be pointless.

The next weekend, I drove four hours from Edinburgh to see Millie, my girlfriend in Yorkshire, and had a frustratingly sex free weekend. The bright winter sunshine and resplendent views over the River Swale were not sufficient compensation.

"You're a bit irritable this morning," she said smugly on the Sunday. That annoyed me, implying that her lack of interest in sex was my fault.

"I'm irritated rather than irritable."

"I just wasn't in the mood."

I nodded, trying to be understanding but realising that I would never be in the mood to come back. Clearly, a girl has the right not to be in the mood for sex but, equally, a bloke has the right to be very much in the mood. There is a need for compatibility in a relationship.

I went to burn off my angst and enjoyed the scenery and sense of space that desolate moors offer the lonely runner. I came in hot and sweaty but exhilarated.

"How was your run?" Millie asked without much

interest.

"Good, thanks. I did about ten miles." She nodded absently whilst taking another chocolate from the box on her knee. I glanced at the near empty box and could not help but notice her developing stomach.

"That's good," she said absently whilst still glaring at a crappy Sunday afternoon soap opera. "I should do more exercise."

The relationship was passed its sell-by date and I spent the rest of the day wondering how to break up effectively whilst limiting the stress. In the end, a clever strategy was not necessary. We went out for supper before I drove back to Edinburgh. The evening went slowly, the rapport between us now jaded.

When I finished eating, I absently but very precisely folded my napkin along its original creases and smoothed it down on the table.

"That's neat," said Millie. I shrugged.

"In a world of chaos, it is nice to have some balance."

"A folded napkin won't save the world." I considered that for a while before replying.

"I know, but at least in the sphere of my immediate influence, order is restored."

I had not actually meant to comment on our relationship, folding the napkin was an instinctive gesture, but there was something critical in Millie's demeanour and I realised that our relationship had already culminated. So did Millie.

"Thanks for supper." She rose from the table, screwed up her napkin and threw it on the table.

I went back to Edinburgh feeling liberated and began to more actively exploit the opportunities that Edinburgh seemed to offer. I met Caroline at a parade in camp at the end of a training course. I was dressed in my best uniform. I had noticed her looking at me through the throng of parents and hangers on at the reception after the parade but paid little heed. Eventually she manoeuvred herself in front of me.

"Hello," she gushed as if we were old friends. I smiled uncertainly.

"Hi," I said holding out my hand. "Billy Hanson, I'm the Company Commander." Caroline brushed my hand aside and leant up to kiss my cheek.

"I know, silly," she said, "I'm Caroline, remember? We met in Rose Street last month[64]." I did vaguely remember having met her briefly in a pub. I had a sudden fright that she might be one of the recruit's mothers although she was not really old enough.

"What brings you here then?" I asked. Caroline took a deep breath and delivered a well rehearsed line.

"Well, my mum works with Maggie Sinclair who is the aunty of Matty Culdrose who has just finished his basic training." Caroline waved her hand about in the direction of seemingly random people in the hall and I was left with the slightly uncomfortable feeling that she had contrived to come to the parade in order to meet me.

I was not sure whether to feel flattered or threatened. Still, she was quite pretty and I had not been laid for a few weeks so I dived in. We got on quite well and soon arranged a dinner date. Caroline was fun and flirty and we dated for a short while but the relationship never quite worked for me; we seemed to lack spark.

Caroline tried hard enough.

"Billy, I have a bed time surprise for you," she said on the phone one day. My mind raced. The possibilities were endless and I was exhilarated that this lady

---

[64] Another of Edinburgh's drinking areas.

understood me, my need to pursue excitement. She seemed to have some FMH potential, after all.

I drove down into Edinburgh in a state of heightened anticipation and then spent a very agitated evening with Caroline trying to elicit from her what she had planned: Girl Friday, Florence Nightingale, Cleopatra? Caroline just smiled indulgently, eluding my interrogation with elegant verbal manoeuvres that simply made the anticipation worse; or perhaps better.

Eventually we got back to her flat.

"Da daa," she exclaimed, indicating a box on the floor. I leapt on it like a six-year-old at Christmas.

"What's this?" I asked, holding up what looked suspiciously like an airbed.

"It's an air bed," Caroline replied, perhaps sensing that I was a little under whelmed. "It's a double," she added hopefully. She had a small flat with a single bed.

"Oh, excellent. Have you got a foot pump or something?" She did not and it took me over an hour to blow the fucking thing up. Once I finished, Caroline tried to recover the situation.

"Come, Billy, let's try it out," she whispered, slowly sliding her dress from her shoulders. It was a good attempt and a better man might have responded accordingly but the exertion of inflating the bed and the disappointment that she was not dressed up as Lara Croft was too much. I was like a whipped dog.

I awoke in the cold hours of the morning, lying on the hard floor. The airbed had deflated and Caroline had crept back into her soft, warm, single bed.

30

In Edinburgh I became an advocate of the *Six Week Rule*. If a girl had not demonstrated FMH potential after six weeks, she was dumped because soon after that the *Eight Week Rule* applied. Under the Eight Week Rule, women invite you to their Parents' house for lunch on Sunday, followed by a trip to Homebase. Mothers look at you appraisingly and thereafter you become marriage fodder, irrespective of any actual compatibility.

This was confusing. There was a plethora of eligible young maidens in Edinburgh and some of them might have qualified to be FMH had they not been quite so obvious about it. I wanted to meet a girl that I could love, with all other considerations being secondary, but I began to feel that I was seen as little more than a sperm and money donor. Mrs Hanson never seemed like she was coming home for supper, even if I was cooking.

"You're quite the Lothario," smiled Johno as I arrived late at work one morning.

"Well, it's not really intentional," I countered, "I just don't seem to meet the right girls." He nodded slowly, deep in thought. Johno and his wife had been very supportive of my quest to find the FMH but after I had test driven two of her friends and moved on, the supply of totty had dried up.

"A reluctant Lothario is a contradiction in terms," Johno said with much amusement. It was, I had to admit, and my search for the FMH was in constant contradiction to the regular acts of copulation with clearly unsuitable women.

Another issue that I had to contend with was that my sexual proclivities were becoming ever more adventurous. Straight in and out sex was just not that interesting for me anymore but finding a girl who could converse with interest about political philosophy, natural history, or whether Rugby Union was better for having gone professional, who would then dress up as a she-bitch dominatrix, or a timid slave girl, and romp around on her knees getting rigorously rogered whilst sucking pussy or another cock, was proving to be difficult.

And it was not just girls that I got into difficulty with.

"What a nice coat!" exclaimed a complete stranger to me as I was walking along Princess Street one Saturday morning.

"Thank you." I was a little uncertain. He stood in front me, preventing me from sidestepping him without undue rudeness.

"Do you mind if I ask where you got it?" His approach was rather abrupt, but he seemed like a decent middle-aged bloke and he was fairly unthreatening.

"Actually, my father gave it to me for Christmas. I think it's from Austin Reed." He smiled a little uncertainly himself then. "There's a store along George Street." He nodded at me and then we both realised that we were not on each other's wavelength.

"Right, thanks," he muttered.

"No worries," I mumbled and we went our separate ways.

So, after six months of failed adventures, I tired of living in the midst of all that trouble with girls in the city and managed to argue myself a Pad[65] close to work. This was my first real foray into the realms of the married folk and initially it was an amusing experience for all concerned.

---

[65] Service Family Accommodation: A house with subsidised rent for families. There is no single servicemen's equivalent.

I would take a bottle of wine and my washing to a colleague's house and he and his wife would wash my clothes and feed me supper. In return, I would amuse their children. I was particularly good at Lego. It was a happy arrangement for a while but the novelty quickly wore off and the Pads became bored of me.

I bought a washing machine and the Pads were friendly again but it still seemed as if I was standing still. My friends, military and civilian, had all bypassed me in some way, earning more money, buying country houses, and raising young families. The laughter they extolled in response to my tales of misadventure developed a distinctly derisory ring to it.

I enjoyed being a Socratic grasshopper but at thirty years old being a career hedonist was not particularly satisfying. It is a sobering moment in life when you realise that, at a relatively young age, you have reached the top of your evolutionary tree. Still, I was quite comfortable on my branch and, whilst meeting the FMH would have been nice, I was not in a rush.

It had been the same all through my life; I had never really joined in the male race to be first to do something new. As boys it had been the first to get a skateboard, as teenagers it had been the first to get laid, as young men it was the first to get a pretty girl to marry and now it was the first to have children and a cardigan.

"There's a definite correlation between a man's hairline and marriage; the sooner that the former recedes, the quicker he'll opt for the latter," declared the ever philosophical Johno over another manly brew in his office. Johno was nearly bald and his wife was lovely.

But my hair never began to recede so I carried on playing the game to the same rules although the paying fields had changed from pubs and clubs to friends' dinner parties.

"Would you like to come around for supper on Saturday night?" the Pads would ask. "After supper we usually gather around the piano and sing together."

Hey, that sounds like fun, maybe I can stick needles in my eyes to really liven things up.

I would dutifully wear *smart casual* clothing and go around with a bottle of wine and bunch of flowers.

"Thank you, they're lovely," the wives would gush before turning on their husbands. "He never buys me flowers."

Perhaps you should suck his cock more often then.

I always wanted to defend my harangued mates but since discretion is supposedly the better part of valour, I usually just smiled sweetly. Besides, the wives would no doubt argue that if they received flowers regularly they might be more accommodating. I suppose it was a "chicken and egg" argument, or perhaps more pertinently, "flowers or fellatio", as to which comes first.

Such evenings could be fun and there was always the remote possibility that the wife's single friend would not be too much of a behemoth. It was actually them, rather than the wife, I was hoping to impress with the flowers.

The inevitable interrogation of my persistent single status did become rather wearisome but it seemed like the penance for a free meal and a possible introduction to a woman. It was also worth it just to observe slightly drunk women who had forgotten that they were no longer single twentysomethings try to turn the conversation a bit risqué.

"Have any of you heard about the *Rabbit*?" asked Amy one evening. She was ten years and a bottle of wine on the wrong side of such dinner party chat. There were a couple of smug smiles around the table but little direct response, which seemed to disappoint Amy.

There was at least one more sheltered woman, giving Amy the platform she so clearly wanted.

"What's a *Rabbit*," asked Rachel cautiously.

"It's a vibrator," gushed Amy amidst unflatteringly girly giggles, "with *ears* on the side for extra stimulation." Her husband looked suitably embarrassed.

"Come on," interjected Phil Swain a robustly handsome man who probably was very familiar with women and should have known better. "There's no way a vibrator can be as good as a man!" I was not sure if he was being serious or deliberately contentious.

"Are you kidding me?" roared Hannah, the wife's single friend, like Billy Connolly on a Glasgow stage. "To compete with a *Rabbit* you'd have to be nine inches long, permanently hard and last for as long as a girl likes it. You'd have to frig me whilst you fuck me as well," she added in case we had not realised by then that she owned a *Rabbit*.

There was an awkward silence over the table but at least I now knew why Hannah was single.

"How are you getting on with finding a girlfriend, Billy?" came a pointed question intended more to divert attention from Hannah by highlighting my failure in getting married, than actually enquiring about my welfare. All eyes looked at me and I sipped my wine slowly, contemplating the mood of the evening.

"It's difficult," I replied evenly, "girls in their late twenties or early thirties seem to think that a potential husband can be secured in the same way as a lucrative job, complete with company car."

"Don't you want to get married, Billy?" asked Claire, a rather drunk and very annoying wife. "You don't even seem prepared to discus it." I sighed inwardly. I hated this line of conversation. I did not want to become defensive because that would make me a little spiteful but the woman's smugness was overpowering.

"Eventually, when I meet the right woman."

"But don't you get bored of meeting girls and starting new relationships all the time?" she persisted. I shrugged to evade her inquisition.

"A little but then folk don't keep the first car they buy for very long, do they?"

"That's a bit obscure, Billy," said one of the guys, moved to mischief.

"What do you drive now?" I asked him.

"Volvo estate, I'm a pad," he replied smiling.

"But what was your first car?"

"Some old boiler." One of the girls caught on at last.

"Are you suggesting that girls are like cars?" she said, flushing slightly.

"Not just girls," I said in lame recovery. "Relationships. I doubt that you drive the same car you first bought."

"Very illustrative analogy," another chip from one of the blokes.

"We've got kids, and only one car," ventured one of the girls, rather missing the point. "We have to share."

"That's what I've heard about Pads," I said. Some times you just can't stop yourself. There were coughs and giggles around the table.

"For goodness sake, Billy," one of the other girls began to remonstrate but some of the blokes seemed to quite like the idea.

"Perhaps you're having an early midlife crisis," said Claire. This was not the first time such an opinion had been ventured in my direction and it usually came from a wife feeling threatened.

"What's a crisis about having younger girlfriends, a sports car and your own skis?"

"Nothing, I suppose," she replied, "until those girlfriends are only interested in you for money, then it would become rather sad."

I felt too provoked to be cautious.

"Well, I am only interested in them for sex so at least its an honest relationship." My quip was met with stony silence. Even the blokes looked offended. We had finished eating and the group began to move from the table. I had been too indiscrete for any valiant recovery, so I went home.

I left trying not to think about Hannah with her *Rabbit*. Despite her pugnacious attitude, she did have a degree of physical charm[66] and the thought of tying her up and digging her burrow with her own *Rabbit* was quite appealing.

Whilst the search for FMH continued, I lived my life. I realised that you could actually buy most things, including female company. This I already knew, of course, but I had consistently failed to be a whoremonger so decided that was unlikely to be a satisfying solution. The answer was strip clubs. There is still a sense of delicious depravity about a strip club.

One of my married colleagues had a beer fund. He volunteered to do the shopping and other petty cash chores so that he could add the change to his fund. When he had enough beer tokens we went for a night out. We had worked together previously and we once spent an expensive night in a Parisian brothel where the champagne was more expensive than the women, which tells you something about Gallic priorities, but that was long before he met his wife.

"Will Emma be cross if she finds out?" I asked whilst we were watching a rather clumsy pole dance.

"No," he smiled, tilting his head to ogle the girl's upside down tits. "She's been to see the Chippendales a

---

[66] Big tits.

couple of times. Truth is, I just want to have some secrets. This is as close to having an affair as you can get without actually having one."

I smiled at that.

"Aye, a man needs some space. I just like to see lots of tits." He smiled at me.

"Private dance?" a very leggy and smiley girl asked my friend, draping herself over the arm of his chair. He had three children and his beer fund really only covered the cost of beer.

"On me," I said, proffering twenty quid. "Happy birthday." She led him away by the hand. They were both smiling.

"Hey, stranger, what about you?" smiled Isabella, my favourite girl[67]. She gyrated lazily in front of me, just grazing my nose with her soft breasts. We were not supposed to touch but I did not mind and just sat on my hands and let her abuse me.

"Bella, keep your knickers on," I urged as she swooned past. Somehow, that seemed more intimate. She smiled and carried on dancing.

"Any other requests, Honey?" she breathed in my ear as she knelt over my lap, creasing my shirt with her tits. I had been out drinking for a while and did want something special. I slid another tenner into her knickers.

"I'd love a brew." Bella smiled and led me to the bar. She stood bare-chested and poured me fresh coffee from the girls' own machine. There is something comfortably perverse about drinking coffee with a near naked woman in a strip club.

---

[67] I don't think it was her real name.

31

"I need a big, strong man," said a girl with a quiet grin. I looked around but there was no one else in the car park except me.

"What do you need a man for?"

"Well," she said in that peculiar way that women do when they're about to launch themselves into a contrived and complex explanation for some spurious idea. "I've bought these new racing boots and they are ever so stiff. I can't fasten them on my own."

I had gone to the Cairngorm ski centre early one morning to beat the queues and was unpacking my kit in nervous excitement. Skiing in Scotland is not for the casual skier; only an enthusiast can endure the near constant drizzle and patches of heather waving through the broken piste.

However, on this particular morning, the early sun was bright in the sky and the Highlands had a thick cover of snow. It was a day to rival the best that the Alps could offer and if I were quick, I would be one of the first on the slopes, enjoying a couple of hours skiing before the hordes descended. I was certainly not expecting trouble with girls.

Still, fastening the lady's boots was not an onerous task and she was very pretty so I knelt to the task. Her boot clips were very stiff.

"I need to you to lean forward," I said, holding the back of her knee to support her. "Do you mind me holding your leg?" I asked, suddenly conscious of how intimate the situation had become.

"Feel free," she smiled happily. So I did. She had lovely legs, very firm; she was probably quite a proficient skier. I told her so and she said I was very gallant. My hand unintentionally reached a little higher up her thigh as I struggled to fasten the clips. She leant on my shoulder as I made her bend her knee. She giggled. I finally managed to fasten the last clip on one boot.

"Ooh, it's very tight, you must be ever so strong." She was smiling broadly at me. I was not sure where she was going, racing boots can be difficult to fasten so her request for help was simple enough but the cheeky grin was a bit odd.

"I need to do the other one," I said. She nodded.

"A man's got to do what a man's got to do."

Kneeling in front of a smiling girl with your head between her legs is rarely a bad thing but I wanted to go skiing and had not anticipated being held back by some dizzy chick, no matter how pretty. I fastened the other boot more quickly and stood up.

"Well, I'm afraid that this man's got to go up the mountain." I smiled apologetically.

"Oh, good," she said casually, "I'll come with you." There was no hint of a question in her voice so I picked up her skis and we stomped off to the chair lift.

"I'm Jane. " She offered a gloved hand.

"Billy," I replied slowly, looking into her ski glasses.

"Where are we going skiing," Jane asked as if we had planned the whole day together.

"I was going to try the Wall, it's never had enough snow before." My response was fairly reflective as it was reputedly a very difficult run. I also wondered if skiing such a black run would put her off.

"Ooh, yes," she gushed with excitement, "it's great when it's fully snow covered." She was certainly persistent. We skied away from the chairlift together and turned down towards the slopes. Jane moved with an easy grace on her skis and she turned efficiently without straining. She stopped effortlessly on the hard packed snow, which was icy in the early morning.

She leant on her poles looking over the edge of a slight cornice. The gully of the unmarked East Wall was deep in shadow and looked dark and a little foreboding. I slid in beside her.

"Shall I go first?"

Jane smiled, gently mocking me.

"No big, fellah, you've not done this run before." She dropped off the edge of the cornice, landing expertly about ten metres down the slope. She ran on in a powerful arc turning back down the hill. I could hear her skis clattering on the ice but her slender legs absorbed the pressure of the turn with ease and her skis held such a tight edge that a plume of incandescent powder was thrown high into the air, just catching the early sun above the hill.

It was a beautiful effort and I was not sure I could match it. Now I understood her mocking smile, a cute way of countering my presumption that I was the better skier. I wondered if she was hoping I would fall so that she could laugh gently and ski off with an "I told you so" sort of triumph.

But Odin smiled on me and I absorbed the drop and held the edge of my skis as proficiently as Jane had done. In fact, as I drove the turn back in towards her, I added a pirouette to the run and carried on past her slowly cruising down the gulley.

"Show off," Jane laughed and let her skis run down the slope to keep up with me. We skied as one and, as the gulley narrowed, we skied short swings in parallel with each other as if we had practiced together many times before. It felt like dancing.

We slid out of the run in casual arcs, laughing together with exhilaration. I was slightly lower down the slope and Jane was too casual, losing her edge slightly and sliding into me accidentally, I thought. I had to catch hold of her to stop her knocking me over.

We were both panting and laughing.

"Wow," she said, "that was fun." Her excitement was infectious. As I held her upright and looked down at her smiling face she seemed to relax into my arms. She kissed me warmly like a long-standing lover. It felt good.

"Wow, indeed," I responded breathlessly, "that was fun." Jane smiled and escaped my embrace to run into the draglift.

"Can't catch me!" she teased as the lift pulled her up the slope. For the rest of the morning we chased each other around the mountain in a blur of snow and smiles; I had not had so much fun for a long time.

By midday the crowds and queues denuded skiing of any fun so we mutually decided to quit. After such a connection, shagging Jane was inevitable but I had not expected to do it in the car park.

"What's the plan now?" Jane asked as we stomped down to the car park. I shrugged.

"I was going home to Edinburgh but, since the forecast is good, we could come back and ski tomorrow as well," I was musing, since I did not really have a plan.

"Excellent idea, but it's not worth driving into Edinburgh. Let's find a hotel," she said. Then she climbed into her car, turned up the heating, put Bon Jovi on loudly and starting taking her jacket off. I got in and closed the door. Jane was nearly naked by then and she knelt over my lap and kissed me passionately whilst helping me undress.

We got on well. Jane shared my sense of adventure and our relationship consisted of skiing, exploring castles, going to strip clubs and having very exciting sex; often all at the same time, or at least in the same day. It was good to discover a woman who genuinely enjoyed adventure.

"Oh, hello!" I said with genuine surprise as Jane walked into the lounge with a bottle of champagne one evening. "What's your name?" She was wearing a French maid's outfit, with high heels and bright red lipstick. The outfit hugged her figure enthusiastically, lifting her breasts as if a pair of loving hands was holding them up for adoration.

"Violet, sir, from the scullery." Jane role-played instinctively. She poured the champagne, which bubbled over the glass like an innuendo.

"Cook says you are all alone and so I have to keep you company," whispered Violet with a coy seduction that reached my inner being.

"Well, that's true, Violet, Cook is very considerate." I took the proffered champagne glass and held it away from me whilst the bubbles subsided. Violet leant forward and gently licked the spilt wine from my fingers.

"What did Cook suggest you do to keep me company?" I asked tentatively, worried that my taste for adventure might be too threatening. Violet glanced shyly at the floor, looking very much like a timid wench.

"Whatever, you want to do, sir." She lifted her gaze to look me in the eye with as much challenge as submission. I drank some champagne and then kissed Violet with the bubbles still in my mouth. She responded with an ardent passion as I stroked her with my spare hand. I cupped a breast then ran my hand down her back and over her leg.

I put my champagne down and started to undress. Violet helped, kissing my skin wherever it became exposed and when I lowered my trousers she knelt down to do Cook's bidding with expertise. I twirled my fingers in her hair with one had and had to hold myself up on a chair with the other.

"Violet, that's good," I gasped, "do you get much practice in the scullery?" She paused in her duty to respond.

"Yes, sir," she said whilst stroking me smoothly, "Cook gives me to the stable boys if I am bad."

"What do you do that's bad?" I queried, fascinated by her willingness to play this game.

"Once I forgot to clean the grate in the kitchen so cook spanked me and took me out to the stables." She spoke with a quiet, high pitch that drove me to a near frenzy. I pulled her up and pushed her forward over the arm of the sofa.

"Spanked you like this?" I slapped her arse and ploughed into her from behind.

"Yes, sir," she squealed, pushing back forcefully. I was fucking her hard now and she was panting.

"The boys used me for ages, laughing whilst they took turns." Jane was very convincing in playing Violet.

"How many stable boys have I got?" I asked, not certain that I wanted to know.

"I'm not sure, sir," panted Violet, "I lost count because some were using my mouth. At least six, I think."

I took Jane to meet Isabella.

"Wow, she's gorgeous," enthused the dancer as soon as we walked in. Isabella took Jane by the hand into a private booth, and began dancing without being asked. I just followed in the wake of intense sexuality.

Isabella danced slowly in front of Jane, waving her nipples, stroking Jane's arms and hair as she danced, getting closer and closer to her face. Jane sat and smiled and ran her hands over Bella's thighs and when she got close enough, Jane's tongue snaked out and licked Bella's nipple slowly. This was well beyond the rules but no-one could see and I just kept stuffing tenners into Bella's thong to keep the adventure going.

It ended prematurely when an angry bouncer came over to see why we had been so long. We stood to leave and Jane had to pull her skirt down to cover her pussy, which was knickerless since they had both been playing with it. We ran out into the Edinburgh drizzle and were lucky to get a black cab straight away.

We fell into the back snogging furiously. I removed most of Jane's clothes and she sat, legs akimbo, on the back seat rubbing herself some more whilst sucking my cock. The cabby's eyes were staring into the rear view mirror more than the road and I had a sudden image of myself in a magistrate's court but he read my mind and winked encouragement. I gave him a very large tip.

Jane and I developed a relationship that pushed the boundaries of even my own sense of adventure. We drove to the Alps before Christmas when the snow was thin and icy and the weather cold and unforgiving but when the slopes were empty and we spent a week charging down black runs and sitting naked in the sauna.

On the way back we stopped in Paris and went to a sex club. It had not been on the agenda as such but we had read about the Partouzes[68] and each assumed the other wanted to go.

"I'm a bit nervous," I admitted as we went through the heavy panelled doors like naughty schoolchildren.

"Me too," she beamed, eyes wide with excitement, looking anything but nervous.

"Come, come," urged the hostess in halting English as she lead us up some dimly lit stairs. The place was quiet and a little disappointing for the lack of naked

---

[68] French sex club.

bodies.

The hostess led us into a small parlour with a bar at the end. Two couples were there already and they smiled politely as if we had just gone into a parents' evening at a primary school. The complimentary drink did not last long and I took my wallet out to buy another. This drew looks of disapproval, as if I had committed an unforgivable faux pas in orgy etiquette.

"You should not have brought this in here," declared a Frenchman slowly, carefully considering his words.

"I'm sorry," I replied with equal uncertainty, "why is that?" The Frenchman looked perturbed, unsure how to explain.

"Well, if you need to leave it somewhere it will not be safe," he managed eventually. I looked around for help.

"Why would I leave it somewhere?" I asked the stupid question. The Frenchy smiled.

"Well," he said gently, "if you want to take your trousers off and leave them for a while..." I nodded slowly, getting his drift, and the Frenchies all smiled their exasperation that the stupid Brit prude had worked out why he was in a sex club.

"Come," he gestured, moving towards a door, "I will show you. I am Emil." He proffered a hand and led us into a large room full of swirling naked bodies.

In the centre of the room was an enormous round bed and in the middle of it there was a naked woman lying on her back as she took cock from every angle possible. There was a queue of blokes waiting for a chance to abuse or pleasure her; I was not sure which.

She was a mature woman, a matriarch, and she wore nothing but stockings and an armour plated suspender belt. Whether the belt was intended to hold her stockings up or stomach in was not clear since it did not achieve either effect very well. This did not seem to detract from her attraction to the group of adoring people; she was the queen bee in a hive, surrounded by dedicated workers.

Around the sides of the room were a myriad of blokes being attended to by women as if they were being prepared for the queen. There were women knelt down giving head or stroking cock, women sorting each other out and at least three smaller groups where one women was receiving the attention of two or three men.

There were a lot of spectators, people just watching, and that was how Jane and I participated. I thought beforehand that I would be driven to engage like a horny Viking running amok in ancient Britain. But, in the event, I was a little overwhelmed and maybe my ego was finally taking precedence over my libido. In that context, abstaining was almost liberating.

A bloke came and stroked Jane's arm, leaning to kiss her. She responded instinctively, closing her eyes and opening her mouth to allow his tongue to slide in. I was a bit stunned and just watched as he pulled her closer, dropping one hand to stroke her bum. Jane's hips tilted forward naturally so that she was rubbing herself against the stranger's thigh and as he slipped a hand down to her breast I saw her whole body tense and then relax as she moved into the zone.

The stranger tried to lead her by the hand into the fray and she began to move, smiling with anticipation. Then she looked at me for support. I nodded encouragement but was unable to move, so Jane smiled at the man and shook her head, declining his offer to get group fucked by strangers.

"I'm sorry," I whispered, feeling like I had let her down.

"That's okay," she replied, "I understand." Then she

kissed me and I imagined I could taste the stranger's tobacco in her mouth. We ran out into the Parisian drizzle and I fucked her roughly up against a wall as if reclaiming my woman. Jane seemed to understand my need to do that and did not demure, although when we got back to the hotel she pushed me onto the bed and rode me hard, as if to redress the balance.

The drive home was a little stilted. Whether that was because Jane was disappointed that I had not lived up to the adventure, or I was disappointed that Jane had been so enthusiastic about getting gang-fucked by unknown Frenchmen was not clear so we ignored the issue.

We stopped in London to visit one of my old army friends and break the long drive up to Edinburgh and the issue of sexual adventure was resolved there. We got drunk on champagne.

"Let's go to a strip club," suggested Mark, which we all thought was a splendid idea although it did not immediately occur to me that two blokes and one girl in a strip club had inevitable consequences. It was quite a good joint as strip clubs go but a little lacking in Isabellas.

"I could do better than this," declared Jane and she immediately began to pirouette provocatively, sliding her hands up her thighs to raise her skirt enough to be indecent. Her delicate fingers began to pull her knickers down and the punters in the crowd began to shift their attention to her so much that we were asked to leave by a big man who did not seem to expect any dissent.

We got back to Mark's flat and carried on. I raised Jane's hair, kissed the back of her neck and slowly lowered the zip of her dress. I expected her to wriggle free and playfully chastise me but she did not and the zip came all the way down so that the shoulders of her dress began to slip forward. Jane was swaying gently to

297

the music that Mark had put on and her hip movements became more exaggerated as she got into the rhythm.

She raised a hand to hold the dress against her breasts as she slipped her shoulders free so that she was bare backed. Her other hand ran into her hair and tousled it as she turned her back on us and let the dress slip completely to the floor. She peered at us over her shoulder and smiled a challenge that made us both step forward to reach her. Jane wagged a finger, eluding our grasp and she stood on the sofa, turning towards us for the finale.

She danced in front of us wearing nothing but her stockings and thong. That did not last long and, once she was naked, Jane allowed us to start kissing and mauling her with frenzied excitement. Mark kissed her deeply, roughly squeezing a breast. She responded enthusiastically and soon she was lying on the sofa with her legs over Mark's shoulders and my cock in her mouth.

"Fuck me somebody, please," she urged and Mark was at her with indecent haste. He humped her with abandon and little consideration but Jane seemed happy enough, this perhaps not being the occasion for sensitivity. Then we took it in turns and Jane seemed not to care, or even know, who was riding her. As long as she had a cock banging into her and one in her mouth she was happy.

It was intensely exciting at the time but afterwards I was uncertain. The etiquette of a threesome was unclear but I did feel that it would have been good manners to let me shag my own girlfriend first. I was not sure whether Mark's urgency was driven simply by an ardent desire for Jane or a vehement wish to avoid seconds but his approach undermined our friendship, somehow.

However, it was Jane's enthusiasm that knocked me

off balance. I had initiated the idea of a threesome and Jane had been a little reticent but she had overcome that quickly and for her it had been absolutely satisfying. For me it was clearly a case of "be careful what you wish for".

We survived the incident but our relationship never quite gathered enough momentum to carry it through the increasingly frequent sticky patches. This was exacerbated when my parent regiment in Yorkshire received a warning order to deploy to the Balkans. I wanted to join that party and I managed to arrange to leave my post in Edinburgh early. Jane and I were prematurely forced to consider our relationship. It was not promising; perhaps I was just too difficult to love.

"What are you doing?" Jane asked me gently one evening when she found me sat on the bed contemplating the future.

"Sitting in my cave," I responded since Jane had bought me yet another copy of *Men are from Mars* and I thought she would accept the notion. Actually, I just wanted a break from her chatter, which seemed increasingly like nagging.

"Can I come in?" I considered this for a moment; no one else had ever been in my cave.

"Well, okay, since it's you." I moved up and she sat down next to me.

"What happens in your cave, Billy?" I shrugged my shoulders and looked out of the window and Jane sat there too, quietly, without talking.

Whilst girls were fond of buying the book, they seemed reluctant to read it themselves. If they did, they would realise that *sitting in a cave* is a metaphor for *time on my own* and therefore not something they can participate in. Perhaps, however, they did read it and considered it a euphemism rather than a metaphor and therefore not really something that a man should be allowed to do. That was how Jane seemed to see it.

"Shall we come out now?" she said eventually.

"Later," I replied. Jane bridled at what she probably saw as rejection. She got up and went downstairs, leaving me to contemplate the world outside my cave. Perhaps if I had gone for a long crap with the newspaper I might have caused less friction.

The next day Jane went to visit friends in London so I went to Edinburgh Castle. I enjoyed the solitude of being lost amongst the tourists. I also enjoyed the irony that one of the icons of Scottish independence was actually built by English monarchs to subdue the Picts. Moreover, the castle always reminded me that one of the greatest Scottish heroes, Bonnie Prince Charlie, was actually an Italian drunk who was principally supported by the French.

I sat sipping espresso in a bay window in the café with a stunning vista over the Firth of Forth. I watched the city come to life as it got dark.

"Hey, Billy!" Two girls joined me at the table. It was Sandy, my ex-flat mate, and Mary, who had climbed under my duvet one night. They were very smiley.

"Would you like some wine?" Mary sat next to me and began to pour.

"Thanks. So, how's things?" I smiled at them and they giggled.

"Things are merry," said Sandy, sitting on my other side. "I'm single now," she said, resting a hand on my thigh.

"Me too," said Mary, taking possession of my other leg. I smiled.

"I'm not," I said, perhaps with a little regret.

The trouble with girls is that they always want what they can't have. Mary looked around the table.

"Where is she then?"

"In London for the weekend."

"Then she won't know," smiled Sandy, her hand sliding higher up my leg.

"And what she won't know, won't hurt her," whispered Mary, her hand also sliding higher. I thought she might offer me an apple.

The trouble with girls is that you can't resist them, certainly not two, and they were tempting. With infectiously high sprits, gleaming eyes and big tits, they were tempting. It was true, Jane wouldn't know but it would always be there.

They were pressing closer to me now, firm breasts rubbing on either arm, hands almost rubbing my crotch. They were so very tempting. If I did not succumb I would always wonder what I had missed. If I did succumb I would always be demeaned by my own lack of strength.

Mary's fingers gently turned my chin to face her. She kissed me slowly. Then Sandy turned my face and she slid her tongue softly into my mouth.

Sweet Jesus, help me.

I stood up. With a strength borrowed from my Grandfather's memory, I stood up.

"Ladies, I can't." I was whispering, disbelieving myself.

I left and got in my car almost panting for breath. I was not sure how I felt. I think I was pleased. As I drove away, I began to see what I had been missing for so long. There would always be another Eve. I would never be immune from temptation, no matter how beautiful and gracious my current girlfriend might be. Resisting temptation was part of the test of being with another person. This was a revelation, even liberation.

When Jane got back I loved her with an urgency that surprised us both.

"What's got into you?" She asked. I did not know

how to explain.

"Nothing, I just wanted to get into you." Our relationship seemed to have moved on a little and the future seemed to hold more promise: until Jane and I were invited to a supper party.

I had a bona fide girlfriend so was not subjected to inappropriate matchmaking, inquiries about my lack of marriage or latent homosexuality. The party was still dull, the conversation focussed on when to get married.

"What about you, Alex?" one of the harridans asked a bloke at the end of the table. "You've been a bit quiet." Alex Rennie looked up from his crème caramel with a degree of innocent surprise.

"Me?" he asked as if the preceding conversation had passed him by.

"Yes, you?" she demanded. "Why did you get married?"

"I met the right person." He smiled at his wife across the table with a warmth that filled the room. His wife smiled back and such total empathy between two people stilled the party. I suddenly realised why I was still single.

Next morning Jane and I went for a walk. The atmosphere was tense, as if we had exposed a truth that neither of us wanted to embrace. The unspoken but undeniable reality was that skiing and shagging were not sufficient basis for an enduring future together.

We tried to enjoy the autumn sunshine, wandering along the lanes kicking up leaves in mimicry of a happy couple. The veneer finally began to peel when we walked through some horse chestnut trees.

"Wow, look at these conkers!" I said, unable to contain my boyish instincts. Jane looked uncertain. I picked a couple of big, shiny conkers out of the fallen leaves and offered them to her.

"What are you going to do with those?" she asked

with pointed sarcasm. I was disappointed that she could not at least pretend to be impressed, but that is the trouble with girls, they have no sense of the true value of a really big conker.

32

It was good to be back in God's Country, in the green rolling hills of my youth. In Yorkshire the ever-present birdsong was like the melody of life and folks were less hurried and seemed to smile more. I could run swiftly through the countryside with a deep sense of contentment and, sometimes, when the clouds parted and the sun shone through in thick columns, it looked as if the sky was held up on shining pillars of light.

I also found myself alone once more. Before I moved up to Edinburgh one of my colleagues' wives who had been to university there told me of the myriad of young women there was in the city.

"You'll come back to us married," she said, as if I had a disease that only marriage could cure. But Edinburgh had not been the Promised Land for me. Still, I had come to accept my fate as a single man and I was surprisingly comfortable with it.

The discomfort that I felt at being back in my parent regiment was less surprising.

"Billy, good to see you," enthused Chris Myers, an old hand and friend who was holding the fort whilst the Regiment were in Bosnia. He took me to his office and gave me a coffee.

"I'm glad you'll be in charge," he said, "it's been hard going on my own." I looked at him uncertainly.

"In charge of what?" I replied. "I'm deploying to Bosnia to Command C Company?" It was his turn to look uncertain.

"You've not been told then?" Chris was treading carefully now, realising that he was delivering bad news. "There has been a restructuring in Theatre," he explained. "The Regiment only needs two Rifle Companies. You're to stay here and assume command of the rear party and control of the recruiting effort."

He paused to let it sink in. "I'm sorry I had to tell you."

I was gutted. The Army Bitch was having a real laugh at me now. I had prematurely left a job I was really enjoying and, in so doing, had forced the end of a relationship that still had some life in it and now I was stuck on my own in a near empty camp looking after the sick, lame and lazy who could not deploy on operations.

Bastard.

I went out to Bosnia briefly to see the Commanding Officer and to see the Rifle Company that I was eventually to command. The company had been split up to provide troops for other companies whilst on operations in the Balkans. As I visited them, I tried to enthuse about the future but I realised there was no corporate body that I would inherit in the form of a company of men. I would have to pull together a collection of individuals who had grown feral whilst languishing under the command of other officers who had made no real investment in my soldiers' future.

The announcement that the regiment would deploy to Cyprus the following year lifted my mood. A tour in Cyprus was unlikely to enhance my career profile since the infantry role of guarding the RAF whilst they played volleyball was very sedentary, but I had fond recollections of the Island. Jane and I had holidayed there enjoying a lot of adventure.

"Hold it there, Sweetheart," I instructed as I fished my camera out of the bag. "Okay, now smile." I clicked away whilst Jane faked a few cover-girl poses. She looked very sexy in her wide sun hat and long shirt. We were leaving the beach and the evening sun had dropped quite low which gave a soft lighting effect. Jane was knee deep in the sea; the perfect photo opportunity.

I lowered the camera and smiled at her.

"Undo some buttons, sweety." Jane smiled and undid her shirt down the front until her soft brown cleavage was presented to the camera. Obviously, I wanted more. Jane hesitated slightly

"There are a load of blokes playing volleyball over there," she protested. I glanced over my shoulder.

"Well they're obviously too busy to notice," I assured her, clicking away as she swept the shirt aside, revealing one very pert breast.

"They're looking now!" she cried but without trying to cover herself.

"You can't blame them for that," I said, "now drop your bottoms." Jane gave me her resigned look and ran her hands under her shirt. The long shirttails still preserved her modesty but the bikini bottoms floating by her side offered a very provocative contrast.

"Now completely undo your shirt," I ordered, trying to stop my shaking hands ruining the pictures.

"But they're all watching now," Jane exclaimed, possibly near to her limit.

I glanced over at the volleyball players who were indeed all watching. They had moved closer to the edge of the sea, their ball discarded back up the beach.

"Well, you can't disappoint them now," I urged. Jane did a good striptease but she had not previously performed in public. She was hesitant and I sensed she would stop until one of the watching boys whistled loudly. Then they all started to clap as one.

"Off, off, off," they began to chant in mesmeric unity. Jane smiled broadly and I raised my camera again. She turned her back on them and glanced coyly over her shoulder. Then she slowly moved the tails of her shirt aside to reveal her very shapely behind. The clapping increased in tempo.

Jane looked away and lowered her shirt to cover herself. Then she ripped open the last few buttons and dropped the collar of her shirt over her shoulders and down her back. The clapping and cheering became rapturous. She threw the shirt in the water and stood naked and beautiful with her back to the boys. Then she slid the hat down over her front and turned slowly on one leg to face her audience.

Jane smiled over the brim of her hat, clutching it to her like a last bastion of virtue. Some of the boys were wading into the water towards her and I was worried that the situation was out of control. Jane raised a hand and stopped the tide of advancing men so firmly that King Canute would have been jealous. I carried on clicking and she smiled at me through the camera, ignoring all the adoration around her: it was the most intimate moment we ever shared.

Suddenly, everything went still. As if on hidden cue, the boys all stood quietly, silently anticipating Jane's next move. I scarcely dared breathe. My camera was redundant since my hands were shaking so much. Jane looked about her, offering each of the boys a look of direct challenge. Then she simply dropped the hat into the sea and walked naked through the parting crowd.

Jane past me without a glance and kept on walking up the beach into the sand dunes out of sight. I stood with the crowd, transfixed by the sheer sexual audacity of the spectacle. Then I remembered that I could follow her and I ran up the beach like a clumsy puppy.

Back in the real world, I sat in my empty office with my feet on the desk enjoying the long moment of reminiscence. I idly wondered, not for the first time, why Jane and I had not made it together. We got on well but I suppose we both sensed that *Jane Hanson* just did not sound right. Anyway, then the phone rang.

"Hey Hanson," shouted an excited Dan Harley, "do you want to go to New York?"

Part 8 – Proverbs Ch 21 V 19

"I just wanna feel real love, feel the home that I live in."
Feel - Robbie Williams 2002.

33

I ambled along the plane to my seat, glancing around to identify any possible muses. There was limited potential although I did see a dark haired lady who had a vaguely familiar look that I could not place. Her presence evoked a strong sense of recollection but she seemed to be comfortable chatting to the man next to her so it was irrelevant.

Dan was putting his bag in the locker and waiting for me. I checked my ticket and realised I had the centre seat. The dark haired lady was sat directly across the aisle. I caught Dan's eye and then glanced at the lady and then our seats. He smiled as he understood my meaning. He took the centre seat.

The lady laughed gently and lent out of her seat brushing my leg.

"Oh, excuse me," she said with coy confidence. I smiled a little and sat down.

"First contact?" asked Dan quietly. We settled into our seats with an air of boyish enthusiasm: old college friends en route to New York for beer and skittles.

I listened as subtly as I could to the conversation between the dark haired lady and her co-passenger and it quickly became apparent that they were strangers. This presented an opportunity but I sensed that the situation needed to be exploited carefully, lest it was spurned as so often before.

"Fancy a drink?" asked Dan once we were airborne and the stewardesses started to ply their trade. He was looking at the drinks list. I was planning a seduction.

"Champagne? I'm buying." Dan shrugged and smiled acknowledgement. He did not really care for champagne but he understood my intent and was happy to be complicit within it.

"Ooh, I like shampoo," said the dark haired lady

when the stewardess brought the bottle. I looked at her and then I glanced at the stewardess.

"Another glass, please?"

"Thank you. I'm Helena." The lady offered a dainty hand. I squeezed it gently and looked slowly into her face. She was astonishingly beautiful and equally charming and suddenly I realised who she was. Her smiling radiance, elegance, intelligence and humour all revealed themselves to me; she was the FMH.

"Billy," I replied slowly. The man next to her smiled, sat back and picked up the in-flight magazine. He was married anyway.

"Why are you going to New York?" asked Helena, as she nonchalantly opened a packet of nibbles.

"We're going to a wedding." I leaned back in the seat. "This is Dan." They smiled and waved at each other.

"Wonderful," enthused Helena, "I am going to a business meeting. I am in marketing. Very dull."

"I'm a soldier," I replied pouring Helena's champagne rather expertly. She waited until I filled our glasses and then said, "Cheers".

"Do you think," asked Helena whilst munching nibbles, "that it's uncouth to drink fizz and eat mini-cheddars at the same time?"

I wasn't quite sure what she meant.

"It depends how you eat them."

"I suppose so," she said and absently sucked the end of her finger. Dan almost choked on a peanut and the man next to her slapped his palm against his forehead mumbling silently to himself.

Dan cast a sideways look at me.

"Why does this stuff happen to you?" he asked quietly and with mild exasperation.

"Dunno. I gave up worrying about it years ago." I considered the situation for a moment, "Helena

Hanson. Do you think that works?" Dan passed another furtive look at Helena.

"It could do," he said slowly, "she's very nice."

Helena raised her glass again.

"Here's to a good trip."

I smiled back at her and raised my own glass.

And to the rest of our lives.

We chatted and, following another bottle of champagne, Helena agreed to meet me in Manhattan. She came to meet us in a bar in the upper Eastside but was not immediately approachable.

"You may be an officer," she said to me with clearly rehearsed emphasis, "but you're obviously not a gentleman!" I was a little taken aback; she had been so friendly on the plane.

"I'm sorry, what have I done?"

"It's more what you haven't done," retorted Helena enthusiastically. "It would have been nice to have been met at my hotel!" She had a point, I suppose, but it occurred to me that if my negligence was such an issue for her she would not have turned up at all. I let it slide. I liked her a lot and she seemed worth the effort of a long seduction.

I tried not to rush her. Although Helena was clearly keen, she obviously wanted to control the pace of any possible relationship. Dan was a true friend. He showed no indication of being pushed out but remained supportive, knowing how lonely I actually was and how closely and quickly I had connected with Helena.

"I think I'll wander slowly home and watch a movie or something," he said quietly like Captain Oates announcing his departure from the Antarctic tent. He was smiling as he left.

"You've driven your friend away with your lustful intent," admonished Helena with gentle humour. I nodded.

"It's for a good cause, he'll understand. It's your responsibility to make such sacrifice worth the effort." Helena smiled. It had been a wonderful evening of warmth and immediate companionship such as I had not experienced for many years.

"How fickle is fate that we should meet in such unusual circumstances," I breathed in Helena's ear as we stopped outside her hotel.

"You're clearly an experienced charmer, Billy Hanson," she sighed but without reproach.

"I was just practising for when I met you." We embraced with a long, slow kiss that confirmed so much and promised much more.

"Get a room!" shouted a drunken reveller from across the street.

"Sounds like good advice," I suggested to Helena as we finally broke the embrace.

"Major Hanson!" she exclaimed in mock surprise. "If you besmirch me now you'll forget me tomorrow." I shook my head.

"Never."

"Even so," she said gently, "I need more time." She kissed me again with deep passion. "Hang in there, Honey," she breathed, "it's worth the wait." Then she left me standing on the pavement and went into her hotel.

"What shall we do today?" asked Dan next morning as we stirred from the previous nights exuberances. I sat looking out of the window contemplating the idea. Dan was in New York without his wife and kids so whatever we did was likely to involve drinking.

"Let's go to the Seaport on the Eastside. We can see Brooklyn Bridge from there."

The autumn sun was strong and we enjoyed an outdoor lunch watching boats chug past on the East River and tourists milling about like penguins on an ice floe.

"What now?" Asked Dan.

"More exploring," I replied absently as I was more than a little absorbed with the seduction of Helena. Tolerant as he was, Dan's enthusiasm for my mooning was waning.

"Right then," he said emphatically, "let's explore all the Irish bars on the way home."

There are a lot of Irish bars on the East Side of Manhattan and we went to them all. We had lots of fun, not just because we drank a lot, but also because it was Hallowe'en.

"Why are you dressed as a ghost?" asked Helena when she eventually turned up to meet us.

"I am the ghost of East Manhattan," I said as if it was obvious. Helena seemed neither scared nor impressed.

"And what about you?" she asked Dan.

"I am the Brooklyn Skeleton," he moaned in a ghoulish way.

"You're in Greenwich."

"Am I? Then that's because I am forced to wander Manhattan looking for solace."

"Looking for more Guinness more like," mocked Helena looking at our empty glasses. She left us rather abruptly.

It occurred to me then that, whilst obviously amusing to a bloke, being a drunken ghost in Manhattan might not impress a sophisticate like Helena. I was more than a little crestfallen. Helena, however, had her own sense of comic style and she returned moments later wearing a witch's hat and carrying three schooners of something green.

"I am the Witch of Washington Square," she cackled, "and you will drink my potion." She watched us drink one each and then she passed me the third.

"I want you under my spell," she demanded.

"I am already," I proclaimed but she ignored me as one not yet worthy.

"Hocus pocus," chanted the Witch of Washington Square as I poured the potion down my throat, "tomorrow you will buy me a diamond."

That was a little presumptuous, even for a witch, but the idea had some appeal so we met for lunch the next day and went shopping.

"We'd like to look at diamond rings," Helena declared to the jeweller. His eyes lit up like one of his own gemstones.

"Okay, we have plenty of choice. Would it be for an engagement?" He was a balding old man who didn't suit romance; his smile was too thin. Helena looked at me and then back to the jeweller.

"No, we've only just met. The ring is simply an opportunity for Billy to express his immediate affection for me." Helena smiled broadly as she explained this to the bemused jeweller who glanced at me uncertainly.

I smiled as well for I was, indeed, feeling immediate affection for her. Never before had I felt so close to a woman so quickly. Quite apart from her elegant beauty and obvious intellect, a woman who could find a witch's hat in a bar in Manhattan and unswervingly join in a drunken hallowe'en party with two near strangers impressed me.

We returned to the UK and developed our relationship with enthusiasm. I enjoyed being with Helena and knew I would miss her when we were apart. Before we met, I had anticipated posting to Cyprus with excitement but, having become so deeply entwined with her, being permanently away suddenly became a dreadful prospect. Such sentiments were new to me.

"Being with you makes me realise how lonely I

was," I told Helena over supper one evening. She smiled at me warmly nodding her agreement. She reached out for my hand and played with my fingers.

"Being with you makes me realise that I will never be lonely again." I felt a lump in my throat.

"I love you," I whispered in amazement. I had not expected to say that for it had only been a few weeks.

"I know," replied Helena in her beautiful way, "and I love you."

I moved in with Helena for the short period before I deployed to Cyprus and we enjoyed rehearsing what we both knew was our future but did not yet openly discuss. Helena's flat had a functional, eclectic style that reflected her personality and, in many respects, our relationship. It was an elegant apartment in colours of beige and contrasting browns. It was cosy without clutter.

Her two cats caused me to falter slightly since there are allsorts of connotations about girls in their late twenties who have cats. I managed not to tease them, which was clearly an acid test for Helena, and our relationship progressed like a love song.

We stayed in stylish boutique hotels and drank champagne before supper. We had long breakfasts of coffee and croissants, broadsheets and vibrant conversation. We had long walks on the beach and through the countryside holding hands and saying nothing. We had become inseparable despite the paucity of time that we had spent together. I felt like I really had met the FMH.

Once I deployed to Cyprus, Helena came to visit me regularly and the warm sun, starlit nights and serenading cicadas were an intoxicating mix. It is Aphrodite's Island, after all, and love blossomed for us.

One night we drove down to a secluded beach for a BBQ and whilst I was busy making a small fire Helena went to paddle in the sea. I turned to see where she was and noticed her thin dress lying with deliberate casualness on the sand and I watched her walking naked through the shallows.

The moonlight reflected off her pale skin illustrating her stunning beauty yet further and tiny waves caressed her ankles like eager hands running up her legs. She walked towards me slowly with long, languorous strides and held my gaze as the light from the fire took over from the moon in wrapping itself around her in a warm embrace.

We made passionate love in the sand. Years of wanting and waiting culminating in that very moment. It consumed us both so that we were, entirely, as one. Afterwards, I felt such an overwhelming love that I thought Aphrodite herself was holding me in her arms.

"Marry me," I whispered. Helena answered me with a kiss.

We had breakfast in near silence. In the spirit of the moment, we had champagne and fresh fruit; melon and grapefruit freshly picked. There was an awkward tension between us, almost embarrassment. We both knew that this was our destiny but, perhaps, it had come more quickly than either of us had anticipated. At least that was how it seemed to me.

"I thought I'd wait for you to ask me," said Helena, "I figured you'd prefer to be traditional." She smiled as she said it, as if she was giving me a gift, temporarily ceding me a measure of control. I suppressed the slight rankling that I felt for I had wanted this moment for too long to let it spoil.

We decided to arrange our wedding quickly to keep the momentum going. Trying to organise such a major event from a foreign country is difficult and Helena bore most of the burden. We also decided to buy a house and my limited involvement in the details of either event clearly caused some friction. I tried to be engaged with the arrangements but, apart from physical distance, it was difficult to be focussed on house buying and wedding plans, as I was busy getting petrol bombed.

34

I had not expected to get petrol bombed in Cyprus. Aphrodite's Island is supposedly a place of love and beauty and such violence seemed incongruous. Perhaps the Army Bitch was jealous that I loved another and this was her way of seeking vengeance.

The violence erupted when a Cypriot Nationalist politician tried to use the British presence on the Island to generate some publicity for his failing presidential campaign. It started with a seemingly spontaneous protest against the British police station and degenerated quickly into arson attacks, beatings of isolated police officers and focussed vandalism of the police vehicles and equipment.

The Nationalist did have a point. There was something perverse about Britain owning two small chunks of Cyprus, but it was a longstanding agreement between nations. Moreover, at the local level, the British military employed several hundred villagers whose whole lives depended on our presence. It seemed unlikely that they would join the protest but this became a "free Barabbas, crucify Jesus"[69] moment.

The petty politics of small-minded men can cause exponential problems and it certainly interrupted my wedding planning.

"Have you read through the menu options, Darling?" Helena asked me sweetly on the phone. I had not even looked at them.

"No, fraid not," I replied absently as I was trying to pack my kit, "we're a bit busy just now."

---

[69] In three of the New Testament Gospels, Pilate, the Roman Governor of Judea, asked the crowd whether he should free Jesus or a criminal called Barabas as part of the Passover celebrations. The crowd had been paid to cry for Barabas.

"Well, I'd have thought this was a priority for you," she said sharply.

"Helena, it's a little tense over here right now with rioting. We've got folk in hospital." I paused and tried to be gentler. "I've been ordered to deploy the whole company to the airfield tomorrow. I'll be away for a while."

Actually, it was gratifying to leave all the tedious detail of wedding planning behind and go do manly stuff. We deployed to the vulnerable areas of the airfield and took what shade we could whilst we waited for the fighting to begin.

Cyprus in mid-summer is very hot, so dressing in full body armour and helmets and carrying riot shields was uncomfortable. This was exacerbated by the need to wear long cotton underwear as protection against the anticipated petrol bombs. In her meanness, the Army Bitch would not give us the fire-proof overalls that the police wore. We estimated that a man thus dressed was good for about fifteen minutes before he would succumb to the heat.

Once we were in position I had a quick huddle with the Company Second-in-Command and Sergeant Major.

"Phil have there been any orders from Battalion or news from the other companies about the movement of protesters?"

"Nothing," he said absently, "but it is Cyprus so they'll no doubt be late!" He smiled at his own joke.

"Sarn't-major how are the men?" I asked concerned that the young soldiers were struggling with the heat and nerves.

"Fine," he said cheerfully looking over the three platoons, "Smoking a lot but I think that's boredom rather than nerves. It would be good to let them relax a little and take off their body armour." His concern for the soldiers was obvious although he tried to hide it. I nodded and the Sergeant Major stormed over to the platoons.

"Right you lazy fuckers get your armour and helmets off. Put them in neat piles ready to move when ordered. Platoon Sergeants make sure that everyone's water bottles are filled up." The Sergeant Major bulled around amongst the men masking his compassion for them with military bravado. The soldiers smiled to themselves as they responded to his instructions and that just made him more vehement.

"And get your arse into the shade," he yelled at a slow moving individual, giving him a playful boot of encouragement. "We're here to defend Britain's interests not top up your tan you pasty faced bastard!"

Eventually, a handful of black robed old women and one man emerged tentatively from the nearby village and stood opposite us to begin the protest. The old man also brought a mangy dog. We waited, fearing that this was the vanguard of a larger protest aimed at generating sympathy for the world press. They did not turn up either and so we waited a bit longer. The police sat in their air-conditioned coach with the door closed. It was a long wait.

The elderly Cypriots looked more uncomfortable in the heat than we did.

"Colour Sergeant Jenson, please take some bottled water over to those Cypriot folk and ask if they want some tea," I instructed the Company Quartermaster Sergeant. He smiled to himself and crossed the road with one of his soldiers. The atmosphere then became rather convivial.

This seemed to cause the police Superintendent some angst. The door of his coach hissed open and he stomped over to me like some marauding alien newly landed to begin the earth's conquest.

"What's going on, Billy?"

"Nothing much is going on so we've relaxed a bit." I smiled at him. He seemed a little unsure as to the advisability of standing down eighty armed soldiers in the face of such dangerous opposition so I made it easier for him

"I want to conserve my combat power for future action." That seemed to placate him for he offered me a cigar. I did not smoke but it seemed the manly thing to do.

"Strange," he muttered to himself whilst puffing out thick black smoke, "the intelligence on this indicated a much more violent protest." One of the old ladies across the road sat down on a folding chair offered by one of my soldiers.

"Did you get any indication of timing?" I asked him. He glanced across at me.

"Not really, the source wasn't specific."

"Who was your source?" Ordinarily, you do not question the source of intelligence on the assumption that it would be sensitive but I was not convinced that this chap knew what he was talking about.

The Superintendent seemed to consider if I should be trusted before he answered my question.

"One of my policemen's wives was in the hairdressers and she overheard another customer telling the stylist that she'd heard there would be a protest." I inhaled sharply and began to choke on cigar smoke. "Are you alright, Billy?" the Superintendent asked with a frown of concern.

Are you fucking mad? I've deployed my whole company in full riot gear in forty degrees of heat because some fat bitch of a wife overheard a vague rumour whilst having her blue rinse touched up.

Fortunately, however, the politics of the matter pervaded and I managed not to rant at the feckless twat and simply excused myself as an inexperienced cigar smoker.

I excused myself further and went to confer with my Company staff.

"Sarn't-major, please get the men inside but keep them as close as possible and keep them on fifteen minutes notice to move. Also keep a double sentry at the perimeter corners and the gate. The protest will likely not happen before dark." He sucked on his cigarette then stubbed it out on the sole of his boot, putting the stub in his pocket before giving orders to the NCOs.

We waited around all day. The soldiers began to get listless and then bored. I wanted to run some training to occupy their minds but the heat was too draining and I needed to preserve my soldiers' strength. The Company Second-in-Command and Sergeant Major drilled the men slowly in walk-through practices instead.

As dusk began to descend on the scene a sense of anticipation began to develop. The younger soldiers began to get nervous but the older ones who had served in Northern Ireland began to get excited at the prospect of some action.

We still had some time to wait and maintaining discipline was vital to stop very young men becoming scared and older ones becoming aggressive. The Sergeant Major moved amongst the soldiers instilling his presence in the way that only good men can do.

"Sir!" the radio operator called my attention, "message from the OP on the water tower; two motorbikes seen driving towards the airfield, stopped and turned back."

The Sergeant Major overheard the message and looked questioningly at me. I nodded.

"Let's saddle up." The Sergeant Major signalled to the Non Commissioned Officers who quietly and efficiently brought the Company to order. It was gratifying to watch the soldiers silently prepare themselves with shields and helmets without any further instructions. They sat quietly, preserving themselves, waiting for orders.

I took the radio handset from the operator and called Battalion HQ.

"Zero, this is Three-Zero-Alpha: Light switch. I say again: Light switch." I gave the codeword that indicated we were expecting some movement and then went to speak with the platoon commanders.

"Okay fellahs, we're getting close. Keep your men together, keep the shields tight and don't let anyone get isolated." The young officers nodded at me and went to brief their troops again.

Eventually, in the distance, we heard the hum of engines.

"Sir, the OP reports about ten motorbikes moving quickly in our direction," the radio operator relayed the message.

"Stuart, about ten bikes coming our way," I shouted to the Police Superintendent who came over with two of his biggest policemen.

"Right, I am going on to the road," he said emphatically.

"Are you sure? You'll be a bit exposed." He set his jaw squarely and turned to face me.

"The law will not be intimidated," he shouted above the approaching motorbikes and went onto the road.

Ten hairy-arsed bikers will not be intimated either and they roared down the road pulling impressive wheelies. I had eighty soldiers with riot shields and helmets stood by ready to move but there was a balance to hold between demonstrating a presence and provoking a reaction and my orders were to remain behind the wire until absolutely necessary. The bikers roared back again. One waved cheerfully.

In the ensuing lull, the Superintendent came back to the gate seemingly happy with himself.

"Was that it?" he mused to himself.

"Probably not." I nodded at the newly arrived television camera crew nearby. "I think that was just for effect."

"What next then?" he asked. I shrugged.

"More waiting."

It was a good tactic, really. Since the rioters could not gain any surprise, and since the battle was really for media sympathy, drawing out the tension to try and provoke an overreaction from nervous soldiers and policemen was an effective approach.

"Sir," called the Company Sergeant Major quietly, "should we rest the men?"

"Aye, Sarn't-major, sit them down and remove helmets. Ask Colour Jenson to dish some water so the fellahs don't empty their bottles."

We waited quietly until we heard the rising clamour of noise in the distance.

"Sir, radio chat that One-Zero is being stoned by protestors!"

"Thanks, Scally," I said as calmly as I could, "keep listening and let me know of developments, especially if the protesters move." The soldiers from my company remained sat down, resting, but they were starting to fidget as they had heard the radio operator's translation of events up the road.

"Sir! One-Zero reporting the use of petrol bombs." That woke everyone up.

"Scally, check with the OP for sightings of movement in our direction, Sarn't-Major stand the Company to order," I went through the motions of shouting instructions, more to keep idle minds from wandering than from a desire for any specific effect since all the soldiers were already alert, ready to move.

Scally started shouting above the growing din for my attention.

"Sir, One-Zero advancing with shields raised."

"Stuart, Sarn't-Major," I called more urgently now, "the rioters will probably move away from One-Zero and in our direction." That had been the plan, at least, in order to prevent the riot from establishing a presence and it seemed to be working well enough. My soldiers were all stood in their formations. Their shields were at shoulder height and their batons were at their sides as they had been trained.

"Are we good to go, Sarn't-major?" I called to the back so that everyone could hear. I could see him smiling and nodding in the dim light.

"Just like old times," he yelled back cheerfully, meaning Northern Ireland.

The OP was shouting down to us, not even using the radio, and pointing up the road. The protesters were moving towards us. They came quickly but in a tight group as if they were being well controlled. They stopped in front of the gate shouting and gesticulating. Stones and bottles bounced off the fence. The bigger and more aggressive individuals started rattling the gate hard. It was time to move. I gave the signal to open the gate.

"Company," I had to shout above the din, "advance!" The gate was flung open and the forward platoon raised their shields and moved tightly forward towards the road. The protesters were pushed away by the shields.

"Halt!" I yelled as the platoon reached the road. We held the position there whilst the protesters started hurling rocks. Some of the bigger men charged at the shields.

"Hold tight men!" roared the platoon commander,

"shoulder to shoulder," he encouraged and his soldiers responded manfully. Some young men were growing up quickly.

There was not enough room on the driveway to the road for more troops so the first platoon took all the abuse. A few more adventurous, and probably drunk, rioters forced their way through the undergrowth to get behind the platoon. The platoon sergeant was waiting with a small team of stout Cumbrian men.

"Charge!" he yelled and two of them ran forward with shield and baton raised. They engaged the rioters like gladiators.

"Fuck off!" One of the soldiers rammed a rioter with his shield and whacked his thigh with his baton. He was clearly enjoying himself and he came back to stand behind his platoon sergeant with a broad smile.

Unable to get into the compound, the protest moved on down the road alongside the airfield. I ordered the second platoon to move through the first to keep herding the protest away. Scally and I followed the second platoon slowly down the road. It was still only wide enough for one platoon. The company advanced until we reached the perimeter of the airfield beyond which, as soldiers, we had no jurisdiction.

I could not see the police and the rioters, suddenly realising they had nothing to protest about, turned their attention back to us. They started stoning again and quite a weight of rocks was incoming. The missiles bounced harmlessly off the shields. Even in the midst of the chaos, I was pleased that my soldiers kept close ranks and moved slowly forward together, not exposing any individual to harm.

"Sir, how long do we hold this position?" asked Adam the platoon commander who was crouched under his shield.

"As long as necessary," I replied, "Two-Zero should

come and try to disperse the rioters." He nodded to himself.

"I wished they'd fucking hurry up," he muttered loudly as he scuttled back to his men. "Stand fast," he shouted at them above the din of the shouting and stones bouncing off shields.

A tight group of rioters charged suddenly at the shields. There was a huge roar of approval from the crowd. The shield wall held tight but was forced back a couple of metres.

"Seven Platoon," shouted Adam with impressive gusto, "advance!" His soldiers moved forward again recovering their lost ground.

"Dinny, Samson, look left!" yelled the platoon sergeant to his small team. A rioter had crawled through the undergrowth behind the platoon and struck a soldier with an iron bar.

"Bastard!" yelled Samson as he dealt efficiently with the rioter. The fallen soldier was back on his feet and moved to take vengeance against the rioter. Samson stopped him with a bear hug, preventing illegal retaliation. "I've done that for you, Johnny," he said indicating the limping rioter who was now in the hands of the police who had finally turned up.

Then a petrol bomb exploded on the road. It flared harmlessly in front of the shield wall but it was an escalation by the rioters. The smell of the fuel was strong and hung like a threat in the air. I could sense the nervousness in the soldiers in front of me. This was heightened by the increasing noise. The tempo of stones against the shields increased as the rioters tried to intimidate us.

"Steady, men!" called Adam with an authority beyond his youth. "Keep tight and hold fast." The soldiers visibly stiffened.

I took the radio handset from Scally and called all

stations on the company network.

"Charlie, Charlie One, this is Three-Zero-Alpha. Go firm. Hold this position until Two-Zero moves forward." We had reached an impasse then. Legally, we could not move forward and the rioters could not physically move us back. Like most conflict, it had become a war of attrition where the will to engage was the variable factor.

Petrol bombs continued to flash in front of the forward platoon. The flames dissipated against the shields bringing no physical harm but the burning smell of fuel wore on the nerves of my young soldiers. Stones rained down and, likewise, bounced off the shields. We held firm but it was draining.

"Sir, the men in the forward platoon are getting tired." The Company Sergeant Major had come up from the rear. He was sweating and panting hard. He must have run all the way from the rear to offer this advice.

I nodded.

"I know, but we can't disengage to rotate the platoons until Two-Zero relieves some pressure."

He nodded slowly.

"Where the fuck are they?"

"Scally, get on the blower and find out where Two-Zero are," I told the radio operator, "Sarn't-major, ask Mr Fields to come forward to me." The Sergeant Major nodded and spoke to the young officer as he went back past the rear platoon.

"Adam," I yelled at the forward platoon commander, "come here!" The young officer nodded, spoke with his platoon sergeant and then came running towards me in a crouch with rocks bouncing like hailstones off his raised shield.

The two platoon commanders came to my position and knelt down with their shields raised above their heads. Both were sweating hard and looked very tense.

"Adam, how are your men?" I shouted at the forward platoon commander.

"They're good," he shouted between pants, "but tiring quickly, I think." His voice was strained and I noticed his hand was shaking a little. A particularly large rock bounced off his shield with a thud. A flash of anger creased his face. I put a hand on his shoulder.

"Okay, I need you to hang on for while longer. Hopefully Two-Zero are about to engage." I had to shout above the clamour of stones bouncing off our shields. "When they do I want your platoon, Carl, to move forward through Adam's men; forward passage of lines." Both nodded and I hoped they understood for there was no time for further detail.

"Sir!" Scally was waving the handset at me. "Two-Zero are close."

"Move quickly!" I barked at the young officers who scurried off to their platoons.

There was an almighty roar as Two-Zero charged the rioters. The pressure slackened palpably on my forward platoon as the rocks and petrol bombs were focussed on the other company.

"Now!" I yelled at the platoon commanders and the rear platoon moved quickly forward in close order.

"Seven platoon stand clear," I bellowed at the forward troops. They parted smoothly allowing the rear platoon through. It was an efficient manoeuvre. There was still an interminable moment when there was a gap between my troops and the rioters.

The rioters sensed their opportunity and surged through the gap. I held my breath and watched. There was nothing I could do. Eight platoon came steadily forward with shields raised. There was a satisfying thud as the troops collided with the rioters who realised too late that British troops do not yield.

"Forward!" urged Carl in his best Action Man voice and his platoon drove on into the rioters like a Roman Legion defending the Eternal City. I watched with gratification as the troops pushed the rioters back and then stoically held their position.

Scally passed me radio handset.

"It's the CO, sir,."

"Hello, Three-Zero-Alpha," I bawled into the handset.

"This is Sunray, I want you to come to the rear and command the call-sign at Garden-gate." I looked at the handset in disbelief. Garden-gate was the codeword for the antenna site well to my rear. It was being defended by a platoon and should have been commanded by a young officer or sergeant. The Commanding Officer was pulling me out of a riot to go and sit at the rear to guard a static site under no immediate threat; it made no sense.

"I am currently engaged," I yelled back into the handset, "who'll command my troops?" At that moment a petrol bomb exploded nearby; close enough to warm my face.

"Send Three-Zero-Bravo forward," came the CO's reply. That meant my company second-in-command. I still could not see the point in pulling a company commander to the rear and sending a junior officer forward. Apart from the lack of continuity of command, he was completely undermining my position as the company commander. Perhaps that was his intent.

"I'll send Three-Zero-Bravo to Garden-gate," I suggested over the radio.

"Hanson, get your fucking arse back here," screamed the CO, ignoring all radio procedure. Clearly, I had pissed him off. Even so, this seemed like a rather petulant moment for him to test his own authority.

I waited for the second-in-command to come forward. He shrugged at me as I gave some quick instructions. Then I went to the rear.

"Where the fuck have you been?" the Commanding Officer glared at me when I got back.

"Disengaging from a riot," I countered defiantly, then in a more conciliatory tone said, "I came as quickly as I could, sir."

"Well, I needed you back here to cover this exposed flank," he shouted at me, seemingly determined to make a point, "did you stop for a fucking rest." I struggled to resist that challenge, notwithstanding his rank.

"No, I fucking didn't! And an exposed flank is your responsibility! It's your crap plan!"

"Are you going to hit me, Major Hanson?" he asked me with his face pressed close to mine. I realised that my fists were clenched.

"Not until you hit me." We had reached our own impasse then. He was a bigger man than me and likely to win a straight fight but we had gone beyond that and this was now simply a contest of will.

Military judgement suddenly got the better of him and he stood straight abruptly and gave me orders in a more conventional manner.

"Please go and ensure the antenna field is secure, Major Hanson." He walked away. I went to the rear and listened impotently as the riot dissipated itself against my soldiers.

"Tough break, Boss," offered the Company Sergeant Major as he brought my company back to our position the next morning. I had been completely undermined as the company commander but whether that was through poor judgement or deliberate intent was never made clear. It was quickly forgotten for the riots petered out. Nobody was badly hurt and nothing was badly damaged so the media drifted away and the rioters, presumably, went back to the bar.

35

I returned to my wedding plans. I had heard many men complain that their fiancées, and often more pertinently, their future mothers'-in-law, became obsessed with the wedding. I was still surprised by the intensity with which Helena planned ours and I quickly developed a sense that the wedding ceremony was more important to her than actually being married.

Perhaps I was too casual. I certainly did not invest enough interest in the details of the day to satisfy Helena but it seemed to me that the wedding would not be a failure if each member of the congregation did not have their own order of service or table menu. Who remembers what they ate at a wedding?

We married in the Regimental Chapel amid splendid surroundings and an enthusiastic congregation. Standing at the altar before all my friends and family and God to commit forever to one woman seemed like my destiny. I had thought it would never happen but there I was standing tall and straight awaiting my bride. When she came down the aisle I gasped at her beauty.

Many friends had told me of the mixed feelings that they had whilst actually getting married but as I slipped the ring on Helena's finger, I felt a surge of pride and love and I was absolutely certain that this was the right thing. I thought I might cry, but I was from Yorkshire.

The feeling of fulfilment stayed with me throughout the day. It stayed with me throughout the lakeside reception and throughout the supper in the evening until I stood up to pay my dues to everyone for their support. Of all the excitement I'd had in my life, getting married was the biggest rush ever.

"If a red rose is a raven and a white rose is a dove," I concluded my speech, offering Helena a white rose, "then a red rose is my passion and this white rose is my love."

But after dinner I lost sight of my wife. We were swept apart by the tide of well-wishers, I thought. I waded through the throng trying to fight a rising sense of inexplicable panic.

Helena was sat with her mother.

"Hello," I said quietly, feeling very much like I was intruding. "I thought I had lost you." Helena smiled, rather weakly.

"Well, I just wanted to be with my Mum. I don't see much of her." I resisted the urge to say that she did not see much of me either as I had been in Cyprus.

I offered my hand.

"Shall we dance, people are waiting for us?"

Helena stood, almost reluctantly, to take my hand. She left the white rose I had presented at dinner laying on a table and I saw her mother surreptitiously try to pass it to her.

Our guests cheered enthusiastically as we took the first tentative steps of our ritual dance together. It was a bit clumsy.

"I love you," I whispered trying to stimulate a sense of intimacy.

"And me you," she replied although with little enthusiasm and it was not quite the magical moment I had hoped for.

It was a relief to leave the reception and be alone with my new wife in the honeymoon suite of our hotel. Helena appeared rather tense. I kissed her and undressed her almost shyly since she did not really reciprocate, physically or emotionally. She did not actually resist me but she just seemed rather remote; like a stranger.

"You're so beautiful," I whispered as I stroked her arms, trying to be gentle and patient. It was almost as if this was the first time we had made love. I gasped with excitement as I undid her gown. "You've no knickers on, sweetheart," I said with a racing heart and big smile, "did you get married in such a sexy way?"

"No," she scoffed, "but I'd had them on all day and didn't feel very fresh so I took them off!" That was a slap in the face. Whatever the reason for her lack of knickers, her response to me was cold and hard and I was caught off balance. I had so wanted this to be a magical moment but consummating our marriage actually seemed like a chore.

Next morning I set off on honeymoon in naïve optimism. The atmosphere was still rather tense although I could not tell why.

"Are you okay, Honey?" I asked as gently as possible.

"Yes, I am just a little tired and stressed from the wedding, that's all." Her smile was unconvincing but gave me hope that being away from the pressures of the wedding and family would enable us to find each other again.

I had been in charge of planning the honeymoon and I felt great relief when we arrived at the hotel. It was exactly what I had worked so hard for, searching the Internet and travel magazines to find the right place for a dream honeymoon.

It was an idyllic setting. The hotel had a grand façade at the front and a commanding view over the Mediterranean at the back. The staff were cheerfully attentive without being intrusive and the reception arrangements were efficient enough to satisfy my critical mind.

We explored the room, which was pleasant enough, but it was the veranda that created the atmosphere I had worked so hard to capture. It had a dual aspect around the corner of the hotel so we could see over the cliff gardens and down into the bay where the sea gently lapped at the cliff edge. There was a full moon illuminating the scene and below us were fishing boats quietly moving across the dark sea.

As if I had planned it, a mandolin began to play and the atmosphere was near magical.

"Some champagne would be nice," said Helena. Her tone was rather languorous, almost dreamy, although I did detect a hint of criticism as if I had forgotten something. I sidestepped the inference, assisted by Venus, for at that moment there was a knock on the door. I ushered in the black tie-d waiter who set down an ice bucket. I poured us both a glass, gave one to Helena and offered a toast:

"To marriage." I smiled at her, already imagining her resplendent nakedness shimmering in the moonlight. I was filled with love and stepped forward to embrace my wife, to fulfil a lifelong desire. Helena raised a hand to my chest and stopped me.

"I am tired," she said, "I'm going to bed." She undressed very efficiently and lay down, pulling the sheets firmly over her body. I was devastated; standing alone in the moonlight nursing shattered dreams, simmering champagne and a redundant erection.

The dream honeymoon became a nightmare. I had previously had holiday disasters with women but the feeling of being trapped had always been mercifully short. Temporary relief was ever near in a bottle or on a long run. Now there was none: I was married. However, since I was married, I was determined to survive the honeymoon with the relationship intact so that we could make a fresh start at home.

It was not easy.

"Am I expected to have sex just because we're on honeymoon?" demanded Helena one evening when I made a speculative attempt at intimacy.

Yes, of course you are you crazy bitch!

"You're expected to want to make love." I tried to be gentle in my response. It never happened.

It was a relief to return to our newly bought house to begin married life in earnest. I had been excited about that since the prospect seemed to have so much promise. I looked forward to seeing Helena everyday; to seeing her smile and feeling her gentle kiss; to feeling her compassion and warmth; to sharing my life with her.

It was a fine house, ready made to be a home with lots of space and a big garden. I tried to put the honeymoon behind me, to not let it mar our nascent marriage. I assumed that Helena had similar feelings and, in her mind at least, held me to blame. All my life I had been plagued by feelings of resentment when women caused me trouble and I was determined not to let that feeling ruin my marriage in the first month.

Besides, living together in our house for the first time seemed to offer an opportunity for a new start. It was quite a new house and it seemed like a blank canvass for us to paint ourselves into.

"Do you think we should get cream towels or white?" Helena asked in Selfridges at the beginning of a home development expedition.

"White, it's more versatile."

"Oh, I really prefer cream."

"Okay, that's cool, we'll get cream then."

"That sort of attitude is not helpful." Helena looked vexed. I was confused.

"Sorry…what do you want me to do, then?" I could sense the rising tsunami of female contempt but couldn't see how to avoid it.

"I'd like you to show some interest in our home." Her exasperation was palpable.

"I did. That's why I said we should get white towels but, if you want cream, that's fine with me."

"Well, you can't simply agree with me on everything."

"I realise that but in this case I didn't see the point in arguing over the colour of towels."

"Well, we're arguing now," she said emphatically as if that proved her point.

"Clearly, but if I'd insisted on white towels we'd have had an argument anyway, so what could I do? Why don't we get two of each?"

"You're impossible." She stormed off.

I wasn't sure if Helena was trying to be funny and I was being filmed covertly for one of those crappy comedy TV shows. But no-one came to spoof me and Helena was already looking at cushions.

"Beige or brown," she asked between clenched teeth as I joined her.

"Brown, it's more practical."

"Well, yes, but I think beige is more stylish."

Early married life was not quite how I had imagined it but I was committed to making it work and looked for advice. I found it in the book *Men Are From Mars, Women Are From Venus* that several past girlfriends had bought me although I never took the hint. I found it a little confusing, not least because the onus seemed to be very much on me to make the relationship work and that seemed a bit one sided. I tried hard to make an effort with a special dinner.

The meal I would make had become immediately symbolic. If it was nice, Helena would accept it as a token of my commitment. At least that is how my simple perspective developed. And apart from my determination to make our marriage work, I genuinely wanted to do nice things for my wife.

I scrutinised cookbooks, followed the advice on the labels of ingredients and looked up suggestions on the Internet. I even rang my mother. In the end, I decided on simple but stylish reflecting what I thought were Helena's tastes. I shallow fried steak in oyster sauce and garlic.

It was high summer so too light for candles but I did my best to create a romantic atmosphere with fresh napkins on the table, fresh baked rolls in a basket and chilled smooth but light red wine in the fridge as Helena liked it. I served the meat with new potatoes and salad, poured the wine and called my wife with a sense of excitement.

Helena came into the kitchen with a smile of bemusement, which I mistook for affection.

"It looks a little overdone," she said, before she had sat down.

"Oh, sorry, I tried my best."

"I know but I like steak rare," her observation was simply stated but it cut deep.

"Well, you haven't even tried it."

She cut into the meat and hesitantly ate a piece.

"It is a little dry," she said a bit more gently but by then I did not care.

"Sorry, I'll try again tomorrow." We ate in painful silence. I was not certain but I thought Helena hid a smile of triumph. I drank most of the wine and tried not to let my ego stoke my temper.

Ironically, Helena seemed more amenable after we had finished the meal. Perhaps pissing on my bonfire like that was a way of asserting herself. She certainly seemed less reserved; almost flirty.

"Let's go to bed, Honey," she said later with a smile that I had not seen since before we got married.

"Are you sure?" I had got used to carnal disappointment but it did seem that Helena was finally in the mood to develop our relationship physically.

We went upstairs to our bedroom. Then our tentative passion was immediately interrupted by one of her cats, which started to scratch itself.

"Ooh, I almost forgot to put anti-flea powder on you, Sweety," she said to the cat. My libido began to wane in deference to my ego, which was not happy being second priority to a cat.

"Is that necessary, right now? Can't you do it in the morning?"

"Well I might forget in the morning."

I was actually jealous of a cat.

"Perhaps it will remind you when they start scratching."

Helena looked at me with thinly veiled angst.

"That would be really unkind," she said, "they would have a terrible itch."

"Well I've got a fucking terrible itch right now but that doesn't seem to bother you." I had never sworn at a woman before. My Grandfather would have been appalled but I could feel myself losing control as my ego now raged unabated. I could not shake a persistent sense of being trapped in a manipulative relationship that had no end.

The following morning I tried again to smooth things over. I made a pot of strong black coffee and sat hunched over the mug relishing its strength and intensity.

"Coffee, Honey?" I asked as Helena came into the kitchen, "I've got fresh croissant in the oven." Helena shook her head.

"All that caffeine and sugar is too stimulating," she said dismissively.

I looked suspiciously at my mug but it seemed innocuous enough so I took a big gulp, grateful that something was prepared to stimulate me. I munched on a croissant.

It was a beautiful morning with the sun already beaming down over the forest beyond our garden. Deep in the trees would be deer grazing quietly as they moved amongst the shadows.

"Shall we go for a walk in woods?" I suggested. Helena shook her head again and made a brew of nettles or other witch-like infusion.

"I've got work to do," she said, "I have to go away for a few weeks on a big project."

"Is that unexpected?" I hoped it was since the alternative was not promising.

"No, I've known for a while," she said without looking at me. I drank some more coffee.

Helena sat musing to herself for a moment.

"What's up? Are you worried about us being apart?" I asked, trying to be interested. Helena looked at me as if I had farted.

"No, I'm just thinking of jobs for you to do while I'm away."

"What am I, your butler?" My response was, perhaps, unnecessarily vehement but I was getting bored of being controlled like a whipped puppy. I went to run in the forest whilst Helena did her homework.

36

A lonely man has time to reflect and whilst Helena was away I considered the path I was following. I had not really planned my life's route, preferring to wander where fate lead, and it had generally worked for me. Following a determined path, however, had been a disaster and quite why was unclear. Perhaps I had simply married the wrong girl. Perhaps I was too difficult to love as Carla had prophesied.

I had always felt that I was a thoroughbred man, preferring elegant, powerful horses with a long stride and high temperament. I realised then that I lacked the subtlety of technique; thoroughbreds were dull. Riding through the Canadian Rockies or Belizean jungle on sturdy ponies was simply more exciting than a straight gallop along an English paddock.

Dan came to visit me. He had been there when my trouble with girls really started and he had been there when I met Helena. He came now when I was alone to remind me of the value of a true friend.

"How's it going?" he asked proffering his strong, slow handshake.

"Okay," I shrugged, "bit lonely. Work and Church are not really enough to occupy a man." We sat in armchairs looking out over the forest. One of the cats came purring into my lap. Dan smiled slowly.

"You need a good woman," he said sipping his whisky, "it's the best therapy that money can buy." His smile broadened.

"I'm done with philandering," I mused whilst absently stroking the cat.

"Would you rather sit here brooding with two cats?" he challenged in the gently forceful way that only a friend can.

"They're actually good company."

"Come on, man, you'll go mad sat here alone with those two moggies."

"These two moggies are the closest that I've come to any pussy in the last four months."

Dan laughed into his whisky.

"That's ironic after all your previous adventures. Why did you marry a woman like that?"

I raised my eyes to meet his gentle challenge.

"Obviously, she wasn't like that before we got married. I must have pissed her off somehow."

"But she must have known beforehand, you can't change your mind that quickly and if she knew how she felt she shouldn't have married you at all." His vehemence made his speech seemed rehearsed. I nodded slowly.

"I'm sorry," said Dan withdrawing from confrontation. "I hadn't intended to lecture you." He paused. "Has she said why she's been so distant?"

"Not at all," I almost whispered. "She hasn't said anything."

"That's unfair. Why doesn't she end it?"

It was a question I had asked myself many times.

"I think she is trying to push me to do it. So she can blame me to herself and friends." I spoke slowly, testing the logic of the thought as I said it.

"Why would she get married at all if she wanted it to fail?"

"Perhaps it's because being a jilted wife is more socially acceptable than being an aging spinster." We sat in silence drinking our whisky as if it was an elixir for the lonely.

"What will you do now?" asked Dan eventually. I shrugged again.

"Possibly leave the army to stay the course with Helena. I got married because I love her." I spoke to the cat as much a to Dan.

We finished the whisky.

I tried to focus on work, the last refuge of the lonely man. I had been posted as a staff officer to a large headquarters working for a gritty general who was hewn straight from the Charlton Heston School of manliness. He was revered for his straightforward approach and the headquarters began to mould itself around him. Instinctively I wanted to be part of it.

"We've got to balance the risks very carefully," he said in a command meeting in preparation for deployment to Iraq. "I want you to ensure that when my soldiers are in harm's way, they absolutely need to be there." His voice rumbled like a dog's low growl.

"That isn't to say we should pussy about," he continued. "You all know I've danced with the Devil before now." Then he seemed to drift into a personal reverie. "Actually, I've boned the bastard a couple of times."

Invading Iraq caused me some difficulty. I could not see any moral or legal justification for it. Clearly the Kurds had been subject to a form of genocide but this was reflected in many other countries so that seemed an uncertain authority. The nuclear weapons line also seemed vague.

There were other possible factors, oil being one, but it seemed to me that the US drive to invade Iraq was so that it could surround Iran with troops in Iraq, Turkey, Afghanistan and the Northern Gulf. It was sound strategy and worth British support, but it was not the reason that the then prime minister gave as justification to parliament. Such unease added weight to my notion of leaving the army.

I got a call from the chief of staff to go to his office. He was not a big man but he was impressive in manner, exuding the determined confidence of all senior officers. He did not like me.

"Major Hanson," he said whilst studying a map of the Northern Gulf. "We have not found a replacement for you yet so the option of deploying to Iraq is still open to you." He looked at me directly.

"Thanks, sir, I'll think about it."

"What's to think about?" he asked as I left his office and, for a moment, I thought he might pass me a white feather.

In the meantime, I did brood with the cats. They became a means of détente for Helena and I during uncomfortable telephone conversations. We made some tentative progress and agreed to try to sort things out when she came back but, as I started to draw closer to her, she edged away. Imperceptibly at first but with increasing determination until at last she declared that she could not delay her break from work to coincide with mine so she was going on holiday alone.

"What about the counselling that you suggested we have?" I asked her on the telephone.

"Counselling will have to wait until I conclude this deal." She spoke casually, as if it were a trifling matter.

"But I have been warned off to go to Iraq."

"I thought you were leaving the Army?" Her voice had a hint of sarcasm.

"I was but I can't leave ahead of an operational deployment."

"Is it official?"

"No, parliament hasn't decided yet but we expect it will. If I resign now it will look as if I am trying to avoid deployment." Helena considered that for a moment.

"We can't work if you're in Iraq."

That floored me. I had been trying to break free of the Army Bitch since before I joined but now it seemed as if Helena was suggesting I leave at a time when I actually wanted to stay.

I married Helena because I loved her. I thought she was different, with a strong sense of identity and rich character. It turned out that she was as self focussed as every other woman I had met and there was a terrible irony for me that, after all the women I had spurned for being too controlling, I should now be dictated to by the one woman that I thought I truly loved. I felt like I was being emasculated.

"Won't you wait for me?" I asked. Helena gave a brief laugh.

"What do you want from me, Billy?"

I want you to be my wife.

I want you to be the mother of my children.

I want your love.

"Actually, I don't want anything from you but my freedom." I had not intended to say that but it felt good. Helena was silent, though whether that was due to sadness at the final demise of our marriage or frustration that she had lost control, was not clear.

And that was it, the ultimate failed relationship after so many before. I ran: not from anything or to anywhere but for the sheer exhilaration of my legs carrying me through the woods and fields around the house. In the late evening, running swiftly and silently, I would disturb foxes and deer and lovers in an illicit tryst in the woods. It was intoxicating. I was in control.

Helena came back from her business trip and moved out. She took everything, even the bed. As therapy I decided to shred all my pictures of her feet first, hoping it would hurt more.

Then the Attorney General cited a case for war. I had no faith in the contrived legal arguments but not going to Iraq then would have been morally wrong.

Besides, the desert seemed to be the ideal place for a lovelorn man: the Wisdom of Solomon certainly suggested that.

So I abandoned my plans to leave the army and joined the deploying troops. I heard a faint laugh behind me, around me, everywhere. I was still full of self-doubt about the Army Bitch and about Helena but I marched along and the laughter became a mocking litany of my own indecision.

Throughout my life, in the face of opposition from rugby players, senior army officers and women, I had stood up for myself and what I believed in. Now the truth of the Proverb that seemed to have governed my life felt so apt, and not just because we were going to the desert.

The faint mocking laugh became a hysterical howl as the Army Bitch realised that she had won at last. As I marched smiling down the road to Basra, I finally accepted that the real trouble with girls is that you just can't live with them.

Proverbs: Chapter 21, Verse 19:

It is better to dwell in the wilderness, than with a contentious and an angry woman.

Jonny Cox served for fifteen years as an infantry officer, getting into trouble all other the world. The questionable invasion of Iraq finally convinced him that he was in the wrong place. He now lives in the country with a beautiful wife and three happy little boys.

Thanks to David Kinchin at the Writers' Bureau for helping to turn the drunken ramblings of an old soldier into something more useful. And to Mila Blanca at youwriteon.com who provided advice and encouragement. I am also grateful to Foxy, Big Al, Skip D, Barney and Aunty Fifi for feigning interest and lastly to Darin Jewell for pulling it all together.

Lightning Source UK Ltd.
Milton Keynes UK
UKOW041945180313

207849UK00002B/159/P